COBRA CLUTCH

A NEWEST
MYSTERY

Library and Archives Canada Cataloguing in Publication

Devlin, A. J., 1978-, author
    Cobra clutch / A.J. Devlin.

("Hammerhead" Jed mystery ; 1)
Issued in print and electronic formats.
ISBN 978-1-988732-24-4 (softcover).--ISBN 978-1-988732-25-1 (EPUB).--
ISBN 978-1-988732-26-8 (Kindle)

    I. Title.

PS8607.E94555C63 2018   C813'.6
C2017-905217-9

C2017-905218-7

Board Editor: Merrill Distad
Cover and interior design: Michel Vrana
Cover images: istockphoto.com, shutterstock.com
Author photo: Gina Spanos

NeWest Press acknowledges the support of the Canada Council for the Arts, the Alberta Foundation for the Arts, and the Edmonton Arts Council for support of our publishing program. We acknowledge the financial support of the Government of Canada.

NeWest Press
#201, 8540-109 Street
Edmonton, Alberta T6G 1E6
www.newestpress.com

No bison were harmed in the making of this book.

Printed and bound in Canada

2 3 4   20 19 18

For Leonard Schrader

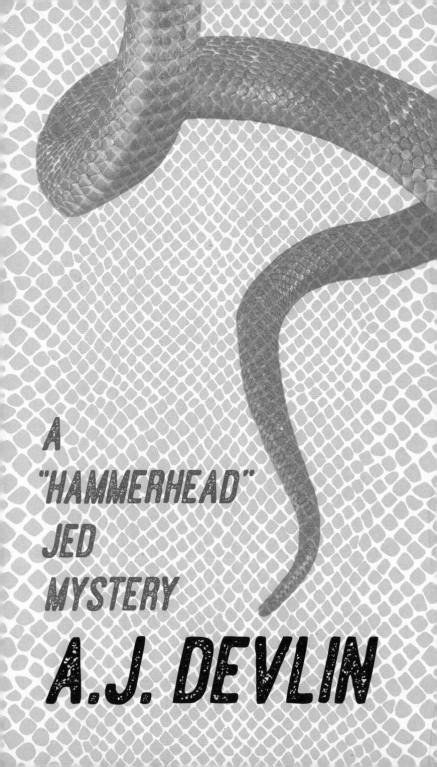

A
"HAMMERHEAD"
JED
MYSTERY

A.J. DEVLIN

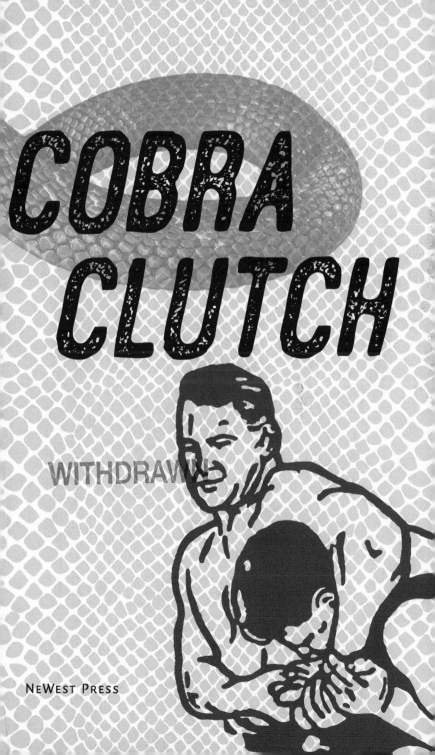

Cobra Clutch:

[koh-bruh] [kluhch]

noun, *verb* (used with object)

1. Professional wrestling submission move. Also known as an arm-trap half nelson sleeper; the wrestler stands behind the opponent and uses one arm to place the opponent in a half nelson. The wrestler then uses his free arm to pull the opponent's arm (the same arm to which the wrestler is applying the half nelson) across the face of the opponent. The wrestler then locks his hand to his wrist behind the opponent's neck to make the opponent submit or lose consciousness as the carotid artery is cut off.

ONE

"Some asshole kidnapped my snake."

"That sounds like a hell of a case."

"I'm serious, man."

"So am I."

"You don't believe me?"

"Not really, no."

"I thought you would. That's why I came to you."

"Just so I'm clear, by 'kidnapped' you mean someone actually stole your pet snake?"

"Yes. And her name is Ginger."

"The snake or the kidnapper?"

"The snake."

"Are you sure Ginger didn't, like, slither off somewhere?"

"I'm sure."

"Seriously, who put you up to this?"

"I can't believe you think this is a joke."

"It was my cousin, wasn't it?"

"You know what? Forget it."

I took another sip of my banana milkshake and glanced around the Dairy Queen in search of an accomplice. "You're videotaping this, right? Declan wouldn't go to all this trouble and not get this on camera."

Johnny slammed his fist down on the table. "Damn it, Jed! I'm not screwing around here!"

"All right, take it easy. I believe you."

"About goddamn time."

"You have to admit, it's not the easiest sell. I'm also not sure which is more disturbing—the fact that someone went to the trouble of kidnapping your pet snake or that you actually named a reptile after a Spice Girl."

My old friend smirked despite himself. "You're an even bigger smart-ass than I remember."

"Fair enough. Now why don't you take me through this thing from the top?"

Johnny plucked a crinkled photo out of his wallet and handed it to me. In the picture he was leaning against the turnbuckle of a professional wrestling ring with a yellow python with brown patches draped over his shoulders. "That's my baby," he said.

"I can see the resemblance."

"Eh?"

I pointed at the tattoo of a yellowish-brown python spiralling around one of his sinewy forearms.

"Oh, yeah. I got inked for Ginger's birthday a few months back. I've had her for three years now, Jed. I make my entrances with her around my neck and keep her ringside during my matches and everything. I can't wrestle without her."

"Any idea why someone would want to take your snake?" I asked, handing back the photo.

"Christ, I don't know. You're the private investigator."

"I'm a bouncer, Johnny. Not a PI."

"That's not what I've heard."

"My old man is the one with the licence. I just help him with some of the leg work from time to time."

"So do some leg work for me now and help me get Ginger back. You should have seen the cops this morning, man. They laughed at me while I filled out the theft report."

"I'm sorry, bub," I replied earnestly. "I can't help you."

Johnny gripped my forearm as I stood.

"Baton Rouge, man."

My heart skipped a beat. "That was a long time ago."

"You owe me."

"You sure you want to play this card?"

"I am. I got nowhere else to go."

I took a deep breath, my mind scrambling to find an alternative solution. "I know some excellent private investigators. Why don't I give you some referrals?"

"So they can laugh at me too? No. I want you."

I sat back down. Johnny let out a huge sigh. "Thank you, Jed. Thank you so much."

I sucked back on my milkshake until the straw made a slurping sound. Some people complain about Dairy Queen and say they don't make quality shakes. I say that's bull. They're the only place that mixes their syrup with real bananas and that makes all the difference in my book.

I set aside my frosty treat and looked at my old friend. It had been a long time since I had last seen Johnny Mamba. Instead of the buff young wrestler I remembered, he now looked nearly a decade older than his thirty-eight years. Although still muscular, he'd lost a lot of mass and his skin now appeared more loose and leathery than tight and tanned. Crow's feet had crept their way around his eyes and his hairline had started to recede. The years he'd spent punishing his body on the professional wrestling circuit had definitely taken their toll.

"Let me see that picture again," I said finally. Johnny slid the photo across the table. "Can I have this?"

"No way," he said, snatching it out of my hands.

I pulled my phone out of my pocket. Johnny clued in and placed the photo flat on the table so I could snap a pic.

"Good enough. Now tell me about the, uh … abduction."

"It was after practice last night. I left Ginger in her sack in the locker room while I showered like I always do. When I came out she was gone."

"How long was your shower?"

"Five minutes or so."

"Who else was there?"

"Nobody. I usually stick around after practice and work with the rookies so I'm always the last to leave."

"Johnny, if this really is a kidnapping then you would have received a ransom note."

Johnny produced a printout of an email. It read:

```
From: thesteelcrab@gmail.com
To: gingerlover69@hotmail.com
Subject: PAYMENT
-------------------------------------------------
Ten thousand dollars or you never see the
snake again. You have three days to get the
money.
-------------------------------------------------
```

Johnny stared at me with saucer plate eyes. "What do you think?"

"I need you to forward me a copy of this. You still have my email?" Johnny nodded.

"What about thesteelcrab@gmail.com? Does that mean anything to you?"

"No."

"I find it curious the kidnapper would send you a ransom note via email, but I guess that might explain why you were given three days to secure the funds instead of one."

"How so?"

"I doubt they would know how often you check your email and they had to ensure they gave you ample time to receive the message. Any idea how the kidnapper got your address?"

"Every wrestler's email is posted on the XCCW website."

"XCCW?"

"X-Treme Canadian Championship Wrestling. Fastest growing professional wrestling promotion in Western Canada."

"I've never heard of them."

"It's a great circuit. Quality talent, awesome schedule, lots of exposure. You ever thought about a comeback? XCCW would be the perfect place for you to —"

I silenced Johnny with a glare.

"I was just throwing it out there," he said quietly.

I let it go and tapped my finger on the printout. "No offense, Johnny, but why would someone in their right mind expect you to pay ten thousand dollars for a pet? Couldn't you just buy another snake for a fraction of that amount?"

"I love her, man. I'd pay anything."

"Odds are whoever took Ginger knew that."

"What are you saying? That the son-of-a-bitch who took Ginger knows me?"

"Yeah, that's exactly what I'm saying. Do you have any enemies? Anybody that would want to hurt you?"

"No way, man."

"Anybody at XCCW?"

"Are you kidding? I'm like Tom Cruise at a Scientology convention at that place."

"How about the money? Can you afford to pay the ransom?"

"I got some coin squirreled away for a rainy day."

"And how many people are aware of that fact?"

Johnny shrugged, tucking his long hair behind his ears. "A bunch, I guess. My Nana died a few months back and left me about twenty grand."

"You never played connect the dots much when you were a kid, did you, Johnny?"

He blinked a few times. After a moment, it clicked. "Oh, shit! You think they knew about my inheritance?"

"No one without intimate knowledge of your relationship with Ginger would waste time with a scheme like this. How many people does XCCW employ?"

"Maybe eighty or so, including wrestlers and staff. I haven't been back since Ginger was taken but I can show you around if you need me to."

"No, I want you to steer clear of there for now," I replied. "Best thing you can do is lay low and let me do my thing."

"You got it, Jed. So what do you charge for this kind of thing?" he asked, cracking open his wallet.

"Just your word that this squares us," I said, sliding out of the booth. "I'll be in touch."

"Are you sure? Isn't there anything else I can do?"

"Yeah. Get to the bank."

I tossed my empty cup in the garbage and ordered another large banana milkshake to go.

TWO

The junkie came out of nowhere. She smashed her fists down on the hood of my Ford F-150 and shrieked like a banshee. I gave my horn a blast and she stumbled backwards, her pale skin illuminated by the glare of my headlights. She smiled, revealing a mouth full of rotted teeth, most likely ravaged by years of crystal meth abuse. She giggled like a schoolgirl, threw her bony arms into the night air, and began to plié and dance herself across the street like it were a stage for a strung out ballerina.

The light turned green. I hit the gas. I sped down Hastings Street past Pigeon Park, where the addicts and vagrants fluttered about in more directions than the birds. The sidewalks were alive with bustling activity, and despite the woeful living conditions of its destitute inhabitants, there was no denying the area crackled with a unique and vibrant energy.

Dozens of street people chatted, bartered, fought, and fraternized. A crazy-haired woman in a polka dot muumuu sobbed next to an overturned shopping cart while a few locals looted her treasure of empty bottles and blankets. A shirtless man held up traffic by running into the street, beating his chest, and roaring like a grubby gorilla.

By the time I had driven two blocks I was outside the radius of Vancouver's Downtown Eastside, a neighbourhood that also doubled as the most impoverished district in all of Canada. The streets were immediately cleaner and the homeless had vanished. I parked in front of a vinyl record store and made the familiar march toward the pub next door. I wasn't but two steps inside when I was assaulted by a thick Irish brogue.

"Get your big arse over here and join me for a pint o'the black stuff, you bollocks."

Declan St. James was renowned throughout Vancouver for his ability to pour the perfect pint of Guinness. But he is damn near legendary for his tendency to pick a fight after downing one too many of his masterful creations. He's also my cousin, on my mother's side, and had been a staple around the pub ever since he immigrated to Canada five years prior. I pulled up a stool at the lacquered oak bar while he grabbed a glass and worked his magic.

"How was the meeting with your old mate?" he asked.

"Unusual." I filled Declan in on the snake-napping. He laughed so hard he almost spilled my beer.

"Did you really think I'd go to all that trouble just to bugger with your head?"

"Are you telling me you wouldn't?"

Declan smirked. "Aye, you're right. I would. I just wish I had thought o'the idea me self."

After letting the pints sit for a minute and a half, Declan topped up the glasses. As a finishing touch he etched a shamrock into the creamy head of my Guinness, the mark of a truly gifted barman.

"Is my pop around?" I asked.

"He's at that security conference, remember?"

"Can you let me into his office? I need to use his computer."

"No bloody way."

"Come on, D."

"I do that, Frank will twist off me nuts and punt them back to the motherland."

"The threat of a scrotal assault never stopped you before."

"Aye, well perhaps if you sweetened the deal a wee bit I might consider it."

We clinked glasses. Once my Guinness had settled I took a big sip, then licked the froth from my upper lip. Damn, it was good. "How about I cover a shift for you this weekend?"

"Think bigger."

"Whitecaps tickets?"

"Just because I like me football doesn't mean I want to watch those bums."

"I'm running out of ideas here."

"Tell you what. I'll settle for a bottle o'single malt and a visit to me flat tonight for a good and proper piss-up."

"Deal."

Satisfied, Declan grabbed a big ring of keys off the wall. Pints in hand, we headed toward the back, passing a few regulars on bar stools and a booth crammed full of film students prattling on about some director I had never heard of. This was hardly uncommon since my old man's pub, The Emerald Shillelagh, was located across the street from the Vancouver Film School and had long been a favourite watering hole for both students and staff.

We trudged up the narrow staircase to my pop's office on the second floor. *Ounstead Investigations* was painted on the frosted glass of the office door and I noticed that the *O* and *V* had started to fade and peel. Declan unlocked the door and let me inside.

"Make it quick, mate. And be sure to clear the web browser when you're done. Wouldn't want to have to explain to Frank all the visits to Me Friend's Hot Mom dot com."

"Not to worry. Besides, everybody knows that you're the one with the MILF fetish."

Declan grinned devilishly. "Aye, I do love me ladies a wee bit mature."

"Thanks again, bub. I owe you one."

"If you really want to make it up to me then you can bloody well spring for the eighteen-year-old Glenfiddich."

Declan left me alone with a desktop full of case folders. I put down my Guinness between an archaic PC and a rotary phone and pushed aside the clutter until I found the keyboard and mouse. After logging onto my pop's preferred cyber-detective website with the same username and password I knew he used for all his online accounts, I ran Johnny Mamba's name through several searches. What I found was what I had expected—a clean criminal record and nothing notable other than numerous former addresses and phone numbers across Canada over the past several years. I knew firsthand this was pretty standard for a struggling professional wrestler still looking to make it big.

I felt a tinge of guilt for checking up on my old friend so soon after our meeting but reminded myself that it had been years since I had last seen him. Even though we went all the way back to pro-wrestling school together, I wasn't about to neglect what my old man calls "Private Eye 101"—*know your client*. People can change and sometimes it happens fast. I knew this from experience as well. However, since the information I found indicated that Johnny had indeed been moving around Canada from wrestling promotion to promotion just like he had said, I did a web search for XCCW.

The league was part of the National Wrestling Alliance and operated under the NWA's Pacific Northwest banner. A flash animation in the top left hand corner of the XCCW homepage advertised a house show at a Russian community centre in West Vancouver the next day. I jotted down the address and then continued exploring the website. The Upcoming Events page promoted a Battle Royale for the XCCW heavyweight championship. The show was also set to be XCCW's first ever online pay-per-view event.

In addition to the Battle Royale, the pay-per-view card also hyped several other bouts including a Bra and Panties match featuring two scantily clad, female wrestlers and a Last Man Standing match for the XCCW Hardcore Championship between Johnny and an obese, barrel-chested, bearded grappler by the name of Brutus Bonebreaker.

I leaned back in the chair and took a big gulp of Guinness. It didn't take long for the memories to come flooding back. My head filled with flashes of gruelling training sessions, endless road trips, and dingy hotels — all of the unglamorous realities that come with a career in professional wrestling. I thought I had left that life behind me for good. Over two years had gone by since I had left. Yet somehow it felt like only yesterday. I found myself wishing that my career had ended for a different reason, like getting hurt. At least with an injury there was a chance for rehabilitation. There was no coming back from what had happened to me.

I downed the rest of my pint and cut short my trip down memory lane. I cleared the web browser history and emptied the cache, careful to leave no trace before logging off the computer. I meticulously recreated my old man's cluttered desktop and buried the keyboard and mouse under the numerous case files, covering my tracks so he would be none the wiser.

Since there was not much else I could do until visiting XCCW the next day, and because I wasn't scheduled to work the door at Tonix nightclub until the weekend, I decided to head off in search of some eighteen-year-old scotch.

THREE

I awoke to searing pain. I cracked open my eyelids, only to have my irises blinded by light. After fighting back a wave of nausea, my vision settled on a near nude figure in the distance.

"Top o'the morning to you, princess. Actually, I guess it'd be top o'the afternoon."

Sporting a jockstrap and a pair of aviator sunglasses, Declan alternated between puffs of a cigarette and spoonfuls of cereal while lounging on his patio that overlooked the hustle and bustle of Vancouver's upscale Yaletown neighbourhood.

"We got right scuttered last night, didn't we, mate?" he said, scratching an itch on his scalp full of close-cropped hair. "I'm telling you, that eighteen-year-old Glenfiddich is the shite." I rolled off the couch and stumbled toward the kitchen. "Hey, if you got to chuff, do it in me bloody toilet."

I ignored Declan and turned on the faucet. I ran the water until it was cold, then washed my face and rinsed my mouth, gargling excessively in a desperate attempt to cleanse my palate of its foul single malt aftertaste. I steadied myself against the countertop as I dried my face with a dishtowel. Declan just grinned and kept slurping up his breakfast. I grabbed the open box of Lucky Charms and held it up.

"You do realize that as a full-blooded Irishman you're only perpetuating a stereotype by eating this crap."

"Sod off. They're magically delicious."

After using the restroom I returned to the kitchen fully dressed to find Declan furiously digging through the box of cereal. "I don't even want to ask."

Declan pointed toward a caption on the box, which advertised a free Batman mini-PEZ dispenser inside. "I want me bloody prize."

My cousin's sinewy triceps flexed as he aggressively searched for the Caped Crusader, causing the prominent tattoo on his arm to move. A rising fist was inked against the backdrop of the green, white, and orange of the Irish flag, and written beneath in Gaelic were the words *Tiocfaidh ár lá*, which translates into *"our day will come."* The tat was an emblem of the IRA. It was also a permanent reminder of Declan's former life, something he didn't like to talk about. I could definitely relate.

Declan cursed in Gaelic, his search remaining fruitless. Despite my headache I couldn't help but smirk as I found the sight of an angry bare-assed Irishman desperately searching for a children's toy quite humorous.

"I swear to Christ I'm takin' this box o'shite back to the market if I've been screwed out o'me—aha!"

Clutching the Batman mini-PEZ dispenser, Declan yanked his hand out of the cereal box and thrust his fist in the air victoriously, littering the countertop with marshmallow yellow moons and red balloons. I grabbed my jacket off the bar stool and raided his fridge for a bottle of water.

"Off to save the day then, yeah?" Declan asked.

"That snake's not going to return itself," I replied.

"Aye, well, if you piss off some hardchaws during your search and need me to rescue your dainty arse, you know where I'll be."

"Good thing I got the number for that Thai rub'n'tug massage parlour you like so much on speed dial."

"Get up the yard, ya Bombay Shitehawk."

"I love you too, D."

I stopped off at home and rooted through my medicine cabinet until I found a Costco-size bottle of Advil. I doubled the recommended dosage and chased it with a litre of water before taking a hot shower. I put on a fresh change of clothes, whipped myself up a turkey–cranberry sandwich, and read the sports section in *The Vancouver Sun*. Finally, after double-checking the start time for the Thursday night show, I left a few hours early for the West Vancouver location where XCCW was based.

I parked on the street and made my way down the sidewalk on West 4th, passing a slew of specialty fashion shops, a yoga studio, and a newly opened doggy spa. I nearly collided with a gaggle of hipsters as they stumbled out of an herbal smoke shop, and I was pretty sure the whiff of cannabis I picked up on wasn't coming from their hemp clothing. All and all it was pretty par for the course for an evening stroll through Kitsilano, which was well known for being one of Vancouver's funkiest and most eclectic neighbourhoods.

The dilapidated building XCCW operated out of was a Russian community centre, and the dated outdoor marquee was just one of several markers that poorly hid the fact that the place had once been a local cinema. My nostrils were immediately assaulted by the scent of musty wood and stale popcorn upon entering the building, and the pungent mix of odours only grew stronger as I made my way down a dark hallway toward the gymnasium. With its bright orange basketball rims and parquet floor, the gym looked as if it had been preserved in a time capsule since the seventies. Several wrestlers were gathered in the centre of the gym, grunting as they assembled a regulation size pro-wrestling ring. A skinny teenager bopped his head to the beat of his iPod shuffle while arranging folding chairs around three sides of the ring. The gym's space was limited, so there was only room for two rows of about fifteen chairs on each side of the ring, making for nearly a hundred seats. The fourth side of the wrestling ring backed onto a stage. A small ramp on a decline angle connected the stage to the ring and served as an entryway for the XCCW performers. It also gave the wrestlers the opportunity to appear before the crowd with some flair, since strutting through the faux velvet stage curtains and down the ramp made their entrances much more theatrical.

"Well, tickle my taint and call me Tania," said a shrill voice. "You gotta be kidding me with this shit."

I looked around for the source of the vulgarity and came up short. Literally. A three-foot dwarf in a white linen suit strutted toward me, his angular face scrunched up in a big grin.

"There a problem?" I asked.

"You're 'Hammerhead' Jed Ounstead."

"Once upon a time, bub."

"Where's your fuckin' two-by-four, bro?"

Back in the day I had earned the nickname *"Hammerhead Jed"* due to my penchant for breaking a two-by-four piece of Western red cedar over my head after pinning an opponent. The crowd used to eat it up. It also might explain why I'm not very good at crossword puzzles.

"Left it in my truck," I replied.

"That's cool, I got ya," the dwarf said. The little man stood on his tiptoes and offered me a fist bump. I returned the gesture and he enthusiastically pounded his tiny knuckles into mine. "Tell me you're joining XCCW, bro." Before I could answer he was hollering across the gym. "Yo, Ula! Get over here!"

The parquet floor vibrated as a mammoth Samoan man lumbered toward us, his belly fat rolling like an ocean wave. I made him for three-fifty and change, easy. He wore a pink T-shirt underneath a crisp blue blazer and white linen pants. Polynesian tattoos covered his neck and cheeks. The Samoan's bulbous face lit up the moment he recognized me.

"Aznuts! 'Hammerhead' Jed! Whassup, brah?" the behemoth bellowed.

The Samoan's thick sausage fingers gripped my hand and pumped it furiously. The little man and the giant were quite the sight, and when I noticed their matching sock-less loafers, I realized their peculiar attire was part of their wrestling gimmick.

"Bro, you're gonna fuckin' kill when you debut," chirped the dwarf. "Crowd'll pop so loud it'll be sick. Let me guess, your coming out party's the Battle Royale, right?"

"I'm still retired."

"Damn, bro, you got me all excited and shit," bemoaned the dwarf. "What are you doing here then?"

"Johnny Mamba's snake," I said solemnly.

Both the dwarf and the Samoan shook their heads and frowned. "That shit with Ginger is whack, yo," said the dwarf. "Me and Ula still can't believe it. Where's Mamba at, anyway?"

"He's taking some time off," I replied. "Do you guys know Johnny well?"

"Hell yeah, bro. We tight. The three of us used to wrestle in triple threat matches till Mamba switched over to the Hardcore division. He ain't never mentioned us to you?"

I shook my head. "Who are you guys, anyway?"

They exchanged a distressed look, clearly upset that I had no idea who they were. The dwarf scoffed and spread his hands. "Uh, only the best tag-team in XCCW and the entire National Wrestling Alliance."

"I don't follow wrestling anymore."

The little man was not impressed. "We're 'Pocket and Tubbs,' bro! Like *Miami Vice* except with twice the spice!"

They were both awaiting my response with baited breath. "That … " I said, pausing for dramatic effect, " is one awesome gimmick."

"Bro, I know, right?" the dwarf said proudly.

"But which one of you is Tubbs?"

They were about as prepared for that question as Kanye West would be for a coherent thought. After a moment, Pocket clued in and got the joke. "Ha! That's fuckin' hilarious!"

Tubbs clasped a meaty paw down on my shoulder. "Dis 'Hammerhead' Jed, he talk funny stories."

"Fuckin' rights," agreed Pocket, before initiating another round of fist bumping.

"Listen, guys, what can you tell me about Ginger's disappearance?" I finally asked.

"We didn't even hear about it till yesterday, bro. I guess it happened after practice or something. But me and Ula, we always cut out early so we were long gone."

"How'd you get word then?"

"Stormy tell us," said Tubbs.

"Who's that?"

"Stormy Daze, bro. Mamba's girlfriend."

"Ex-girlfriend," chimed in Tubbs.

"Shit, that's right," said Pocket. "I keep forgetting they broke up."

"How long ago was that?"

Pocket shrugged. "Not sure. But it was recent."

"This Stormy, is she a wrestler?" I asked.

"Hell, yeah, bro. She's the damn XCCW Women's champ."

I made a mental note to talk to Johnny about his ex.

"Did she tell you that there's been a ransom demand?"

"No, but our boss did this morning. Fuckin' prick screamed at us for half-an-hour cuz he's pissed that Mamba's MIA, especially with the pay-per-view coming up."

"And who's your boss?"

"Bert Grasby," snapped Pocket, spitting out the words as if they left a bitter taste in his mouth. "He's the owner of XCCW."

"Where can I find him?"

"Dat mahu be here somewhere," said Tubbs.

Pocket snickered and slapped Tubbs on a beefy calf. "Yeah, probably backstage greasing up some poor rookie with baby oil!"

Pocket and Tubbs had themselves a good laugh while I bumped Grasby to the top of my interview list. "Were either of you aware that Johnny Mamba recently came into some money?"

"Everybody knew, bro. He's always yapping about how he's gonna buy Ginger some fancy new ... terror-mun? Terry-yum?"

"Terrarium, brah," said Ula.

"That's it!" chirped Pocket excitedly, snapping his fingers. "It's like a giant aquarium for snakes but with no water. Anyways, Johnny was gonna custom build one of those things with all these special plants and caves and shit. I told him he needed to buy himself a sweet new ride but he didn't want to hear it."

"One last thing, guys," I said. "Is there anybody that you can think of who might have a grudge against Johnny?"

Pocket and Tubbs both shook their heads emphatically. "Hell no, bro. Mamba's a cool cat. You know what this business is like. Chock-full of cocksuckers and motherfuckers. But Mamba's different. That guy will beat the shit out of his body in the ring to entertain the crowd, then stick around to work with the rookies, and even help the janitor clean up."

"They don' make 'em like Johnny boy no more," said Tubbs.

I thanked them both for their time and gave them my number. They promised if they remembered anything else they would give me a call. Pocket seemed almost flattered, and I had a feeling I was going to hear from my new knee-high acquaintance one way or the other.

I walked past a sticky-looking concession stand as I left the gymnasium, heading into the bowels of the community centre. I encountered a frumpy woman with a hairnet unloading crates of potato chips and canned soda. I asked her if she had seen Bert Grasby and she grumbled something in Russian before directing me toward an arts and crafts room. I opened the door and ducked underneath numerous paper-mache masks dangling from the ceiling, inadvertently barging in on what I can only describe as a rather vigorous stretching session.

A ripped young wrestler sporting shiny boots, Speedo-style trunks and single-digit body fat percentage lay on a mat while another man stood over him driving his shoulder into the back of the kid's knee. Although I had seen trainers perform this type of hamstring stretch on athletes countless times before, the way this pasty, pot-bellied man with the bad comb-over was doing it made me feel like I had just stumbled into the opening scene of a twenty-year-old gay porno.

"What the fuck, asshole? Ever heard of knocking?" barked the butterball.

"You Grasby?" I asked.

"What's it to you?" The paunchy man adjusted himself, trying to hide the bulge in his velour Adidas track pants. The ripped wrestler sprang to his feet behind his boss.

"I need a word with you," I said. The ripped wrestler crossed his arms and tried to look tough.

"You don't talk to Mr. Grasby unless he says so, dickweed."

I sighed and put my hands on my hips. "Listen, kid, you're pretty built and all, but for future reference, it's a lot easier to intimidate someone when you're not wearing neon tassels around your arms." The kid looked at the colourful shoelace-like tassels tightly cinched around his biceps and blushed.

"Enough," said Grasby. "Dylan, go finish stretching in the break room."

"Yes sir, Mr. Grasby."

The kid glared at me as he strutted by. Maybe if he had been paying attention to where he was going he wouldn't have gotten one of his arm tassels caught on the metal hinge on the door frame, because suddenly his entire body jerked backwards like he was a puppy being leash trained. The kid threw a hissy fit until he ripped the tassel free, then stormed off, slamming the door behind him. I turned back to face Grasby, quite amused with his stretching buddy's exit. That's when I saw the gun levelled at my chest. I didn't find that nearly as amusing.

FOUR

"Give me one good reason why I shouldn't blow your goddamn head off."

"I can give you ten," I quipped, holding my hands in the air.

"I made it clear to Nikolai that I found another supplier," snarled Grasby. "Sending punks like you to disrupt my show is not going to make me change my mind."

"I don't know anyone named Nikolai. And I'm no punk."

"You look like one to me."

I flashed a million dollar smile. "Look at these pearly whites. How many goons-for-hire do you know who get dental?"

"Shut the fuck up." Grasby tightened his grip on his pistol, which looked to be some kind of subcompact Glock. "If Nikolai thinks I'd have a moment's hesitation taking out one of his guys, especially a smug prick like you, then he really didn't do his homework on Bert Grasby."

I couldn't believe this guy. He has the nerve to call me smug then proceeds to refer to himself in the third person? Grasby was definitely a piece of work. He was also getting an itchy trigger finger.

"Take it easy," I said, slowly lowering my arms. "You don't want to do anything stupid, especially since you have me confused with somebody else."

"Is that so?"

"Yeah. In fact, I'm a little surprised that you don't recognize me."

Grasby cocked his pudgy head sideways like an inquisitive bulldog. I could see the recognition slowly creeping its way across his face but decided to help him the rest of the way.

"I'm Jed Ounstead." Grasby blinked twice but still held the gun at my chest. "The former wrestler? Ring a bell?"

"Son-of-a-bitch," hissed Grasby. "'Hammerhead' Jed. I totally didn't recognize you without the goatee."

"Shaved it off after I retired."

"I hear that," he said, stroking his soul patch with his index finger. "I'm always trying to find new ways to keep my look fresh."

"Good for you, bub. Say, how about lowering that gun now?"

Grasby looked at the Glock like it had magically appeared in his hand. "Oh, shit, yeah. Sorry about that." Grasby tucked the gun into his tracksuit's waistband behind his back.

"Who's Nikolai?" I asked.

"Doesn't matter. Let's talk about you, man. Tell me you're thinking comeback."

"Actually, I'm here on behalf of Johnny Mamba."

"You're joking."

"Afraid not. Can you think of anyone who may have had a reason to target Ginger?"

"Ginger?"

"Johnny's snake."

Grasby smoothed out a few creases in his velour tracksuit and swaggered closer. "Let me get this straight," he said. "You, 'Hammerhead' Jed Ounstead, former pro-wrestling superstar, have no interest in discussing a potential comeback or trying to negotiate a contract with my organization."

"Nope."

"And the only reason you're here is to try and find Mamba's disgusting slimy pet?"

"That's right."

"I don't have time for this." Grasby tried to walk past me. I sidestepped quickly and blocked his path.

"Do I need to get out my gun again?" threatened Grasby.

"I just need you to answer a few questions."

"Fuck that."

"I think that's the least you can do for one of your wrestlers."

"Man, I don't owe Mamba shit."

I took a deep breath. Grasby was starting to get under my skin. "Johnny's a good guy," I said. "I know it may be weird, but he loves that snake more than anything and is pretty distraught without it. So how about showing a little respect?"

"Why should I?" snapped Grasby. "He sure as shit doesn't show any to me."

"Not even when he works with your new talent and helps the janitorial staff clean up after house shows?" I countered.

"I don't care what stories you've heard, Johnny Mamba is no saint. That cocky bastard walks around here like his shit doesn't stink just because he had a ten-second run in the WWE. Well, guess what? If it weren't for me he wouldn't even be working."

"He could wrestle for another promotion if he wanted to."

"The fuck he could!" bellowed Grasby. "Did you know he was fired from Pure Power Wrestling? Turns out the snake gimmick was so lame and dated, the crowds in Alberta would heckle the shit out of him before up and leaving during his matches. The only reason I let him wrestle in XCCW is because he agreed to do odd jobs and work as a trainer. So don't go thinking Mamba's going above and beyond by showing the ropes to the rookies and helping clean up. It's his fucking job."

Grasby could see the surprise on my face. I knew that Johnny wasn't exactly top-draw talent in XCCW but I figured he was at least holding his own. The fact that Grasby threw him a bone just by hiring him made me realize that Johnny's wrestling career was in a lot worse shape than I had originally thought.

"But what about your upcoming pay-per-view?" I asked. "He's on the card for a championship match."

"As a last minute replacement. The guy whose slot he filled pulled a hammy last week."

I crossed my arms across my chest and tried to make sense of Johnny's predicament. "Look, even if he's just jobbing, it doesn't change the fact that Johnny is still a fixture on your roster. He has a distinguished pro-wrestling pedigree and is clearly good for your promotion's morale. It's also obvious that only someone associated with XCCW would know about his inheritance, cook up a scheme to hold his snake for ransom, and then actually expect Johnny to pay."

"So what?" said Grasby.

"So this is your house, Grasby," I said forcefully. "Johnny needs your help. You know these people best which means you can probably help me narrow down the list of potential suspects."

Grasby sneered, shaking his head so vehemently his jowls jiggled. "Don't you get it? Mamba bailed on me. The chickenshit sent me a text last night telling me how he can't wrestle until he gets his snake back. A fucking text! Despite everything I've done for him, he's willing to leave me hanging three days before our first ever pay-per-view because he lost a pet. That guy can go fuck himself. He's nothing but a washed up piece of shit anyway. I hope a bald eagle swooped down, grabbed his snake, and tore the fucking thing to shreds."

I drove my forearm into Grasby's throat and shoved him backwards, pinning him against the wall. I plucked the gun out of his waistband with my other hand and tossed it behind me. Grasby flailed around frantically, squashing crunchy paper-mache masks behind him as he pawed at my arm. "You really need to learn some manners," I growled.

"What are you gonna do, Ounstead?" he wheezed. "Give me one of your famous head-butts from hell?"

The *Head-Butt From Hell* was one of my signature pro-wrestling finishing moves. And while it made for entertaining wrestling, in real life I greatly preferred my dukes, which is why I cocked a fist and delivered a modest blow to Grasby's gelatinous gut. He crumpled to the floor, a blob of sweaty flesh and cheap velour.

As I left him lying there incapacitated I found myself wondering where his disdain for Johnny really came from. Was Grasby simply a spiteful bastard who was envious of Johnny's past success and upset over him going MIA after losing his snake? Or was there a deeper reason for his animosity toward my friend? His indifference toward Ginger's disappearance left me with the impression he had nothing to do with it, however, I knew it would be a mistake to overlook his lingering bitterness toward Johnny. One thing was for certain—I needed to know more about Bert Grasby.

I left Grasby gasping for air on the floor of the arts and crafts room and made my way back to the gym. Before leaving the community centre Pocket and Tubbs introduced me to a ditzy blonde wrestler who was able to give me a lead on where I could find Stormy Daze. Apparently no one at XCCW had seen her since earlier that morning. Stormy was also not answering any calls made to her cell, despite the fact she was supposed to be at the community centre with the other XCCW wrestlers prepping for the evening's house show. The ditzy gal didn't have an address for Stormy, but she had the next best thing—her home telephone number and full legal name. I thanked her for her help and headed back to my truck.

I dialed my cousin as I pulled into traffic. He picked up after a few rings. I could barely hear his voice over the clamouring of the happy hour pub crowd.

"How's she cuttin', mate?"

"I got a name here and I need you to run it for me."

"Are you right bollixed? I ain't going near Frank's computer."

"It's important, D. It has to do with Johnny." I had filled Declan in on the details the night before. I heard him take a slurp of what could only be a pint of Guinness.

"I dunno, boyo."

"There's another Glenfiddich coming your way if you help me out."

"Piss off with the Glenfiddich. If I do this, I want me a bottle o'the Balvenie, the twenty-one-year-old Portwood."

Say what you will about my cousin, but the man liked his single malt.

"You're kind of robbing me blind here, don't you think?"

"I'll hang this bloody phone up right now!"

"All right, take it easy. Balvenie it is."

"Aye, that'll do, then. Sorry I got to be such a shite. But after the strip Frank tore off me arse last time, I'm at least going to make it worth me while."

"Fair enough."

A husky intoxicated voice bellowed in the background. "Yo, what's it take to get some service around here?"

"Shut your hole, you mingin' skegrat!" screamed Declan. "I'll be with you in a minute. Okay, Jed, I got me pen."

"Name's Bert Grasby. I'm going to need a full background check. I'm talking public, credit, property—the works."

"Jaysus, would you like me to track down his Ma and find out if he wet his bed as a wee lad as well?"

"Just see what you can dig up."

"What about a criminal records check?"

"We both know who I'm going to have to talk to about that."

Declan grunted in agreement. My pop may have been away at a security conference, but if I wanted detailed criminal records on Grasby I was going to need the old man to call in a favour with his buddies at the Vancouver Police Department. Unlike other types of background screening, all criminal records checks were processed through the Canadian Police Information Centre database that is shared by every city police department and Royal Canadian Mountain Police detachment in the country.

"Okay, mate. I'm on the case."

"Thanks, D."

I heard a rattle and thud, like a phone being dropped, followed by my cousin shouting in the distance. "Hey, Dicky Dazzler!

I'll serve your fancy arse when I'm good and ready!" Ah, Declan. What a prince.

The bloated and endless dark grey storm cloud that had been hovering over Greater Vancouver all day finally stopped its taunting and began to spit down rain. I cranked my wipers up to the max but after a minute the downpour was so heavy it didn't really matter, as my visibility was limited at best. I sought refuge from the torrential assault in the nearby drive thru of a Dairy Queen, and as I ordered a large banana shake it occurred to me that there was a very good chance that I was familiar with just about every franchise location in the city.

I parked and drank my shake slowly, the combination of ice cream and rainfall lulling my mind into a state of tranquility. My mind wandered and soon filled with thoughts of what I had encountered at XCCW. The pro-wrestling lifestyle had once been the most natural thing in the world for me, yet now it felt awkward and foreign. After the misfortune that had befallen me a couple of years ago, just setting foot near a wrestling ring had stirred up some old feelings. And the further I pursued the investigation into Ginger's disappearance, the more exposure I would have to elements of the life I had tried so hard to leave behind.

I was still brooding over my past when the Soundgarden song "Spoonman" started playing in my pocket. I welcomed the distraction and answered my phone immediately.

"Hello?"

"Jed, thank God!" wailed Johnny frantically. "I don't know what to do!"

"Slow down, bub. What are you talking about?"

"The kidnapper, man! He just called me with instructions!"

FIVE

"*Johnny, calm down. Take a deep breath and tell me exactly* what happened."

I heard him suck in a lungful of air and blow it out forcefully. "Okay, I was trying to take my mind off Ginger so I went to the driving range to hit some balls. I was on my second bucket when I got a call from a blocked number. I picked up and it was, like, this robot or Darth Vader voice or something. It told me that if I wanted Ginger I had to bring the money to the Vancouver Flea Market by seven o'clock."

I cranked the wheel and hit the gas, nearly hydroplaning as I skidded out of the Dairy Queen parking lot. I looked at my watch. 6:54 PM. I was a good ten minutes away.

"Where are you?" I asked.

"On Terminal, right by Science World."

"Okay, I need you to pull over immediately."

"Jed, he warned me not to be late—"

"Johnny, you have to trust me. They will not hurt Ginger. If they did, they'd have zero leverage. It's not like she's a child. There's not exactly a black market for stolen pythons so they can't fence her for ten grand somewhere else."

"Okay, Jed. I'm pulling into the train station right now."

I cut off a bus and sped through an intersection. I swerved to avoid hitting a Hummer turning left and sprayed its windshield with puddle water. The driver was less than impressed and blasted his horn for all it was worth.

"Jed? Jed, are you there?"

I straightened out my F-150 and kept my foot on the pedal. "I'm here. Did he say why he was bumping up the deadline?"

"No, man. Just that this was my only chance to get Ginger back otherwise they're going to fucking kill her!"

I glanced at the clock on the dash — 6:57 PM. I was making good time.

"Oh, shit!" Johnny cried. "Jed, it's him. He's calling on the other line."

I had to think fast. "Johnny, what kind of phone do you have?"

"An iPhone, why?"

"Okay, good. Take the call. Then when you're on the other line —"

"Merge the calls!" he shouted, understanding my plan.

I heard a click as Johnny switched to his other line. I thumbed the mute button on my iPhone so the snake-napper wouldn't be able to hear anything on my end once the calls were connected. Five seconds passed. Then another ten. I was starting to get concerned when I heard a click followed by a digitally altered voice that sounded more like a wimpy version of the Batman villain Bane than Darth Vader.

" — the volleyball courts behind the flea market. Throw your phone out the window immediately. We are watching you. If we see the police or anyone else, we kill the snake. Failure to follow these orders and we kill the snake."

I knew Johnny would toss his phone immediately, before I got a chance to tell him I was certain they were bluffing about having him under surveillance. This operation had been strictly amateur from the get-go, and the novelty store quality voice changer had just confirmed it. I hit the button to un-mute the call, hoping to get through in time.

"Johnny? Johnny, you there?"

The line was dead. I pounded my steering wheel in frustration, angry with Johnny for ditching his phone and even more upset with myself for not anticipating such a request. Having Johnny get rid of his phone now was a bush league move, especially since the volleyball courts were only a couple of blocks from the flea market. If this crook had any kidnapping experience or just some common sense he would have picked up surveillance on Johnny in front of his apartment and demanded he lose his phone long before arriving at the destination for the exchange. I calmed myself and focused on the positive, which was that the more inexperienced this person was, the less chance there was of Johnny being in actual danger.

I jerked the wheel to the right, causing my truck to fishtail as it careened around a corner at close to seventy kilometres per hour. The rain was coming down harder now. My driving visibility had become so bad I shouldn't have risked taking my eyes off the road, even momentarily. Instead I opened the glove compartment and dug through several pairs of sunglasses and bottles of bodybuilding supplements until I found what I was looking for — my snub-nosed, thirty-eight-special, Colt Cobra revolver. The lightweight, double-action, six-shot pistol was a restricted firearm that I had a Possession and Acquisition Licence for due to grandfathered privileges from my old man. I popped out the swing cylinder, double-checking that I had left it fully loaded. I spun the cylinder with my thumb, snapped it shut, and looked at the weapon in my hand. It had been a long time since I had fired it. But the training that I received from my old man growing up was the kind that never went away. I didn't know who or what was waiting for Johnny at the volleyball courts so I wasn't about to take any chances.

I tucked the gun in my belt behind me in the small of my back, and then spotted the Georgia viaduct in the distance. I was getting close. I zigzagged across lanes and rocketed across the flyover-like overpass, threading the needle between Rogers Arena and BC Place, the two concrete monstrosities that served as Vancouver's hub for professional sports and big time entertainment.

I flirted with the idea of calling Declan but decided against it. There was still no indication that the snake-napping was anything other than the work of a nonprofessional, and despite his colourful personality, my cousin was not the type of hard ass I wanted to involve unless some serious stuff was going down. Although most people knew Declan as a bartender, few were aware of his time as an IRA operative and that he was just as capable of being as lethal as he was jocular. And drastic circumstances notwithstanding, I generally preferred the less violent version of my cousin.

I glanced at the clock on the dash—7:05 PM. It had been nearly ten minutes since I spoke to Johnny. The elongated and oversized rustic red barn that housed Vancouver Flea Market was now visible and I floored it as I raced down Terminal Avenue. My front tire hit the median and my truck jolted as I took a sharp left turn past the market, then an immediate right, before swerving onto a straightaway. I flipped on my high beams. Fifty metres away, the light reflected off the licence plate of a dilapidated Dodge Omni parked haphazardly next to a gate that served as an entryway to the fenced in volleyball courts. The outdated car chugged as dark grey smoke puffed out of its corroded exhaust pipe. I held my breath as I noticed a prominent bumper sticker on the back of the car. It read: *XCCW WRESTLING—Putting the "X" in X-treme!*

I slammed on the brakes and my truck screeched to a halt next to the Dodge. No other vehicles were in sight. My headlights illuminated the gate, which was wide open, its security chain having been either unlocked or broken. Through the gate, by itself in the sand, was a large burlap sack.

I drew my Colt revolver and exited the vehicle. Cold rain pelted my face as I held my weapon in the Low-Ready position. I cautiously approached the burlap sack and crouched next to it. Whatever was inside was bulky and looked heavy. Grabbing a corner, I yanked the sack upward. There was a dull thud as something large dropped onto the sand.

It was Ginger. The snake was motionless. I tapped it with my foot. Dead. I pulled back the hammer on my Colt, keeping it in the Low-Ready position as I surveyed my surroundings. A lone thunderclap echoed above me in the black sky. I stood there in the sand for several moments, getting drenched by the heavy rain. Aside from the rainfall and the rumbling muffler of the Dodge Omni, it was silent. I pushed wet hair out of my face and started to trudge back through the muddy sand toward my truck. I only made it a few steps before I saw the first drop of blood.

There was more. Much more. I followed the trail of blood to the right, just beyond where the light from my headlights ended. As my eyes adjusted to the darkness, I saw a massive puddle of blood that funnelled away from the Porta-Potty Outhouses. I followed the trickling vital fluid to another pool of blood beneath the middle toilet unit. The door was slightly ajar. I tapped it with my foot, the door's rusted hinges creaking ominously as it slowly swung open. Inside was my old friend Johnny Mamba. He was bathed in his own blood, his throat slashed so deep that his head hung lopsidedly to the left.

SIX

Swirling red and blue lights lit up the volleyball courts,
making the wet sand look like the dance floor of a disco club. Three
Vancouver Police Department squad cars had formed a perimeter
around Johnny's Dodge Omni. The punishing rain had finally let
up just before they arrived. I leaned against the bumper of my
F-150, my jacket draped over my wrists, covering the handcuffs
that had been tightly applied by an overzealous rookie who had
never heard of either my old man or me. Fortunately I had the
foresight to put my thirty-eight back in my truck's glove box before
calling 911, and considering how jumpy the rookie was when he
frisked me, it was definitely a good call. The rookie clipped his
radio back onto his tactical vest and hustled toward me.

"Detective Constable Shepard will be here any minute, Mr.
Ounstead," he said, fumbling with his handcuff keys. "Sorry again
about the confusion but when you were unable to produce an
investigator's licence I had no choice."

"Forget it. You did good, Officer. I'll be sure to mention that
to Shepard."

The rookie puffed out his chest proudly while unlocking my shackles. I knew from my pop that when you first got your badge in the VPD compliments were about as common as spotting a dancing Sasquatch, so despite the inconvenience, I didn't see the harm in making nice. Especially since I planned on hanging around the crime scene for a while.

The rookie struggled to tuck his handcuffs back into the pouch on his police duty belt while I rubbed my wrists and watched two techs from the Forensic Identification Unit trudge across the sand. They joked back and forth as they sidestepped Ginger and prepared to dust the Porta-Potty for prints and snap pictures of Johnny's corpse.

"I'd like to review your statement just one more time, Mr. Ounstead," the rookie said as he flipped through his notepad.

"Sure thing, bub. But I think Detective Shepard would prefer it if you dealt with that news crew over there first." The rookie craned his neck to see his fellow officers heading off a TV News van that was arriving on scene. He cursed loudly before thanking me and hurrying off.

I walked toward the gate to the volleyball courts, passing another patrol cop digging a roll of yellow crime scene tape out of the trunk of his cruiser. He was too preoccupied to notice me as I approached Ginger and crouched next to her. Unlike Johnny's body, there were no immediate clues as to what may have been the cause of death. I leaned back on my haunches and thought things through. How the hell did everything get so screwed up so fast? One minute I'm convinced the whole snake-napping is amateur hour, and the next thing I know both Ginger and Johnny are dead.

There had to be an angle I was missing. Johnny's murder was no panicked kill. He was straight up executed. I pulled out my SureFire flashlight that I had retrieved from my truck's glove compartment when stashing my gun and thumbed the switch. Ginger's scales gleamed under the high-intensity light as I inspected the dead reptile and looked for some indication of how it died. I moved closer to the snake's head, and its black eyes filled with amber tint as the light hit them. I studied Ginger's jaw carefully and noticed what appeared to be bits of silver gleaming between her hook-like teeth. I wiped my hands on my jeans and was about to pry open the snake's mouth for a closer look when a silky voice sliced through the ambient crime scene noise and sent a pleasant tingle down my spine.

"You tampering with my crime scene, Ounstead?"

I caught a whiff of perfume in the air before I turned around. It was the same scent of Burberry fragrance she always wore, except now there was an added hint of citrus. I palmed my flashlight and turned to face Detective Constable Rya Shepard, who stood with her hands on her hips. She was dressed in her usual slim-fitting trousers, however, instead of a matching blouse and blazer, she wore a purple Henley shirt underneath a light leather jacket. I hadn't seen her dressed so casually in a long time. It looked good on her.

"Hello, Rya."

"How do you know the vic?"

"He was a friend."

"And you're here because…?"

I caught Rya up to speed on Johnny's case and the snake-napping. If she was at all amused by the absurdity of a reptile being held for ransom she certainly didn't show it, although I chalked that up to her professional integrity rather than concern over offending me.

"I'm going to need a copy of that ransom note," she said.

"I'm sending it to you right now." I tapped a few buttons on my cell and forwarded the email Johnny had sent me earlier.

"I'm sorry for your loss," Rya said. "We have your statement and I'll update you as best as I can. But right now you need to leave."

"Fair enough," I conceded. "But how about I just make sure you guys don't overlook any evidence before I go?"

"If you're even thinking of dicking around with my crime scene I can always have Constable Adams handcuff you again."

"You could. But I doubt my pop would be very impressed."

"I think Frank would agree that if I of all people tossed your ass in a holding cell then I must have had a pretty damn good reason."

"C'mon, Rya. You know me. I wouldn't waste your time."

She pulled her wavy raven hair back into a ponytail.

"All right, Jed. Make it quick."

I motioned to Ginger and we both squatted next to the deceased snake. I used my flashlight to point out the silver in between the reptile's teeth. Rya snapped on a pair of latex gloves and touched the glinting speck.

"It looks like a piece of foil or something," she said.

"Yeah. And I'm no snake expert, but I'm pretty sure their diet doesn't include Ding Dongs."

"Our tech guys will look into it. If there's something of value here we'll find it."

"Who's going to examine the snake?"

Rya nodded at the Forensic Investigation Unit techs. "The IDENT boys will check it for any evidence."

"Are you going to do an autopsy?"

"On the snake? Christ, I don't know. We might get a vet to look at it depending on what IDENT finds. Right now I'm a little more concerned with your friend's autopsy and following the leads on his death."

"Johnny adored this snake, Rya. The person who took it knew that. It doesn't make sense that they would kill it."

"Maybe it just died. It would explain why they bumped up the time frame for the exchange, since they wouldn't want rigor mortis to set in and then be forced to try and pawn off a stiff snake as a live one in order to get their money."

"I don't know. I can't shake the feeling that whatever caused Ginger to expire could shed some light on all this."

"Duly noted. Is that all?"

"There's one more thing."

I headed toward the chain link fence behind the Porta-Potties. I twisted the switch on my flashlight so the light stayed on and aimed the beam toward the object that had caught my eye while I was waiting for the police to arrive.

"What is that?" Rya asked. I focused the light on the item—a blue racquetball. Rya looked at me quizzically. I motioned for her to take a closer look. As she bent down she saw what I had earlier, a small bloodstain, which contained what looked to be a partial fingerprint. Rya snapped at one of the FIU techs who hurried over and bagged and tagged the racquetball.

"Good eye, Jed. But we would have found it."

"I have no doubt. But my friend is dead and the killer is out there. I want your investigation to be as efficient as possible."

Rya pulled me aside and her piercing green eyes narrowed. "I'm on this, okay? The best thing you can do right now is leave and let me work."

"What about XCCW? I should probably brief you since it's extremely likely that whoever did this was connected to the wrestling business."

"Listen to me. I understand you're upset. But you have to trust me when I say we will conduct the most thorough investigation possible."

"Okay, but—"

"Jed?"

"Yeah?"

"Do you really want to help your friend?"

"Of course."

"Then go. If you do that I give you my word I'll keep you in the loop."

I looked past Rya and saw two men from the Coroner's service arrive and start unloading gear from their van. The finality of Johnny's death suddenly hit me. When you work in professional wrestling, you see a lot of crazy stuff. You learn to expect the unexpected. To believe anything is possible. To never say never.

Except Johnny's death was no scripted storyline. There would be no encore performance. No dramatic surprise return. My friend was gone and he was never coming back.

Rya squeezed my arm, her voice softening. "Go home, Jed."

I left without another word.

SEVEN

Declan poured me my third generous serving of Jameson's Irish whiskey and apologized for it lacking the spiced apple and oaky kick of the eighteen-year-old Glenfiddich we had the night before. I told him I didn't care. It's not like I was drinking for taste.

My cousin had hardly said a word to me since I told him about Johnny. Declan was all too familiar with how to cope with death, and, as a result, he made sure that I had plenty of space at the end of the bar while I did my best to drown my sorrows. He'd appear before me now and then to refill my glass, before returning to serve more tequila shots and Jägerbombs to a raucous group of Vancouver Film School students in the midst of a wrap party. By the time I was on my fourth drink I had succeeded in numbing some of the shock and pain and soon found myself in the mood for some company. Declan appeared as if on cue, topping me up and pouring three fingers worth for himself.

"To your mate," he said, raising his glass. We clinked our glasses.

"He was a good guy, D."

"Aye, he must o'been. Never seen you like this before."

"We were pretty tight back in the day. I can't tell you how many crappy motel rooms we shared while bouncing around North America together from one wrestling gig to another."

"Paid your dues together then, yeah?"

"And then some."

Declan popped several PEZ candies out of Batman's plastic head and we enjoyed them with our whiskey. After a while, I made a decision. "I'm going to find the son-of-a-bitch who killed him."

"You takin' the piss?"

"No."

"Ain't that something best left to the cops?"

"I think I can help. Plus I know I can navigate the pro-wrestling circle a hell of a lot better than they can."

"Aye, I believe that. And you definitely got the chops to dig up some shite. You are Frank's son, after all. It's just that going alone on something like this, well, there's a fair chance it might require a bit more o'the rough and tumble than you see at the nightclubs. Things could get ugly."

"Then it's a good thing I've got you around, isn't it?"

Declan smiled. "Aye, I guess it is."

I nearly spilled my whiskey when a skinny twenty-something kid hopped onto the stool next to me, drumming his fingers on the bar.

"What's up, Jed?" he asked excitedly.

"Not now, Billy," I grumbled.

"What's the matter?"

"Feck off, boyo," said Declan, waving his hand like he was shooing away a fly.

"Feck off?" questioned Billy. "Don't you mean fu—"

"I mean feck off! For shite's sake I'm tryin' to be polite, ya wee guttersnipe."

"Okay, relax," said Billy, throwing up his hands in submission. "I'll get out of your hair as soon as I buy me and Jed a round."

I sighed and shared a tired look with my cousin. Neither one of us were in the mood to deal with Billy's usual enthusiasm.

"What's that you're drinking?" he asked.

"Whiskey."

"Yeesh. How about a Guinness?"

"Not tonight, kid."

Billy Nickens was a med student at the University of British Columbia who happened to live a few blocks north of The Emerald Shillelagh. After joining my gym six months ago, he immediately recognized me from my professional wrestling days and pestered the crap out of me until I agreed to show him some mass building routines. He'd been a familiar face around the pub ever since.

"All right then," said Declan. "Time for you to get your brainy arse back to your table."

"Can you bring me another pint when you get a chance?" Billy asked.

"Aye, piss off already and I will in a few," snapped Declan.

Billy slid off his stool and gave me a pat on the back. "You hitting the gym tomorrow, big guy?"

"I'll let you know."

"Cool."

Billy strolled off toward a nearby table that was stacked with anatomy and physiology textbooks. Declan smirked as he topped up my glass. "I think that lad's got a wee crush on you."

"Just call me McDreamy."

I pounded back my drink and stifled a burp.

"Should I call Connie to come pick you up?" asked Declan.

"No."

"You sure? After the day you've had, seeing that lovely lass might do you some good."

I paused before responding. Declan waited me out. "We broke up," I said finally.

"Jaysus Christ," Declan said, shaking his head disapprovingly. "I liked her, Jed. She was a posh gal. Better than the usual slappers you run around with."

I stared into my empty glass, trying to focus my inebriated vision and stop the ice cubes from moving. "I liked her too."

"What happened?"

"Another time," I said, tapping my glass for a refill.

Declan obliged and poured more Jameson's. More celebratory film students entered the pub and Declan ambled off to tend bar. I nursed my booze, my mind swirling with a medley of thoughts. Johnny's murder. My failed relationship with Connie. Even skinny Billy Nickens and the way he looked up to me. I looked across the bar and saw my sallow reflection staring back at me. It took all the restraint I could muster to keep from throwing my old-fashioned tumbler glass into the mirror.

EIGHT

My hair was as it is now — a bit shaggy but still a far cry *from the lion's mane I sported back in the day. My torso was tanned and toned and shined under the spotlights, magically lacking the spare tire my abdominals had been burdened with over the last few years. Adrenaline coursed through my veins as the ravenous crowd roared all around me, yet somehow everything outside the wrestling ring was shrouded in darkness.*

I crouched in a staggered wrestling stance in the middle of the ring, shifting my weight back and forth on the balls of my feet, anxiously awaiting my opponent to emerge from the shadows. Cloaked in a robe, my challenger slipped through the ropes. He untied the knot in his belt and revealed himself.

It was Johnny.

He was sickly pale and covered in blood that was flowing freely from the gash in his throat. He reached out to me, desperate for help, but before I could take a step toward him I was attacked from behind. My unseen adversary tied me up with a monstrous bear hug. I looked down, seeing my attacker's thick sweaty arms as they squeezed me with tremendous force. I fought to break free with all of my might, but the more I struggled, the tighter the hold became. Soon I was completely immobile.

Johnny tried to speak but his voice was drowned out by another sound.

A horrible sound.

Hissing.

Panic surged through my chest like a jolt from a defibrillator as hundreds of snakes began slithering out of the dark and into the wrestling ring. Cobras, mambas, and pythons of all shapes and sizes glided across the mat, baring their fangs and flicking their forked tongues. I watched in horror as the snakes slithered upward around Johnny until he was no more — just a lump beneath an endless amount of slimy scales. The crowd's cheering turned frenzied as the snakes made their way toward me. Desperate to escape, I thrust my head downwards toward my assailant's massive arms, strained my neck, and tried to bite his wrists. My heart seized in my chest when the huge arms began to morph into a familiar yellowish-brown python. I collapsed to the mat as Ginger constricted around my entire body, squeezing every last bit of air out of my lungs.

I awoke gasping for air. It took a few moments for the disorientation to wear off before I recognized the familiar surroundings of my bedroom. I slipped on a pair of gym shorts and went to the bathroom to wash my face. After dabbing my brow with a musty towel and swearing to do laundry the next day, I went to the kitchen and grabbed a can of Moody Ales Affable IPA out of the fridge. I took the beer over to the La-Z-Boy recliner in my living room and eased myself into the chair. I touched a finger to my neck. My pulse was racing. I took a pull of the beer and tried to forget the hissing sounds that lingered in my head.

I surveyed my home's decor in the darkness, trying to preoccupy myself with potential ideas for unnecessary furnishings. Eventually I accepted the futility of trying to distract myself from the nightmare. Johnny was dead. And I had no idea who killed him or why. The only thing I knew for certain was that there must have been a catalyst that caused the killer to bump up his deadline for the exchange. Otherwise why give Johnny seventy-two hours to check his email and arrange his funds only to demand the ransom sooner and without warning? It didn't make sense.

I went to my den, turned on my iMac, and started surfing the web. After checking the box score for the Canucks game I punched in the address for xccw's website. I scrolled aimlessly through the bios of the current roster hoping that someone or something would jump out at me. Eventually I came across the bio for Johnny's ex-girlfriend, Stormy Daze. She was a striking woman and from what I read she appeared to be a seasoned performer as well, having previously wrestled in Japan and several prominent promotions based in Nashville and Florida. I wondered why Johnny hadn't mentioned her to me when we met.

I closed the web browser and the xccw homepage disappeared. But it wasn't enough. I was angry for allowing myself to get dragged back into the unsavoury world of professional wrestling. Deep down I knew I was only kidding myself by thinking that I could somehow escape my past by avoiding anything wrestling-related. The truth was I couldn't even admire the ocean view from the window of my downtown Coal Harbour townhouse without reminding myself that it was the money I made in professional wrestling that had allowed me to buy the place.

Desperate for a distraction, I left my den and started sifting through my Blu-Ray collection until I came across *The Dark Knight*. I put on the movie and knocked back a few more IPAs, enjoying the hoppy brew while I lost myself in the glorious madness of the Joker's anarchy. I knew exactly why I had selected the movie, too. Declan and his damn Batman PEZ dispenser.

NINE

The next afternoon the sun finally punched through the
overcast sky that had been lingering above the city for nearly a
week. I rolled to a stop at the intersection of Hastings Street and
Windemere, and found my truck cast in the towering shadow
of Playland Amusement Park's archaic wooden roller coaster.
The out of commission rickety green and yellow cars were still
slick from the last rainfall, shimmering in the sunlight as they
sat perched on an incline of the track, patiently waiting to start
their slow mechanized climb to the top.

By the time I reached Mondeo Heights, a low-rise condo-
minium building a couple of blocks up the hill on a trendy strip
that bordered Vancouver and North Burnaby, I could still see
the top of the venerable coaster winking at me in the distance.

I parked on the street and made my way down the walk
toward Stormy Daze's residence. I sucked back on the last of my
banana milkshake, making a deep and prolonged slurping sound
that I followed up with some lip smacking and a burp.

"Let me guess. Banana, right?"

I spun around to see that Detective Constable Rya Shepard had sidled right up to me without me even noticing. "Well it sure as hell isn't vanilla," I replied.

"What did I tell you about staying away from my case?"

I crumpled the cup in my hand. "I don't know what you're talking about," I lied, before tossing the cup into a garbage can.

I had found Stormy Daze aka Stephanie Danielson's address by using the home phone number the ditzy blonde at XCCW had given me and doing a quick reverse look up online. I also didn't feel the need to volunteer that information.

"Get out of here, Jed," she scolded.

"Can't."

"Why not?"

"Got an appointment."

"What kind of appointment?"

"Guitar lessons."

"Where's your guitar?"

"I, uh, use my instructor's."

"How convenient."

"Well, I just started. But apparently I'm a natural."

"You are so completely full of shit."

"My goal is to learn to play 'Sweet Child O'Mine'. Is that still your favourite song?"

Rya stared at me. I couldn't tell if she was flattered that I still remembered or was about to clock me in the jaw. "Listen to me," she snapped. "You leave Ms. Danielson alone. She's been through enough already and the last thing she needs is to be grilled by an amateur."

"Don't you think my roguish charm makes up for my lack of credentials?"

"Roguish charm?"

"Yeah, you know. Like Han Solo?"

"Try Chewbacca."

"Did you just compare me to a Wookiee?"

"Yes."

"In my defense, I don't gargle with mouthwash anymore. I've also recently taken up manscaping." A sly grin escaped from beneath Rya's professional façade. I matched it with one of my own.

"Can you at least tell me if she had an alibi for last night?" I asked.

"You think I'm going to discuss an ongoing investigation with you? Come on, Jed. Frank taught you better than that."

"He also taught me that sometimes you have to toss the by-the-book bullshit and trust your gut. I can help you, Rya. I have an understanding of the pro-wrestling world that you can't match. And we both know Johnny's killer is connected to XCCW."

Rya crossed her arms and considered my words. "I'll tell you one thing."

"What?"

"There's a lot more at play here than just some ransom exchange gone wrong."

That threw me for a loop. Then I remembered my case of mistaken identity with a certain gun-toting creep the day before. "You're liking Grasby for this, aren't you? What exactly is it that he's into?"

"I'm surprised you haven't figured that out for yourself."

I wanted to tell her I was working on it but decided against it. "What about the racquetball?" I asked. "Did you get a hit on the print?"

"This isn't CSI, Jed. We haven't even run it yet."

"Can you at least tell me when you're doing Johnny's autopsy?"

"I'm done sharing," she said sternly. "Are you going to leave Ms. Danielson alone or do we need to take a trip downtown?"

"Fine," I muttered begrudgingly, and headed back toward my truck.

"Jed, wait."

"Yeah?" I said, turning around quickly.

She stared at me for a few seconds, and then ran her fingers underneath the trickling water of a two-tier fountain near the building's entrance. "The autopsy is scheduled for first thing

Monday morning, but things have been slow and the ME owes me a favour. He promised he'd try and bump it up."

I nodded, then slid behind the wheel and drove off without looking back. Half-an-hour later I was inside Stormy Daze's apartment and learned something about Johnny's ex-girlfriend that even he didn't know.

TEN

After ditching my truck in the crowded parking lot of a nearby McDonald's, I doubled back on foot and ducked into a café. I asked the barista if they had any milkshakes, but instead had to settle for some kind of banana infused macchiato. It tasted like crap.

I took a seat by the window and waited. Twenty minutes later I watched Rya exit the Mondeo Heights building and drive off in her unmarked sedan. I crossed the street. I knew Stormy must be home due to the amount of time Rya spent inside the building but didn't want to give her the chance to pretend to be out or not buzz me in. As a result, I faked a phone call and loitered around the building's entrance until I saw an elderly lady with a Bichon approaching the door from the inside. I timed my walk and slipped past her into the building. The elderly lady barely glanced at me before fumbling with her plastic poop bag and getting ready for her dog to do its business. A short elevator ride later and I was at Stormy Daze's door. I knocked loudly. I could hear a rustling behind the door but no one was answering. I knocked again.

"Just a minute, goddamn it," a throaty voice said.

A few seconds later Stormy Daze appeared before me, looking a little worse for wear. She was a tall woman, nearly six-feet, but our closeness in height only gave me a better view of her red-rimmed, crystal blue eyes and puffy nose. She wore tight, ripped jeans and a halter top with a plunging neckline that showcased ample cleavage. Her wavy, chemically treated hair was pulled back in a scrunchie and rife with split ends. But despite her unpolished appearance, Stormy Daze was an attractive woman who was clearly in great physical shape. She was not nearly as impressed with me.

"Jed Ounstead. Some fucking detective you turned out to be. You should have stuck with wrestling. At least you were good at that."

"I'm sorry. I had no idea things would escalate the way they did."

"I told him to hire a professional, you know. A real PI. But Johnny swore you were up to the job. He really believed you were going to get Ginger back."

"I, uh—I did my best," I stammered.

"Your best? Losers are always whining about their best. Winners go home and fuck the prom queen. The way I see it, you're either a shitty private dick or you thought Ginger's kidnapping was a joke, just like the cops."

"Look, Stephanie—"

"It's Stormy. Stormy Daze."

I sighed. Wrestlers and their ring names. "I can see that you're in pain. But don't think for a second that I didn't take Johnny's case seriously. We may have lost touch there for a while but Johnny was still my friend. And I know you don't know me, but that's not exactly a term I just throw around, because I sure as hell don't have a lot of them."

That seemed to take some of her edge off. She invited me in, and I took a seat on a scarlet couch inside the red themed one bedroom suite. Candles were lit on the mantle above a burning gas fireplace and smooth jazz played on a music station on the TV. If it were any cozier in her apartment I'm pretty sure I would have taken a nap. Stormy made her way to a makeshift wet bar she had set up on her unit's granite countertop.

"Drink?"

"Sure."

"All I got is scotch."

"That'll work."

"Rocks?"

"However you take it is fine."

She scooped ice into a couple of glasses and poured three fingers worth of Johnnie Walker Black Label into both. So let's see—so far I had determined that Stormy Daze was a busty, cantankerous, scotch-swilling babe who was chock full of moxie. It was a good thing Declan wasn't with me otherwise I'm pretty sure he would have proposed.

"To Johnny," she toasted, clinking her glass against mine before flopping onto the couch next to me. I nodded and raised my glass. We both took long sips. "So what now?" she asked. "You go all Joe Friday on me or something?"

"Not quite." I took another hit of scotch and decided upon a different approach. "Did Johnny ever tell you about the Indian strap match we had in Baton Rouge?"

"Nope."

"This is years ago, back when we had both just signed with the WWE. We were just a couple of naïve kids at the time, eager to pay our dues while dreaming of superstardom. Anyway, after a failed stint as a tag-team, we were told to work the cold-open dark-matches at every show. We hadn't even been on TV yet because the creative team was still trying to come up with gimmicks and story angles for us. In the meantime, our job was simple. Warm up the crowd. Just give them a solid, no frills match while they're still filing in, buying their hot dogs and beers and finding their seats.

"So Johnny and I had been doing this for about a month. One night we find ourselves at a house show in the heart of Louisiana. We're a couple minutes into our match when we notice that this particular crowd, for whatever reason, is all jacked up. I mean, they're popping for us like we're on the upper card or something. I'm just enjoying the attention, but Johnny, he sees an opportunity. Next thing I know he darts underneath the apron, jumps back in the ring, and ties a leather strap to both of our wrists.

"The ring announcer looks at us like we're nuts. Johnny yells at the guy to ring the bell, he does, and all of a sudden our simple little warm-up act has turned into a weapons-based stipulation match. Johnny springs into action and starts lashing my back with the slack from the leather strap. I don't even get the chance to lock him up in the middle of the ring and ask him what the hell he's doing. The guy's literally whipping my ass like a rented mule. So I do the only thing I can think of. I do what I've been trained to do. I quit worrying about the consequences for going off script and throw myself into the match completely. I start selling the pain and hamming it up. Now that I'm on board, Johnny gives me an opening. I take it, gain control of the leather strap, and start dishing out the punishment on him with a vengeance.

"It was a hell of a reversal and the crowd ate it up. So we did it again. And again. Suddenly the entire crowd was on their feet going absolutely nuts for a couple of no-name punks in a dark-match, because they knew we were giving it our all."

I paused to wet my whistle with some more Johnnie Walker. Stormy was enthralled, leaning forward on the edge of her seat. "Go on," she said.

"We're totally in the zone at this point. I mean, Johnny and I always had great in-ring chemistry, but this was just one of those nights when you're completely in sync with your partner. I'm talking every cue, every bump, every move — it was like we were reading each other's minds.

"By now we've already gone a good few minutes over our allotted time, but we didn't care. Still, we knew we had given the crowd a hell of a match and that it was the perfect time for our finish, which called for me to put Johnny over. So he climbs up to the top rope for a high spot when all of a sudden he slips. He tumbles outside the ring, and the goddamn leather strap, it gets tied up on the turnbuckle. I get yanked forward in the ring, but as Johnny falls the strap snaps back his arm and dislocates his shoulder. Of course, I start scrambling to undo the strap, ready to break kayfabe because my friend's arm is dangling out of its socket like a wet noodle."

I killed the rest of my drink. Stormy retrieved the bottle of Johnnie Walker and refilled my glass. Maybe she sensed that the next part of the story was harder for me to tell. "I try and yell for help. But Johnny, God bless him, he stops me. The son-of-a-bitch wants to finish the match." Stormy chuckled softly, her blue eyes sparkling as they filled with tears. Something told me she was more than familiar with Johnny's fierce passion for his craft.

"The crowd's still buzzing but doesn't realize what's happened. Mindful of his shoulder, I toss Johnny back in the ring, turn on the flair, and deliver a few stylish finishers before pinning him for the win. The crowd erupts. I sell the victory, basking in the glory while the ref helps Johnny out of the ring. I finish my celebration and hustle backstage, where I'm shocked to find that instead of getting our asses chewed out, Johnny and I are congratulated for showing initiative and putting on such a great match.

"You see, that impromptu Indian strap match — it changed everything. It put Johnny and me on the map. The creative team threw their full support behind the both of us. The difference was that while I was fast-tracked as a babyface, Johnny's shoulder put him out of commission for months. By the time he was healthy enough to return, the creative team had all but forgotten about him while I was making my first run at the Intercontinental Championship. I went on to bigger and better things within the company, while Johnny kicked around as a jobber for a year before eventually being sent back to the developmental territories." I slurped an ice cube out of my glass and crunched it between my teeth. I looked deep into Stormy's eyes.

"The reason I'm telling you this is because even though he ended up getting the shaft, even though he had every reason to be bitter and jealous, not once did Johnny ever express anything other than genuine happiness for the fame and fortune that came my way. Johnny watched me have the career he could have had, the one he should have had, yet he was as proud of my success as he would have been if it were his own.

"That's the kind of guy Johnny Mamba was. That's the kind of guy that was taken from this world when he was murdered. And that's why when I find the person or persons responsible for his death, I'm not just going to have them arrested. I'm going to make them pay. I'm going to make them suffer. I'm going to punish them so badly they will rue the day they thought they could kill my friend and get away with it."

A wailing saxophone gently faded away as the jazz song on the television ended. The room was suddenly silent, save for the sound of the ice cubes in Stormy's drink clinking loudly against glass. Her hand was shaking. Stormy broke eye contact and cleared her throat. She downed the rest of her scotch, dribbling a little on her chin. Either my words had touched a nerve or Stormy Daze had suddenly developed a case of the jitters.

"I, uh, had no idea you and Johnny had that kind of a bond. He never really talked much about his time in the WWE."

"It was a long time ago."

She topped up her drink and took a quick swig before fumbling with the cap as she screwed it back onto the bottle. This gal was rattled, all right. Now I just had to find out why.

"To be perfectly honest with you Stormy, I'm not really sure what to do next," I said, lying between my teeth. I sighed dramatically and did my best to channel my inner Columbo.

"As much as I'd love to get my hands on the bastard who killed Johnny, I don't really know how to go about it. I mean, I have a couple of questions I'd like to ask you about XCCW, but that's about it. It's not like I'm a seasoned investigator."

"Are you working with the cops?" she asked.

"No. They don't exactly take me seriously."

Stormy was quiet for a moment. I glanced at her hand. Not as twitchy. "Fuck 'em," she said.

"I guess."

"I mean it. All that matters is that you're trying to honour your friend."

"What was it you said before? Losers do their best but winners nail the prom queen?"

"That's just a line from some Nicolas Cage movie. Plus, I was being a bitch. If Johnny knew what you were trying to do he would be grateful."

"You think?"

"Definitely."

I gave her a sheepish grin and raised my glass. "I'll drink to that."

She smiled softly and we slurped our scotch in unison. Nothing like coaching a chump through a bout of insecurity to ease one's own nerves. That Peter Falk sure knew his stuff. Now that I had established a sense of comfort between us I decided to do a little probing.

"You know, Johnny never mentioned you when we met," I said. "But I can tell that the two of you must have been a great couple."

"We were," she replied quickly.

"How long were you guys together?"

"A year and a half."

"I'm so sorry you had to lose him this way."

"If I had known how much I would miss him, I don't think I would have ended things between us."

"I thought you two were still an item," I said, even though I knew differently. "That was the impression I got from the people at xccw, anyway."

"No, we broke up a few weeks ago."

"Must be tough." Her eyes glazed over as she became lost in her thoughts. "Stormy?"

"Yeah?"

"I said that must be tough. Breaking up like that so soon before his death."

"Yeah, well, we didn't really have a choice. Our lives were headed in different directions."

"Tell me about it. My girlfriend and I recently called it quits for the same reason."

"Really?" she purred, before sliding a little closer to me on the couch.

Yikes. I did not see that coming. I had to douse the spark quickly, as I could already see a twinkle forming in her eye. "Yeah. But I'm in the same boat as you, you know? Not ready to move on yet. That's why I still have a lot of her things kicking around my pad, like you do with Johnny's stuff here."

A befuddled expression crept across her face. "What are you talking about? What stuff?"

"Little things. Like those fantasy novels on your shelf over there. Johnny used to read them all the time on the road. And I see you still have his toothbrush by the sink."

I motioned toward the open door to the bathroom behind her. Stormy looked over her shoulder at the matching pink and blue Oral-B brushes side by side on the counter.

"Oh, yeah. I guess I do."

She was lying. Johnny may have loved his fantasy novels but he needed a toothbrush about as much as Declan did a tutorial on pouring a pint. Johnny had worn a set of false teeth since before I knew him. He had knocked out most of his original teeth at seventeen when he attempted a flying elbow drop off of the roof of his parents' house during a backyard-wrestling match.

"Would you excuse me for a moment?" she asked.

"Of course."

Stormy slipped into the bathroom and I heard the click as she locked the door behind her. Maybe she was in there covering up more evidence of her new boy toy's sleepovers. I didn't really care, especially since an interesting opportunity had just presented itself.

I quietly placed my drink on the coffee table and grabbed the Android mobile phone that Stormy had left sitting on the arm of her sofa. I tapped the screen. No password lock. I quickly selected SMS messaging and perused her recent texts. There wasn't much aside from a couple of condolences over Johnny's death and several nasty messages from Bert Grasby threatening repercussions if her grief caused her to miss the upcoming pay-per-view. I switched over to the call log and scrolled down until I came across three missed calls from earlier that morning, all made between 11 AM and 11:15 AM. But it wasn't the number of missed calls that caught my eye. It was the name of the caller that had been previously entered into the phone — Melvin Van Lowe. Melvin was one of my old man's chief business rivals. Except he didn't provide competition in the pub business. Melvin Van Lowe was a private investigator.

I heard a flush and had the phone back on the sofa arm before the toilet had finished gurgling. By the time Stormy took her seat again my nose was touching an ice cube as I drained my glass of the last of its scotch whisky goodness.

"Sorry," she said as she honked into a tissue and dabbed phantom tears from her eyes. "I'm a bit tipsy."

"That's the beauty of a good scotch."

Stormy chuckled and leaned forward, showcasing tremendous cleavage. I couldn't help but notice and was certain her top had covered more of her chest before she entered the bathroom. "I've never lost anyone close before," she said softly. "It kind of hits you in waves, you know?"

"I know," I replied earnestly. We sipped scotch in silence. After a while, I spoke. "Do you mind if I ask you just a few more questions?"

She nodded and I quickly launched into a series of standard investigative queries. According to Stormy she had been at a spin class at the time of Johnny's murder. Suspect or not, I knew that confirming Stormy's alibi would be at the top of Rya's to-do list so I moved on. Interestingly, when I brought up Bert Grasby's name Stormy immediately dismissed him as a potential suspect. She claimed that although her boss was definitely a shady bastard, he was a big enough mover and shaker that trying to hustle Johnny out of ten grand would simply not be worth his while. With none of my other questions generating anything other than the expected responses, I thanked Stormy for her time and showed myself to the door.

"Will you keep me posted on what you find out?" she asked.

"Sure."

"Thank you."

Stormy leaned in to hug me. I patted her softly on the back with one hand while my other reached for the doorknob. She stopped short as she pulled out of the embrace, bringing her face inches from mine. Her lips were glossy and glistened with a hue of purple, while the scent of lilacs wafted up and into my nostrils. I realized that the lowering of her halter top wasn't the only glamour adjustment that had been made while she was in the bathroom. Stormy pursed her lips and began to cock her head, leaning forward ever so slightly.

"Stormy," I said softly.

"Yes," she cooed.

"You're no prom queen."

She gawked at me, momentarily confused. By the time she processed my comment I was halfway down the hall. The door slammed loudly behind me.

ELEVEN

Crisp autumn air bit at my cheeks as I made my way down a street that ran between historic Gastown and the drug-addled Downtown Eastside. The trees lining the sidewalk were bleeding fiery reds and deep pumpkin oranges, and the street gutters were littered with an endless amount of plum and maple leaves. The fall foliage blended nicely with the bright orange, square building on the corner of Main and Powell, which not only housed one of Vancouver's premier gentlemen's clubs but also happened to be only a few blocks from The Emerald Shillelagh. I walked past the No. 5 Orange strip club and peered through the large front window of the smaller building next door.

As far as Vancouver private investigators go, Melvin Van Lowe was definitely the ying to my old man's yang. Whereas my pop was a retired VPD detective with a small office above a quaint Irish pub, Van Lowe was a disbarred former criminal defense attorney who operated out of a sizable studio adjacent to striptease central. Van Lowe had taken over the workspace from a gothic punk art gallery that had gone under a few years back. Since he never bothered to paint over the murals of bosomy vampires wielding broadswords, and because he had a rep as a sleazy PI who specialized in even sleazier cases, it was safe to say the majority of Melvin's clientele were the type of sketchy characters my father had no interest in working for anyway.

Melvin's entire office was illuminated by a neon glow emanating from cheap stick-on stars that were scattered across the walls above the bloodthirsty woman warriors. The lights were off and *Van Lowe 'Vestigations* (seriously, that's the actual name of his agency) had closed up shop for the night. Of course, anyone familiar with Melvin could tell you that if he wasn't in his office he could be found nearby racking up the lap dances.

I had worked the door at the No. 5 Orange in the past, so I wasn't surprised when I recognized the pair of bodybuilder bouncers who were safeguarding the front entrance. After catching up quickly and sharing a few laughs the guys wished me well and let me slip inside without having to pay the cover.

My vision darkened as my eyes adjusted to the minimal lighting. Pulsing techno music cross-faded with sirens wailing as a busty stripper in a latex firefighter costume climbed down a ladder from the ceiling and onto a catwalk. It only took me a moment to spot Van Lowe's distinctive weasel-face in "gyno row," the seats located directly in front of the main stage.

"Evening, Melvin," I said as I pulled up a stool next to him. "You celebrating the closing of a big case or just the fact you're all alone on yet another Friday night?"

"Alone my ass," he snapped. "I just haven't decided which one of these sluts I'm taking home with me yet." Having overheard Melvin, the busty firefighter sneered at us as she wrapped a leg around a pole. Seeing her reaction, Melvin whipped a thick wad of bills out of his pocket. "Like you wouldn't let me lay some pipe for all this, Sugar." Melvin snort-laughed while I avoided the stripper's scornful glare. The music switched to Foreigner's "Hot Blooded" and the stripper turned her back and started peeling.

"I don't think you're getting any private dances from her," I said.

"What are you doing here, Ounstead? Shouldn't you be working the door with the other beef monkeys?"

"Not tonight. I'm on a case."

"Wow, old Frank's giving you your very own assignments now? What do you get if you do a good job? An ice cream?" Melvin snickered, his long nose scrunching up into a snout, which made him look even more weasel-like. Even worse, his snide remark started to give me a hankering for a banana milkshake.

"Why did you call Stormy Daze this morning?" I asked.

Melvin flinched, his long, ladylike eyelashes fluttering. "I don't know what you're talking about," he spat.

"Bullshit."

"Look, give me a break, will you? Do you know where I've been for the last eight hours? Hiding in the goddamn bushes with a telephoto lens waiting for some chubby-chasing prick to show up and pork the fattest, horniest housewife I've ever seen. It was fucking disgusting. My knees ache, my skin itches, and I can't get the image of that sea donkey's O-face out of mind. All I want to do is get drunk and see some snatch, so how about you fuck off already and let me enjoy my night."

Melvin slurped his Jack and Coke. I leaned in close.

"You're going to tell me what I want to know," I said firmly.

"I can't tell you what I don't know. And even if I did know something, haven't you ever heard of a little thing called investigator–client confidentiality?"

"Melvin, you'd rat out your own mama for fifty bucks if you had the chance. You called Stormy Daze three times this morning. I want to know why. Is she a client?"

"Blow me, Ounstead."

I gritted my teeth. I had had enough. Between Grasby's attitude and Stormy's lies I was fresh out of patience. My friend was dead and I wanted some answers. I grabbed Melvin's cheap necktie and yanked.

Wham!

His face rebounded off the stage-side ledge like a bouncy ball. The busty firefighter, now topless, momentarily halted her routine and stared.

"Just teaching him some manners," I said.

The stripper beamed and resumed her act with a renewed vigour. Melvin whimpered and clutched his nose. "What the—you fucking fuck!"

"Start talking."

"My nose!" Melvin checked his hands and saw blood. "I'm bleeding!" he squealed. Melvin looked around the strip club for help. Nobody seemed to care. Most probably didn't even see me do it.

"I'm losing patience, Melvin."

"I'm losing blood, asshole!"

Wham!

I jerked on Melvin's tie again, this time causing his forehead to hit the ledge. He howled like a werewolf that had just been shot in the nards with a silver bullet. Taking notice of the commotion, one of the bouncers I knew from the door approached. I put up my hand, indicating I had things under control. Seeing that the guy I was roughing up was Melvin, the bouncer smirked and nodded his approval. Something told me Melvin wasn't exactly considered a high-value customer.

Melvin machine-gun rubbed his forehead and glared at me with wounded eyes. "Are you fucking crazy? You can't do this to me. I'm—I'm gonna tell your Dad!"

I slid the knot of his tie upward, constricting his throat. Then I slowly wrapped the extra necktie slack around my hand. "I can do this all night," I said calmly.

"Okay, okay!" he pleaded. "Just quit with the roid rage for fuck's sake."

"Let's hear it," I said, loosening my grip.

Melvin took a hit of Jack and Coke and composed himself. "All right, so, this Stormy chick, she called me up a few weeks ago and hired me for a surveillance job."

"You got her case file next door?"

"Of course."

"Take me to it."

"You don't need the actual file, dumbass. It's right here," he said, tapping his index finger on the side of his temple.

"I want to see the file, Melvin."

Melvin sighed and threw his hands up in the air in defeat. "Okay, fine, we'll go to the office. But can we at least wait until she finishes her dance?" Melvin motioned toward the busty firefighter, who was now buck-naked on stage and grinding against an inflatable fire axe.

"No." I palmed the back of Melvin's pencil-thin neck and pulled him to his feet.

"Come on, man!" he begged. "She puts fire-retardant pasties on her nipples then lights her tits on fire. It's fucking awesome."

I glanced at the stripper, then back at Melvin. "Flaming nipples, eh?" Melvin's face broke into a huge shit-eating grin. We stayed for the rest of the dance. It was the best decision I had made all day.

TWELVE

Melvin retrieved a large manila folder out of a filing cabinet and tossed it onto my lap. "That's why I called Stormy Daze this morning," he said, before stuffing more tissue up his nose to stop the bleeding.

Inside the file were two-dozen eight-by-ten black and white photographs of Johnny Mamba. The first few pictures documented him dining with a cute, willowy, red-haired woman on an outdoor restaurant patio. As I kept thumbing through the photographs, a more detailed story emerged: Johnny and the woman walking to a SUV, kissing in the parking lot, driving away in what I assumed to be the woman's Acura MDX. I stopped flipping through the pictures when I got to the last batch that included grainy, long-distance snapshots of Johnny and the red-haired woman in bed together.

"Check out the pic second to last," crowed Melvin. "Total full frontal, man. Look at that bush. It's like a fucking fur trapper's hat."

A big smile spread across Melvin's weaselly face, causing the tufts of tissue to protrude from his nostrils like tiny tusks. I sighed and flipped quickly past the aforementioned photo. Spending this much time with Melvin made me feel like I was in a *Porky's* movie.

"How long ago did you take these photos?" I asked.

"A few weeks."

"And when did she hire you?"

"Couple days before that."

I nodded slowly. The timing fit exactly with Stormy and Johnny's break up. "Did Stormy say why she wanted you to follow Johnny?"

"She had a feeling he was out parking the pink Cadillac around town."

"Say again?"

"You know, leading the llama to the lift shaft."

"What?"

"Visiting the stench trench? Slipping it in the pink velvet sausage wallet? Pounding some poontang?"

"Jesus Christ, Melvin. Can't you just say he was screwing around?"

"Where's the fun in that?"

I sighed and closed the folder. "Why did Stormy come to you in the first place?" I asked.

Melvin interlaced his fingers and slid them behind his head. "I assume she heard that I happen to specialize in these types of domestic scenarios," he said proudly.

"You know, with the way you get off on this sleazy shit, I think Stormy should have charged you."

"Whatever, Ounstead. Like you even know the first thing about surveillance. Maybe if you actually had an investigator's licence I'd consider your point of view. Until then I need your opinion like I need a diamond-studded dildo up my ass."

I opened the folder and flipped through the photos again. There was something about them that was bothering me. Somehow Johnny looked different in the pictures, and I couldn't quite put my finger on it.

"So you think Stormy murdered Johnny and that these pictures are the reason why?" I asked.

"Duh!" snapped Melvin. "What the fuck did you think she was gonna do with them? Post them on Facebook?"

I didn't like it one bit, but Melvin was right. These snapshots rocketed Stormy to the top of the motive list. And when you factored in her behaviour at her apartment and the lying, Stormy was quickly emerging as the prime suspect in Johnny's murder.

"How did Stormy react when she saw the pictures?"

"Bitch was ice cold, man. Didn't say a word. She just paid me on the spot and left."

"How'd she pay?"

"Cash."

I looked at the pictures again and then I saw it—the intangible element that I couldn't put my finger on before. In every photo with the waifish redhead Johnny was either smiling or laughing. That's why he looked so different. He was happy. The last time I had seen him like that was in Baton Rouge after our match had stolen the show.

"Have you spoken to her since then?" I asked.

"Nope. But after hearing about her boyfriend getting whacked, I tried like hell to get a hold of her."

"How did you find out about that so fast, by the way?"

"None of your fucking business. Just because I gave you that file doesn't mean I'm going to give up all of my connections."

I let it go but kept pressing Melvin. "Why did you call Stormy when you found out?"

"Cuz I wanted her to keep my name out of the inevitable shitstorm that's coming her way," he said matter-of-factly.

"So you were just worried about covering your own ass."

"You're goddamn right I was. You think I want the cops to have another reason to harass the shit out of me?"

Melvin had a point. With his criminal defense lawyer background and unscrupulous reputation as an investigator, he was as about as popular with the cops as an ex-con who calls 911 at two in the morning because McDonald's has run out of Chicken McNuggets.

I held up one of the pictures. "You see this guy here, Melvin? He was my friend."

"Look, I'm sorry," he said earnestly. "But what my clients do with the information I provide after they leave my office is out of my hands. I'm not some goddamn cowboy like your old man and I don't make a habit of getting mixed up in my clients' business. I'm just a regular Joe providing a simple service. That's it, that's all."

"What about the redhead?" I asked.

"What about her?"

"You get a name?"

"Nope. But I got a couple of clear pictures of the plates on her Acura so she should be easy enough for you to track down."

"I'm taking this with me," I announced as I stood up and slipped the folder under my arm.

"Fine," aquiesced Melvin. "But if you talk to the cops, just leave my name out of it, okay?"

"I can't make any promises."

"What the fuck, man? I gave you what you wanted."

I walked past a mural of a scantily clad lady astronaut hoisting a Gatling gun while standing in a crater on the moon. I shook my head, opened the door to leave the office, and answered Melvin without looking back.

"Melvin, if I got exactly what I wanted, that stripper would have lit your hair on fire instead of her nipples."

THIRTEEN

After my encounter with Melvin I headed over to Tonix night-club to work my scheduled shift. Tonix was located in the pedestrian-friendly entertainment district of Granville Street, nestled in between several other popular clubs and social spots. As per my routine, I left my truck at The Emerald Shillelagh and walked several blocks southwest until I was weaving my way through a lively crowd filled with the usual yuppies, hipsters, busking guitarists, and street vendors. Numerous oversized neon signs bathed the stretch of street in front Tonix in a rainbow of psychedelic light, and the chilly air was thick with the smell of roasted nuts and alcohol. By the time I reached the club I had counted four homeless people camped out in the cold but only stopped to give a handful of loonies to a frail bearded man who was sitting cross-legged next to his equally malnourished dog.

The door was quiet for a Friday, and the only trouble I had was with some dumbass kid who tried to pass himself off as a VFD in order to receive the "firefighters courtesy" so he could bypass the lineup. The kid lipped me off and peacocked for the crowd after I tossed him, but all it took was a quick one-handed shove to his sternum to send him stumbling backwards and on his way without another word.

Since it ended up being a slow night I was able to cut out early. I was jonesing for a banana milkshake something fierce, but the closest Dairy Queen was in a food fair in the Pacific Centre shopping mall, which had been closed for hours. I settled for some banana sugar crepes at a European café instead, but even with a generous slathering of syrup it did little to curb my craving. I made it back to The Emerald Shillelagh in time for last call. Most of the patrons had cleared out for the night except for some film school geeks and a couple of tired-looking cougars who looked like they needed some chamomile tea and calcium supplements more than another round.

"Here you go, mate. And just so you know, I busted me arse on this one," said Declan. He slid a pint of Guinness and a clear-front duo-tang folder across the bar top, in that order. I savoured the first sip of my frothy treat before diving into the folder like a teenage boy with a nudie mag.

As per my request, the duo-tang contained the basic background check information for Bert Grasby, including provincial, medical, and housing records, as well as a previous employment screening. Although there was nothing particularly noteworthy relating to his property ownership or vital statistics, Grasby's work experience was colourful. His varied employment history included stints as a used-car salesman, travelling carny, failed porn-website manager, and just about everything in between. There were also records of him filing incorporation documents for X-Treme Canadian Champion Wrestling with the provincial government under the *Business Corporations Act of British Columbia*. Finally, while Grasby had taken out several substantial business loans in order to get XCCW off the ground, he had already paid off the majority of the debt over the three years the independent wrestling promotion had been operational.

By the time I had finished skimming through the documents, the pub was nearly empty, I was on my third pint, and Declan had pulled up a stool next to me with a Guinness of his own.

"Anything?" he asked.

I took a sip and closed the folder. "Not much, aside from the fact that the guy paid off his business loans awfully fast."

"The fella is pretty savvy then?"

"In a way. Grasby's clearly got something going on the side because there's no way the profits from an indy wrestling league could get him out of that much debt in such a short amount of time."

"So what? You think he makes the extra cabbage by boosting pets?"

"I doubt it. He's into something. I'm thinking it might be drugs as he mentioned something about a supplier when he pulled a gun on me."

"He bloody what?"

"Did I forget to mention that?"

"This bloke sounds like a gombeen man. It's a shame you don't have yourself a criminal records check. I'd wager it'd be a wee more telling."

"I'm following a more promising lead at the moment." I updated Declan on my encounters with Stormy and Melvin.

"You're definitely onto something, mate. But if I were you I'd still follow up on this Grasby fella."

"I'll talk to my pop as soon as he's back from his conference, okay? Just lay off with the meddling."

"Me? Meddle?"

"Oh, please. You're worse than Dr. Phil with your pointed little remarks."

"Careful, boyo. You can say what you want about me self. But I'll be goddamned if I'm just going to just sit here and let you insult Dr. Phil. The man's a national treasure."

"He's from Texas."

"Ah, sod off! You know what I mean."

"You really need to start doing more with your days other than nursing hangovers and watching talk shows."

"Aye, and you need to quit being such a stubborn bollocks and just ask your Da for help already."

"Touché."

We quietly nursed our pints for a few minutes. Finally, I broke the silence. "Hey, D?"

"Yeah?"

"I always figured you for an Oprah kind of guy."

"Janey Mack! Give me some credit, eh? I've been off o'her ever since she endorsed *The Secret*. Jaysus, what a load o'shite that book was. Three months o'positive thoughts about shagging hot trollops and all I got for me effort was one night in the sack with a shite-faced, chubby gal."

"I guess it's safe to say you're no longer a member of her book club?"

"If I had me one o'those books I'd rip out the pages and use'em as toilet paper. Speaking o'which, I hear the loo calling me name." Declan slid off his bar stool and sauntered off toward the restroom.

"Have a good one," I said. "I'm going to hit it."

"Toodle-oo, mate."

I killed my pint, tucked the folder under my arm, and spun around on my stool to find myself face to face with Billy Nickens, the uppity med-student turned gym rat.

"What's the deal, Jed?"

"What deal?"

"I left you, like, three messages. Don't you want to lift with me anymore?"

"Relax, bub. I've been working."

Billy tossed his bulky knapsack onto the bar and hopped onto the stool next to me. "Do you mean bouncing? Did something go down on Granville tonight?"

I checked my watch. It was almost two in the morning. "Christ, kid, don't you ever go home?"

"I have an exam next week," he said, nodding toward his over-stuffed book bag.

"You can't study at home?"

"I like it better here. So? Did you get to mess some guys up at the club or what?"

I sighed. "No, Billy. Everything was fine."

"Yeah, they'd have to be crazy to start something with you."

I made my way toward the door, Billy nipping at my heels as I walked. "At least tell me when you're hitting the gym again," he begged. "I really need you to show me some new routines because I've seriously plateaued. I mean, I'm eating close to three thousand calories a day and I'm still not putting on any weight."

I stepped outside, the cold night air biting through the sleeves of my faded thermal shirt. I zipped up my North Face vest and rounded the block, sidestepping the rising steam that was escaping from a nearby manhole. "Look, kid, you need to get yourself a girlfriend or something. There's a hell of a lot more to life than just pumping iron and drinking beer."

I paused momentarily, considering the hypocrisy of my words when compared to my lifestyle. My self-reflection was cut short, however, the second my Spidey-sense started tingling over the sight of several large shadows being cast on the sidewalk in front of me. A moment later I spotted four thuggish-looking individuals angling toward us in my peripheral vision. I rolled up Grasby's folder and tucked it into my waistband behind my back, then grabbed Billy by the scruff of his hoodie and pulled him to my other side, using my body as a buffer between him and the approaching men.

"What the hell, Jed? That hurt."

"You want a ride home?"

"For sure!"

"Then shut up and stay close."

Billy nodded obediently as I kept my focus on the thugs. Their collective chatter became hushed as they crossed the street and the lack of loud, late night, drunken banter was all the confirmation

I needed to know these guys weren't coming my way to ask for a light.

I dug my keys out of my pocket and jingled them. Assuming that I was nearing my vehicle, the thugs picked up their pace, just as I expected. They were about thirty feet away and closing ground fast. Billy saw them approaching and went rigid beside me. Although their faces remained cloaked in darkness, the streetlight behind the thugs cocooned them in a dim light that accentuated their bulky frames. I timed my next move carefully, waiting until they were a little over fifteen feet away. I spun my keys on my index finger, and then let them slip out of my grasp and down onto the curb beside me, as if by accident. I crouched to pick them up and hoped at least one of them would take the bait.

"Get him!" a deep voice ordered.

The group charged. As soon as the first thug's knees appeared in my field of vision I rocketed upward with a jumping uppercut that would have made Little Mac of Nintendo's *Punch Out!* proud. My fist drove hard into the attacker's sternum and lifted him a good foot off the ground. I regained my balance just as two of his accomplices each grabbed me by a shoulder and rammed me backwards against the cement wall of Vancouver's lone Church of Scientology building.

I braced myself for impact and despite the force with which I slammed into the wall I was somehow able to prevent the wind from getting knocked out of me. I wasn't sure if it was dumb luck, the fact that I tightened my core muscles, or that Xenu the galactic dictator himself reached down and protected me — all I knew was that I could still breathe and was better off than the thug I had nailed with the uppercut, since he was convulsing and vomiting in the gutter.

I stole a glance at Billy and saw him getting worked over pretty good by a guy in a shiny leather jacket with perfectly mussed blonde-streaked hair. I tried to yell at the son-of-a-bitch to leave the kid alone, but before I could form the words the two thugs on either side of me started raining blows upon my midsection. For once I was actually thankful for the spare tire around my stomach as the extra layer of insulation helped me better absorb the hits.

I targeted the thug on my left, clenched my hands into tightly balled fists, and boxed his ears as hard as I could. The guy stumbled backwards, giving me the opening I needed. I squared up to the thug on my right, but in doing so opened up my torso and made my solar plexus an even larger target. I took a couple of hard kidney shots that caused my sides to explode, but it wasn't enough pain to stop me from dipping my head and thrusting forward with a ferocious head-butt. I felt a warm spray on my neck as the thug's nose split open and splattered me with blood. He howled in pain, his hands instinctively covering his face in an attempt to stop the gushing.

It was only then that I recognized my attacker as Dylan, Bert Grasby's pro-wrestling prodigy and stretching partner who I had met the day before. Unfortunately, before I had a chance to finish off the buff little bastard, the tanned thug with the douchebag hair cracked me on the back of the head with the blunt end of something hard and metal.

"Fuck yeah, Julian!" I heard one of the thugs cry victoriously. "You got him!"

Julian hit me again and I dropped to my knees faster than a victorious Björn Borg at Wimbledon and fought to stay conscious. I heard Julian and his pal barking back and forth with one another while my surroundings spun around me.

"Lyle ain't breathing, man!"

"Oh, Jesus!"

"His face is red as fuck!"

"What do we do?"

"Try raising his hands over his head!"

Billy whimpered behind me. He was curled in the fetal position, sobbing quietly. Julian and the remaining thug I hadn't taken out were hunched over their buddy Lyle, who was still wheezing heavily from my uppercut. Lyle continued to gurgle up puke, despite extending his hands over his head.

"Fugg me! Fugg me!" Grasby's buddy Dylan was hopping up and down on the sidewalk, freaked out by the volume of blood that was still pouring out of his crushed nose. "My fugging dose is fugged ub!" he screamed. "Id's dodally fugged ub!"

I tried to climb to my feet but before I could Julian connected with an ace roundhouse kick to my cheekbone that knocked me back on my ass. "I don't think so, motherfucker," he said.

Julian slipped into a low front stance and bounced on the balls of his feet, eager for me to try something. I spat blood onto the street and dusted off my jeans, figuring that sitting on my butt was as good a place as any for the moment.

Dylan squealed something unintelligible and started running in circles, dripping blood behind him. Julian snapped his fingers at the thug whose name I didn't know and jerked his head toward Dylan. "Shut him the fuck up," he ordered.

The thug left Lyle mid-heave to tend to Dylan. Julian squatted in front of me. Shiny steel glinted in front of my face as he produced a butterfly knife in a flurry of clacking metal. He ended his impressive flipping showcase by levelling the six-inch blade with my eye.

"That was a dirty move, sucker punching my boy like that," hissed Julian.

"I don't see how it's any dirtier than jumping a defenseless kid," I said, nodding toward Billy.

The unnamed thug tapped Julian on the shoulder. "You're gonna want to see this." He held up the duo-tang folder that contained Grasby's background check. Julian flipped pages and quickly got the gist of its contents.

"You got a real hard-on for Mr. Grasby, don't you Ounstead?"

"You're mistaking me for Dylan. I'm not really into the whole homoerotic guy-on-guy stretching thing."

Whack!

Julian backhanded me across the cheek. "Mind your manners."

He slipped the duo-tang into his jacket and yanked me to my feet, sticking his blade in my face again. "Did you really think you could just strike Mr. Grasby and not face any payback?"

"Actually, I did. And what's with all the 'Mr. Grasby' talk? Did he tutor you guys in math or something before recruiting you into his goon squad?"

Julian flushed with anger, and his red face only made the frosted tips of his spiky hair appear blonder. "I'm really going to enjoy cutting you up, do you know that? I mean, I'm going to fucking savour it. Every single mo—"

The crackling boom of a gunshot interrupted him. Julian's hand exploded. Bits of flesh and bone showered down from above as I shielded my face and ducked. The butterfly knife landed at my feet, but I barely heard the sound of it clattering on the sidewalk because my ears were still ringing from the ear-splitting gunshot.

Poised in a shooter's stance in the middle of the street was Declan, lit cigarette dangling between his lips, Browning Hi-Power 9mm gripped firmly between his hands. The smoke from the gun barrel drifted upward and mixed with the swirling fumes smouldering from the tip of his Benson & Hedges butt. Julian's face drained of colour. Seeing their no-longer-fearless leader gaping at the bloody stump where his thumb used to be, the other thugs froze. Time seemed to slow as Declan took a long drag of his cigarette and shifted the 9mm's aim to Julian's accomplices.

"Which one o'ya fuckin' bitch bags wants to be next?"

They started scrambling. Julian scooped up his thumb. The unnamed thug picked up Lyle and threw him over his shoulder in a fireman's carry. Dylan, perhaps unable to see clearly due to his swollen nose, took off in the opposite direction of his cronies. By the time Declan had lowered his gun the street was empty and we were alone.

"The lad looks right banjanxed," Declan said as he crouched next to Billy.

"Let's get him inside," I replied.

Declan put his combat training to good use as he went to work on Billy's wounds. Aside from a possible broken rib and some nasty scrapes and bruises, the kid wasn't actually in that bad shape. However, I could tell he was pretty rattled because he hadn't uttered a word since taking the beating, which for Billy, had to have been some kind of record. Declan set him up at the bar with an ice pack and a pint before joining me upstairs in my pop's office with two glasses and a bottle of Crown Royal.

"Nice to see you haven't lost your accuracy with the BAP," I said.

"Actually, I was aiming for his head."

"Is that right?"

"Aye, that chutney ferret's shiny hair made for a great target." Declan poured the whisky. We clinked our glasses in a silent toast.

"Hey, D?"

"Yeah, mate?"

"What you did back there—"

"It was nothin'."

"I mean it, Declan. I, uh, I want you to—" I sighed, struggling to find the right words. "I just hope you know how much—"

"Hey!"

"What?"

"No bloody girly moments."

I smiled. "Fair enough. Just as long as you know what I'm trying to say."

"Jaysus, what is it with you Canucks and your need to share your feelings all the time? Back home, if you want to say thanks to a bloke, you just buy his arse a pint."

"Or some very expensive single malt scotch?"

"Aye."

We enjoyed a quiet moment, exchanging with looks what we couldn't say with words.

"You think the kid will be okay?" I asked.

"A bit o'action will probably be good for him. Put a bit o'hair on his wee pigeon chest."

"I'm not so sure. I've gotten to know him some from the gym. He's a sensitive little dude."

"Then take him to a fuckin' poetry reading, for shite's sake. I already patched him up and gave him a pint. What more do you want?" I swirled the whisky in my glass. Declan was right. There wasn't much more I could do for Billy, despite the guilt I felt over him getting caught up in my investigation.

"Those were Grasby's boys back there," I said.

"I figured as much."

"They got away with that background check."

"Bollocks!"

"Don't worry. I'll be prepared next time."

"Who said I was worried? I worked me arse off compiling that report. You want another, you can damn well do it yourself."

"The only thing I want to see is Grasby's rap sheet. And not because I think he necessarily had anything to do with Johnny's murder. I'd just like to have an idea of the kind of company he keeps and resources he has access to." I finished my drink. Declan had the cap unscrewed off of the bottle before I had lowered my glass. "There's one thing I do know," I said, as Declan topped me up with more Crown. "And I don't need any type of records check to be certain of it."

"What's that?"

"Grasby's a vindictive son-of-a-bitch. He's going to take a run at me again, and when he does, he's going to come at me with everything he's got."

"I sure hope so."

"Excuse me?"

"Sorry, mate. But I do."

"Why's that?"

"Cuz it turns out that shooting off some poofy bastard's thumb, well, it just ain't that satisfying."

FOURTEEN

*I spent the rest of the weekend laying low around my town-*house recovering from my scrap with Grasby's goon squad. The right side of my face had swelled up and my rib cage felt like it had been pounded on more than a slab of frozen meat in a Rocky Balboa training montage.

On Saturday morning I called Russell, the manager of Tonix nightclub, and told him I wouldn't be able to make my shift that night. I apologized for the short notice and agreed to pick up an extra shift the following Tuesday for ladies night. Declan called on Sunday. When I asked him if he had seen any sign of Grasby's crew or suspicious faces around the pub he sounded deeply disappointed.

"No bloody luck, mate," he said dejectedly. Apparently shooting off Julian's thumb had whetted Declan's appetite for some good old-fashioned gunplay. He complained that it had been far too long since he had shot someone and was itching to do it again. I assured him that plenty of violence would be coming our way once Grasby made his next move. That seemed to lift his spirits a little.

At halftime during the Ravens-Steelers game I cracked open the file Melvin had given me and went over the photographs of Johnny and the redhead again. Eventually I flipped ahead to the photos of the couple leaving the restaurant and jotted down the licence plate of the redhead's Acura. Then I grabbed myself a can of Red Racer IPA and made a phone call I really didn't want to make.

"Hello?" said the familiar perky voice.

"Hi there."

"Jed?"

"Yeah."

Click.

I was anticipating a hang up. That's a standard ex-girlfriend move. The real question was whether or not Connie would answer when I called back. I took a pull of beer and redialed.

"What do you want?" she asked, the perkiness long gone.

"I need some help."

"You're kidding, right?"

"A friend of mine has been murdered."

"Oh my God. Who?"

"An old wrestling buddy. You didn't know him."

"I'm sorry."

"Thanks." Awkward silence. I struggled to find the appropriate segue.

"I'm looking into the murder, Connie."

"Wow."

"Wow?"

"I just can't believe your Dad finally convinced you to get your PI licence."

"He didn't."

"But you said—"

"Look, I'd really rather not get into the details. Can you help me?"

She sighed heavily into the phone. "What can I do?"

"I have a plate I need you to run through ICBC."

The Insurance Corporation of British Columbia's database contained records of all auto insurance and vehicle registration for the province. Connie worked in the collections department and had a surprising amount of access to all kinds of personal information.

"I don't know," she said. "Why can't you just leave it to the cops?"

"Because I've uncovered evidence that they haven't and I don't quite feel like sharing just yet."

"I always said you'd make a good investigator, Jed."

"Will you run the plate?"

"It's not the killer's, is it?"

"Just a potential witness."

Another sigh. "Give me the number," she finally said.

"KSM 742."

"Okay. I'll run the plate when I get into the office tomorrow and email you."

"Thanks."

"Goodbye, Jed."

"Connie, wait."

"Yes?"

"Maybe when this is over we could grab a drink or something?"

There was a long silence. "Are you asking because you want to see me again or because you're just grateful for my help?"

I hesitated before answering.

"I, uh—both." She heard the indecision in my voice. There wasn't much to say after that. I tried to thank her again for her help but the line went dead before I had even formed the words.

FIFTEEN

Wendy Steffen's face drained of colour. She withered into the overstuffed leather chair and clutched her hands close to her chest.

"When?" she asked.

"Thursday night," I replied.

She valiantly fought the quivering of her bottom lip before the tears began welling in her eyes. Wendy's red hair was even more vibrant in person than it was in the photos that Melvin had taken. She was dressed similarly, in a flattering pantsuit and blouse combo that was both stylish and professional.

"You'll have to excuse me for a moment," she said as she slipped past me toward the washroom.

Wendy had agreed to meet with me at a coffee shop that was near the downtown RE/MAX office she shared with several other realtors. I sipped my green tea and looked out the window next to our table. I could see the Vancouver Art Gallery across the street, and a production assistant with a bullhorn struggled valiantly to wrangle a herd of extras from the front lawn over to the neoclassical building's concrete steps for whatever film or television show was in the midst of shooting.

Wendy had responded to me promptly after I had contacted her using the phone number that Connie had emailed me earlier that morning. I wanted to share the news of Johnny's demise with her in person, and witnessing her emotional reaction was all I needed to be certain that she truly had feelings for my old friend.

"Sorry," Wendy said as she sat back down in the leather chair and stirred her latte.

"How did you come to know Johnny, Ms. Steffen?"

"It's Wendy, please. I met him at one of my open houses a couple months back."

"He was looking to buy a house?"

"Condo, actually."

I nodded politely. It made sense that Johnny may have planned to put his inheritance toward a down payment on property. "So you and Johnny just sort of hit it off then?"

"I thought he was cute," she said, blushing slightly. "Especially how concerned he was over whether or not the den in the one-bedroom unit would be large enough for a deluxe terrarium."

I couldn't help but smile. "Are you telling me that Johnny managed to parlay owning a snake into a successful pickup technique?"

She smiled softly. "Yes, I guess he did. Of course, it probably didn't hurt that I shared his passion for exotic pets."

"Let me guess. Pot-bellied pig?"

"Albino iguana."

I nodded and mentally ticked off the question of why such an attractive upscale woman might take a chance on a past his prime pro wrestler and snake enthusiast.

"Tell me Mr. Ounstead," said Wendy, her eyes narrowing. "Have they arrested her?"

"Arrested who?"

"Johnny's ex-girlfriend. Surely she's the one responsible for his death."

"You're speaking of Stormy Daze?"

"Yes. It has to be her. That woman's psychotic."

"What makes you say that?"

"The enormous red wine stains on my crème cashmere sweater, for starters."

Wendy proceeded to tell me how a few weeks ago Stormy had confronted both her and Johnny at an Italian restaurant. According to Wendy, Stormy was clearly intoxicated and deep in the throes of a jealous rage. After dousing Wendy in vino, Stormy smashed their entrées on the floor and threatened to kill them both. She then grabbed a fork and attempted to stab Johnny, but he was able to disarm her.

"At that point the manager informed the bitch that he was calling the police," Wendy said. "She fled pretty quickly after that."

"How long until the cops showed up?"

"They never did. Johnny smoothed things over with the manager before he placed the call."

It also meant that there was no official record of the incident, which made it unlikely that Rya would have learned of the public fracas during the course of her investigation. My mind was racing. Between the drunken tantrums, hiring of Melvin, and the death threats, Stormy Daze was looking guiltier by the minute.

"Needless to say," Wendy continued, "I found the entire incident very unnerving. I told Johnny I needed some time. He apologized profusely and promised that he wouldn't call until he had resolved the situation with his ex."

"So that night was the last time you spoke with him?"

"Yes. Mr. Ounstead, if that woman hasn't been arrested yet, then shouldn't I be contacting the police and informing them of what occurred at the restaurant?"

"You could. But for now it might be best if I pass on your statement myself. The authorities will contact you in time."

"Are you sure? I mean, believe me, the last thing I want is to get involved in such a mess, but if my story can help put that woman away for what she did ..." She trailed off as her emotion got the best of her.

"Let me take care of it for now, Wendy. I happen to be working closely with the lead detective on the case."

Wendy seemed pleased with that. I was pleased for a different reason. Between Melvin's pictures and Wendy's story, I now had something that I didn't have before. Leverage.

SIXTEEN

I tried calling Rya on her cell phone but the number that I had was no longer in service. A quick call to the VPD Homicide Unit and a little dropping of the Ounstead name later, and I learned that she was on her lunch break. I also had a pretty good idea of where.

Since retiring from the force my old man would have brunch with Rya once a week at a gritty diner called The Red Wagon Café. It was located on the edge of Commercial Drive, a funky roadway outside of the downtown core. The Drive was a veritable hodge-podge of ethnic stores and alternative shops, and featured nearly a hundred unique restaurants crammed into just a few city blocks. Not exactly the kind of place you would expect an old-school cop and his protégé to break bread regularly.

However, since The Red Wagon Café offered the most amazing pulled pork pancakes in all of Western Canada, and because my old man would rather dress up as a brawny leprechaun and do the Irish Jig while marching in Vancouver's annual St. Patrick's Day Parade than not get his regular fix of maple syrup on non-kosher flapjacks, every Sunday morning Frank Ounstead made his way down to the heart of Vancouver's raw urban underbelly to dine in the company of oversized Filipino families and glittery stiletto-wearing transsexuals.

I knew from my father that Rya's particular vice was The Red Wagon's pulled pork sandwich, so when I found her chomping into a loaded Portuguese bun in a corner booth next to kitschy pale wood panelling and frosted pendant lights I was hardly surprised. I slid across from Rya and her cool expression only conveyed the slightest bit of confusion while she used a napkin to dab barbeque sauce off of the corner of her mouth.

"Do they have anything else besides pork?" I asked, before cracking open a menu.

Rya's gaze lingered on the puffy shiner beneath my eye. "Makes me look like a badass, doesn't it?" I said.

"More like a dumb ass."

I helped myself to one of the French fries next to her sandwich.

"Touch another and I pistol-whip your good eye."

"Fair enough. Take a look at this." I placed the envelope containing Melvin's photos on the table. She started flipping through the pictures in rapid-fire succession.

"Are these supposed to mean something to me?"

"They will if I tell you who commissioned them to be taken three weeks ago." I saw the light bulb flash above her head.

"Stormy Daze."

"Too bad you already ruled her out as a potential suspect."

"We never ruled out anyone."

"No, you just tried to give me the impression that you had."

"So what if I did? I already told you I didn't want you sniffing around my case."

"Well, I'm not letting this one go. Which is why I went ahead and saved you the trouble of having to track this lady down," I said, pointing at Wendy in one of the photos. "Turns out she's got quite an interesting story."

"Goddamn it, Jed. Start talking."

"Quid pro quo, Detective."

Rya glared scornfully. "Fine," she said. "I suppose you'd like me to go first."

"If you wouldn't mind."

"What is it you want to know?"

"The print on the racquetball."

"Ran it through CCRTIS. No hits."

"How about Johnny's autopsy?"

"It was performed this morning."

"I want a copy of the report."

"Can't do it."

I tapped my index finger on the photos. "Then good luck finding out where these came from."

"Hold on. I said I couldn't get you a copy of the report. But I can tell you exactly what's on it."

"Good enough."

"Official cause of death was a deep knife wound to the throat. No surprise there. Slash severed his carotid artery. Mamba was probably already dead before he was dragged over to the Porta-Potty."

I tried to imagine what must have gone through Johnny's mind while he bled out. I wondered if he had discovered that Ginger had died. I hoped for his sake he didn't.

"Were you aware that 'Johnny Mamba' was your friend's real name? He had it legally changed and everything."

"Yeah, I know. We were at wrestling boot camp in Calgary together when he came up with the snake gimmick. He wanted to be a hardcore version of his childhood hero, Jake 'The Snake' Roberts. Johnny was pretty psyched. I drove him to the Vital Statistics office."

"I don't know what it is with you wrestling people. Can't you just show some respect and be grateful for the name your parents gave you?"

"Rya?"

"What?"

"Can we get back to the report?"

"Oh, I'm sorry," she said, her voice dripping with sarcasm. "My apologies, Mr. Hammerhead." I sighed. Rya scooped up some shredded pork with a French fry.

"Body temperature, rigor and livor mortis, and stomach contents approximate the time of death between seven-thirty and nine o'clock, which fits with your timeline of events."

"Toxicology?"

"Negative. There were no traces of narcotics in his system and his blood alcohol level was zero."

"Any evidence of previous drug use? Cocaine? Steroids?"

"Nope. Not recently, anyway. The Coroner even mentioned that he appeared to have been living a very healthy lifestyle."

That was mildly comforting. I'd never known Johnny to have ever had any issues with substance abuse, but I'd also known people in the business over the years who were awfully good at hiding some pretty addictive habits. Pro-wrestling promotions often had their own narcotics hookups—both performance enhancing and recreational—and with a guy like Bert Grasby at the helm, I wouldn't expect XCCW to be any different. It also meant that the chance of Ginger's kidnapping being used as some kind of cover for a drug-related murder was pretty slim.

"Okay, Ounstead. Time for some pro quo."

"Hold on. What about Johnny's mobile? Did you trace the call that came in from the kidnapper?"

"Dead end. We figure it was a burner."

"Was the snake examined?"

"Yes, the silver in its teeth was just aluminum foil."

"Then how did it die?"

"Who cares? It was examined for evidence. There was none."

"What happens to Ginger now?"

"Enough questions, Jed. I've been more than generous. Your turn."

"Last question, Rya, I swear. I just want to know what happens to the snake."

"The SPCA disposes of it."

"When?"

"Whenever they pick the damn thing up from the morgue."

Maybe I was getting sidetracked, but that scrap of aluminum foil in Ginger's teeth was bothering me. I reminded myself that just because Johnny fawned over the reptile it didn't mean that the kidnapper would have. They could have kept Ginger locked up in a pantry for all I knew.

"That pistol-whipping is becoming more enticing by the second," Rya said.

I pushed my thoughts aside and filled her in on my interview with Stormy and her hiring of another private investigator. Without mentioning Melvin's name, I explained that I convinced the PI to give me copies of the photos and how I used them to track down Wendy Steffen. Rya was clearly irritated that I had beaten her to a potential witness. I gave her Wendy's contact information and reminded her that nothing I had done was damaging to her case.

"You left out the PI's name," Rya said.

"Don't worry, it'll come to me," I replied, knowing full well that I wasn't ready to give up my last bargaining chip just yet.

Rya stood up and grabbed a cardboard sleeve for her latte. "I'll make you a deal. I'll give you a lift back to the precinct if you tell me the name of the PI when we get there."

"What's your plan? To bribe me with donuts?"

"Actually, I thought you might like to hang around the cop shop for a while."

"And why would I want to do that?"

"Because an arrest warrant was issued for Stormy Daze one hour ago. She's being brought in as we speak."

SEVENTEEN

The traffic light turned yellow. Rya blipped the siren and flashed the reds and blues on the Crown Vic's rear-view mirror and visors as we zoomed through the intersection.

"What do you have on Stormy?" I asked.

"Not much. The ITO was a little thin."

An ITO, or Information to Obtain a Search Warrant, is a police compilation of all the information regarding a case and its relevance to the location they wish to search.

"How'd you get the Justice of the Peace to sign off on it?"

Rya smirked. "Rumour is he's a pro-wrestling fan."

"You know, they're never who you expect," I replied. "I once got asked for an autograph at the Toronto Symphony."

"You went to the symphony?"

"Is it so hard to believe that I'm a little cultured?" Rya's eyebrows jerked upward like they were on fishhooks. "It was a special *Music of Star Wars* concert, okay? The guy who plays C-3PO was there as a special guest. I got my picture taken with him and everything." Rya smiled softly, although I couldn't tell if it was because she thought I was cute or a dork.

"There still had to be enough circumstantial evidence to issue the warrant," I said.

"There is. Her alibi is bullshit."

"No spin class?"

"Stormy had a friend at Fitness World doctor the logs to make it look like she swiped her gym card around the same time Mamba was killed. We also have the testimony of her neighbour, who was getting ready to take out the trash when he witnessed Stormy shrieking at Mamba in the hallway outside of her condo. The nosey bastard watched the entire thing through his peephole."

"What were they fighting about?"

"The neighbour only got bits and pieces. But he swears he heard Stormy threaten Mamba's life right before he got in the elevator and left. Two weeks later he was dead."

Johnny had probably gone to talk to Stormy about the altercation at the restaurant. But instead of resolving things with his ex he wound up receiving another death threat. I held up the envelope containing Melvin's photographs. "So these pictures —"

"Are a crucial piece of evidence," Rya said, cutting me off. "They give us a clear motive, and along with the testimony of Wendy Steffen, will be a lynchpin in the Crown Counsel's case."

"Can't you just submit the pix without knowing where they came from?" I asked.

"We can, but unless we are able to locate and identify the source it's unlikely they would carry much weight in court. The defense would simply argue that the photos are hearsay evidence. That's why I need you to honour our deal, Jed. I don't want run this upstairs only to have you screw me over later."

"I wouldn't do that."

"Oh, really?"

"Well … not without at least buying you dinner first."

Rya cranked the wheel, turning off Cambie Street into the underground parkade at VPD Headquarters. Things seemed to be lining up nicely for Rya and her case, and all signs clearly pointed to Stormy as Johnny's killer. But I wasn't sold just yet. Instead, a single question kept kicking around the inside of my head — *why kidnap the snake?* As a smokescreen perhaps? A way to divert suspicion from the pre-meditated murder of a lover? If that was her intent, then why do it so soon after the incident at the restaurant? Stormy had to at least be smart enough to realize that publicly threatening the life of one's intended victim just weeks before their murder would be a surefire way to get your name to the top of the suspect list. I tried to point this out to Rya but she paid it no mind, instead saying something about how such stupidity was often seen in crimes of passion.

Maybe she was right. Maybe Stormy just wanted to hurt Johnny in the worst way possible and saw the snake as her ticket. I suppose the thing that gnawed at me the most was that Johnny had withheld his deteriorating relationship with Stormy from me when we met. I even asked him point blank if there was anyone who would have had motive to hurt him but he drew a blank. Which meant Johnny had either lied to me or he truly didn't believe that Stormy was capable of kidnapping Ginger.

As I followed Rya through VPD headquarters toward the Homicide Squad bullpen, I felt a white-hot spark of anger ignite within as I considered the ramifications of Stormy Daze actually being the person responsible for Johnny's death. If it were true, then she was already in police custody, which meant any chance of me getting my hands on her first was gone. I felt a slow burn inside at the thought of being denied a chance to confront the murderer myself. Until now I had been content to compartmentalize my feelings and focus on the investigation. But if Stormy really was guilty, then it was all over. All I could do was wait for the lawyers to do their morally ambiguous tap dance and hope that the traditionally lenient Canadian criminal justice system delivered a verdict that was just.

Rya took Melvin's photos and went to find her boss. She instructed me to wait at her desk where I proceeded to engage in some subtle snooping. Her desktop was bare save for a stack of files, a password protected computer, and a framed five-by-seven photo of her and my father at his retirement party. In the picture they were wearing party hats and smiles, yet I could see a hint of sadness in both of their expressions.

Upon her promotion to the Homicide Squad, Rya was partnered with my pop and the two spent six years together working high profile murders in Vancouver. But before the legendary Frank Ounstead hung up his blues, he dedicated his last years on the force to grooming Rya as his protégé. I think he intended to pass on his experience and wealth of knowledge to an adept replacement. I doubt he expected to wind up developing a father's love for his young female partner.

I put the picture down and tried to sneak a peek at some of the files on Rya's desk but stopped when I caught the eye of a grizzled detective who was meandering about the office. He tugged his pants up and under his sagging belly and started toward me. That's when the yelling started.

"Quit fucking pushing me, asshole!"

Her hands cuffed behind her back, Stormy Daze stood toe-to-toe with one of the arresting officers who was escorting her through the bullpen. The overweight cop forgot all about me and shuffled over to lend a hand. Together he and the uniformed officers directed Stormy toward the hallway that led to the interrogation rooms. But not before she spotted me.

"Hey! Ounstead!" I stared blankly at Stormy, who was bucking against her restraints like a busty bronco. "You gotta help me! I didn't do this!"

"Shut up," growled overweight cop, as he dragged Stormy forcefully by the arm.

"You saw me that night! You know I loved him!"

She continued to beg for my help as the officers ushered her away, her panic-stricken voice echoing throughout the corridor long after she had faded from view.

EIGHTEEN

Inspector Richard Cornish didn't like me. Maybe it was because he had never cared for my dad. Maybe it was because I was a civilian who had dug up evidence on a case before his detectives did. Or maybe it was because after invoking her right to counsel, Stormy Daze had requested that I visit her in her interrogation room.

"No way," barked Cornish. "I'm not going to jeopardize the Crown's entire case just so this bum can play cop."

"Don't let the shaggy mop and designer stubble fool you, bub," I said. "This is a carefully crafted look."

Cornish looked at me like I had just spoken Klingon. Rya kept pressing him. "She already said she'd sign a waiver. There's no risk."

"There is if he does something to set her off," said Cornish. "You saw the state she's in. Her lawyer could argue she was not of sound judgment at the time of her request."

"I trust him, Inspector. More importantly, Stormy seems to trust him. Who knows what she might let slip to a friendly face before her counsel arrives?"

Cornish crossed his arms and shifted his gaze to me. "This isn't a night club, bouncer boy. Can you play it cool long enough to see what she has to say?"

"Inspector, my old man used to make me memorize the Reid technique's nine steps of interrogation and quiz me on family road trips. Believe me, I'll be just fine."

Cornish begrudgingly gave Rya the go ahead. While she went about ensuring Stormy's request would be properly documented, I observed Johnny's possible murderer through the two-way mirror. Gone was the cynical sexpot I had met before, replaced by an anxious woman shifting uncomfortably on a plastic chair. When I entered the cramped interrogation room ten minutes later, I could see the relief wash over her.

"Thank God," she huffed, as I took a seat across the desk from her. "You have to get me out of here."

"Why would I want to do that?"

Stormy looked at me like I had just slapped her across the face. "Because I'm innocent."

"You are?"

"What the fuck, Ounstead?" she screamed, leaping up and pounding her fists on the desk. "You think I killed him too?"

"Honestly? No, I don't." Stormy nodded triumphantly and eased back into her chair. "But there's an overwhelming amount of evidence that suggests otherwise."

"Bullshit."

"I know about his new girlfriend, Stormy. I saw the photos you hired Melvin Van Lowe to take of Johnny and her together."

I glanced at the two-way mirror, knowing that behind it Rya would be pleased that I finally revealed my source's name. Stormy slumped in her chair. She was silent for several moments.

"I never knew the little slut's name," she finally said.

"That didn't stop you from threatening her life. Or Johnny's. And you did it in a public restaurant."

"He was cheating on me!" she bellowed.

"Which makes for one hell of a motive," I replied.

"Look, I lost it, okay? I was upset and said some stupid shit I didn't mean. Since when does having a bad temper automatically make someone a murderer?"

"So when Johnny came to see you at your apartment and you threatened his life again, that was what? Just another tantrum?"

"How do you know about that?"

"It doesn't matter. One time is a slip up, Stormy. Anything more is a pattern."

Stormy crossed her arms defensively. "I don't think I should talk any more without my lawyer."

I leaned forward, gravitas seeping into my voice. "I can buy that the death threats were you blowing off steam. I can understand you having an affair of your own and lying to me about your new lover's toothbrush in your bathroom." She gasped slightly, a stunned look on her face. "But what I can't figure out," I continued, "is why you would go to the trouble of concocting a fake alibi if you truly are innocent." Her tough exterior finally cracked. Stormy let out a stifled sob, pinching the bridge of her nose as she quietly wept.

"I want to believe you, Stormy. But you need to tell me where you really were the night Johnny was killed."

"I was with someone else," she blurted out.

"Who?"

"You have to swear you won't tell anyone. And you have to promise me that they won't either!" she yelled, jabbing an accusatory finger at the two-way mirror.

Rya slipped into the room and took a seat beside me. "Ms. Danielson, I assure you, anything you reveal with regards to a homicide investigation will remain confidential." Stormy wiped her nose on her sleeve and eyed Rya dubiously.

"You can trust her, Stormy." Stormy sniffled and nodded begrudgingly.

"His name is Eddie Grist. He's a talent scout for Border City Wrestling."

Rya glanced at me with a raised eybrow as she jotted down the name in her notebook. "It's an independent promotion based out of Windsor, Ontario," I explained.

Rya scribbled that down as well. I leaned forward in my chair and looked Stormy in her bright blue eyes, which due to all the tears seemed to almost be sparkling.

"Are you thinking about leaving XCCW?" I asked.

"Are you kidding? BCW is a springboard for the big time. They have connections with ROH, TNA, New Japan, even NXT. When I get on with them I'm set."

"So it's a done deal?"

"Just about. They're very interested in signing me as soon as my contract with XCCW expires next month."

"Wait a second," Rya said. "If this is true then why did you lie?"

"Grasby," I said, finally piecing it together. Stormy nodded emphatically.

"If he knew I was in negotiations with Border City he'd go ballistic. They're his main competition on the east coast and he absolutely hates them. A wrestler named Chet Wilson tried to leave XCCW for Monster Pro Wrestling in Edmonton six months ago. When Grasby found out, Chet's car was suddenly stolen and his apartment was mysteriously set on fire. The poor guy went bankrupt and lost everything."

"There's no mention of this in Grasby's record," said Rya.

"You don't get it, do you?" pleaded Stormy. "He's crazy vindictive. There's nothing he wouldn't do to ruin me if he found out I was leaving."

"Did Johnny know?" I asked.

"I wasn't going to tell him until our deal was official. But by then it didn't matter."

"Our deal?" Stormy smiled sadly.

"It wasn't just my contract that I was negotiating. BCW is hurting bad for female talent. I used that to my advantage so they also agreed to take Johnny on as a jobber."

Now it made sense. Melvin. The fights. The death threats. Stormy hitched Johnny's wagon to her star only to find out the man she loved had betrayed her.

"Is there a chance that Grasby could have found out about your negotiations with Border City Wrestling and that's why Johnny was murdered?" Rya asked.

"Then why am I still here?" Stormy replied. "Besides, Eddie and I were extremely cautious. And I'm pretty sure if Grasby knew about our meetings he would have taken out his frustration on the other wrestlers just like he did after the last time with Chet."

"So you really don't have any idea who killed Johnny?" I asked.

"I wish I did," she said softly, choking back tears.

Rya proceeded to ask Stormy several follow up questions about her relationship with Eddie Grist and Border City Wrestling. When she finished I said goodbye to Stormy and followed Rya out into the hallway where Inspector Cornish was waiting with two uniformed cops by his side.

"Officers, please escort Mr. Ounstead off the premises immediately."

The cops swooped in and grabbed me roughly by the arms. Since I've never been one to take kindly to being manhandled, I slipped my arm out of the first officer's grip and shoved the other cop away from me. The cops drew their batons and were about to go to town when Rya jumped in between us.

"Enough!" The cops backed down. Rya glared at Cornish. "Richard, what is this?"

"I want him out of here."

"Did you not just see what he did in there?"

"I saw exactly what he did. Because of him we now have no suspect and a Crown Counsel en route that's going to be mighty pissed we wasted his time."

"But Richard—"

"I don't want to hear it, Shepard. This is your fault for bringing him here in the first place."

"Aren't you forgetting something?" I said, irritated with Cornish's bureaucratic concerns. "Stormy is innocent. That means the real killer is still out there. You need to be working the case, not wasting time worrying about whether or not some hotshot prosecutor might have to make an extra stop for gas."

Cornish got in my face. With his bristly mustache, small knot tie, and hands on his hips, he reminded me of an angry high-school principal who had caught me smoking in the boys' room.

"Do you really think I'm going to stand here and let you tell me how to do my job?" he hissed.

"My friend is dead," I said solemnly. "I'm just trying to do right by him."

"You mean like you did with your buddy Max Conkin?"

Hearing that name felt like a dagger to the heart. My pulse quickened. My breath shortened. I swayed slightly on my feet as I fought off light-headedness. I glanced at Rya, who was looking at me uncertainly. She had no idea what Cornish was talking about. Cornish smirked, knowing he had scored a blow.

"Oh, yeah," he continued. "I know all about you, Ounstead. I know why your wrestling career ended and I know what you did before resurfacing here in Vancouver."

I pulled myself together, not wanting Cornish to think he had unnerved me more than he already had. "Are you referring to my stint as a performer in *Puppetry of the Penis*, Inspector? Because I still have connections and you strike me as the kind of guy who likes to play with himself."

One of the uniformed officers let slip a chuckle. Rya sighed and shook her head. Cornish stabbed a finger in my chest and glared at me with fire in his eyes. "Solving your friend's murder can't make up for the past, smart ass. Stay away from this investigation. Otherwise I will come after you with everything I've got and won't let up until you're serving time for obstruction and your daddy's little pub loses its goddamn liquor licence." I looked to Rya for support. There was none.

"Get out of here, Jed," she said.

It wasn't until I was outside the precinct that I remembered my truck was back at the café. A crisp breeze swept stray blood red autumn leaves past my feet while I stood on the sidewalk. I zipped up my jacket, buried my hands in my pockets, and started walking back toward Commercial Drive. The city was quiet and other than the sounds of distant traffic and the crunching of foliage under my feet I was alone with my thoughts. By the time I had walked three blocks I had made up my mind about my next move. The only thing I was uncertain of was whether or not what I was about to do would be considered an indictable offence.

NINETEEN

I called Declan to see if Billy was at the pub. Apparently the kid hadn't been around since Grasby's thugs had laid a pounding on him. I had given Billy enough rides home from the gym to remember where he lived. His apartment complex was located on the outskirts of Yaletown, next door to a 7–11 and right below the Granville Street Bridge. I searched the directory until I found his unit number. He sounded surprised that I was there but buzzed me in right away. Billy's studio apartment was pretty basic, his furnishings consisting mainly of a futon, plasma TV and enough Xbox games and medical textbooks to open a store on eBay.

"How you holding up?" I asked, as I stepped over an empty pizza box into the living room. Billy tenderly touched his ribs and avoided eye contact.

"Okay, I guess."

"Good. Because I could really use your help."

"For what?" I told Billy my plan.

"You're joking," he said, when I had finished.

"I'd do it myself if I could. But I need someone qualified."

"I'm not qualified to do that!"

"You're close enough."

"I don't think so, Jed."

"Tell you what. You do this, I'll make you my full-time training partner."

"For real?"

"I do a push-pull split four days a week. If you work out with me and stick to the diet plan I give you I guarantee that in three months you'll be stretching out every one of your T-shirts." Billy touched his ribs again, thinking it over. After a moment, he smiled.

During the car ride Billy fidgeted with the passenger seat controls, visor, heating, and rear window de-mister. By the time he reached for my radio I had had enough.

"Settle down, bub."

"Sorry."

"Something on your mind?"

"No. I don't know." Billy crossed his arms and we drove in silence for a minute. "Can you really help me get bigger?"

"Absolutely."

"Do you think maybe you could show me a few self-defense moves too?"

"Sure."

Billy nodded approvingly. "It's just, you know, after the other night—"

"I know."

"I don't care about being a tough guy anymore, Jed. I just want to be able to protect myself."

"Good for you, kid."

We neared our destination and I pulled into a pay parking lot.

"It's not like it is in the movies, is it?" he asked.

"What?"

"Fighting. In real life it happens so fast."

"Wasn't exactly glamorous, was it?"

"No. It was just ... scary. And it hurts like hell. Is it always like that?"

"Every time."

"So then why did you piss off guys who would come looking for trouble?"

I parked in a stall and turned off the ignition. It took me a moment before I came up with an answer. "Because I'm good at it."

We got out of the truck and walked inside. The city morgue is located underneath Vancouver General Hospital, the second largest hospital in the country. I happened to be all too familiar with the hallways of the medical facility, particularly the leukemia and bone marrow transplant wing. I had spent many late nights there with my mother, watching her endure one failed treatment after another before finally succumbing to her disease in the comfort of her own home.

We took the elevator down to the morgue level and I readied the item that I would need next. One of the perks of being a cop's son is that you have access to certain things a normal civilian would not. Like a former police officer's badge, for example.

"vpd Homicide," I announced, as we approached the bookish morgue attendant behind a desk. Seeing my pop's golden badge, the attendant instructed me to fill out the sign-in sheet. I obliged, except I wrote my name as Inspector Dick Cornish and dotted each lowercase "i" with a big girly heart.

Billy shivered as we followed the attendant inside. The cold sterile air filled my nostrils and smelled strongly of disinfectant. The body of a deceased middle-aged man rested on a slab in the centre of the morgue, his upper torso exposed and revealing a freshly stitched Y-incision. We followed the attendant through a maze of stainless steel until we reached a chrome gurney in the rear corner of the room. The attendant pulled back a sheet to reveal the scaly remains of Johnny's pet snake Ginger.

"Jesus," groaned Billy, shooting me a look of uncertainty.

"Ugly looking thing, isn't it?" said the attendant.

"We can take it from here, thanks," I said, snapping on a pair of latex gloves. The morgue attendant shrugged and took the hint. Once we were alone with Ginger I gave Billy a nudge.

"Autopsy time."

"Necropsy."

"What?"

"Autopsies are performed on humans. It's called a necropsy when you examine an animal or reptile post-mortem."

"Billy, I don't care if it's called the Funky Cold Medina. Let's slice this snake open and see if we can figure out how it died." Billy grimaced and dug a small surgical kit out of his messenger bag. He opened the kit and withdrew a scalpel handle to which he then fastened a new blade.

"I'm going to need you to stretch it out," he said, putting on his own pair of gloves. I did as I was told and gripped Ginger by her throat and tail, utilizing my long wingspan as I pulled the snake taut. Billy made his incision about ten inches down from my hand, on the upper torso where the snake's body became meatier.

"What exactly are we looking for?" asked Billy.

"Stomach contents," I replied.

"Do you even know where a snake's stomach is?"

"Above its middle there," I said, pointing. "Just don't cut too far to the left or you'll hit its gallbladder." Billy stared at me bewilderedly.

"How do you know all this?"

"I googled python anatomy earlier. Got a picture on my phone and everything." Billy shook his head.

"You better get me really ripped," he said, resuming cutting.

Ten minutes later Billy had successfully opened up Ginger. He used several retractors to spread her scaly skin and began probing through the reptilian innards with the aid of a hemostat and forceps. We used the picture on my phone as a reference and were eventually able to identify the snake's stomach. Billy made an incision into the pinkish sack and we immediately found something unexpected. Ginger's stomach was full of strips of tin foil and a variety of brightly coloured pills. Dozens of cherry red, lime green, and electric-blue tablets, some partially digested, were bunched together in clumps.

"What the hell?" said Billy.

I picked up several of the tablets and examined them closer. Each one was either inscribed with an *R* or *WY* logo.

"Son-of-a-bitch," I said.

"What?"

"This is yaba."

"Yaba?"

"It's a type of methamphetamine."

"How do you know that?"

I clutched the tablets in my fist. "After I left professional wrestling I did a little backpacking. Spent a lot of time in Asia, particularly Thailand and the Philippines."

"You were doing drugs?" he asked, the disappointment evident in his voice.

"I was finding various ways to numb myself," I replied. "And if you knew what had happened to me you might not be so quick to judge."

"Sorry, Jed."

I held up a purple tablet between my thumb and index finger and showed it to Billy. "Yaba is very popular over there," I continued. "It's a meth-caffeine cocktail that's especially favoured by the rave and techno crowd. In recent years it's made its way into some party scenes in LA and Northern California, but up until now, I've never heard of it being in Vancouver."

"So what's a bunch of rare methamphetamines doing inside your dead friend's snake?" asked Billy.

"That's the million dollar question, bub."

Just then the morgue attendant marched in, flanked by three hospital security guards and a woman in a tan uniform. Upon seeing Ginger lying dissected upon the gurney, the woman shrieked and ran toward the reptile.

"You sick bastards!" she screamed. "What did you do?"

"Calm down, lady," I said, pulling out my pop's badge. "My colleague here is a herpetologist and we're performing an official necropsy on this reptile as it pertains directly to a murder investigation." I gave Billy a knowing nod, and was quite pleased with myself for correctly using the term *necropsy*. He wasn't as impressed.

"You can save the bullshit," said the morgue attendant. "We already know you're a couple of phonies."

Billy's face went white. I did my best to stay in character. "There must be some misunderstanding," I said, as the hospital security guards unfastened handcuffs from their belts.

"This woman is from the SPCA," said the attendant. "As per their request, she placed a call to the Vancouver Police to inform them she had arrived at the morgue to collect the reptile's remains. Imagine their surprise when the cops heard that one of their officers was already here, to see a dead snake that has already been examined and ordered to be disposed of." The morgue attendant grinned with smug satisfaction. The SPCA woman glared with disgust and the security guards puffed out their chests.

I held up the red and green tablets I still had in my hand. "Any chance you guys like to party?"

TWENTY

For the second time that day I was in a police interrogation
room. Except this time I was the one in the hot seat. It really
does make a difference. After twiddling my thumbs for an hour
Rya entered the room and took a seat across from me. She stared
at me for an eternity, waiting for me to say something. I didn't.

"Are you sure your pro-wrestling name wasn't 'Shithead' Jed
Ounstead?" she finally asked.

"Pretty sure."

"You know you're fucked, right? I mean, there's nothing I can
do for you now."

"You could dial down the profanity. It's not very ladylike."

"What the hell were you thinking, Jed?"

"I was thinking that it was about damn time somebody got off
their ass and tried to make headway on your murder case."

"You impersonated an officer of the law in order to gain access
to the city morgue where you proceeded to violate the remains
of an animal."

"Reptile."

"Whatever! How the hell does what you did help my case?"

"Did you hear about the pills in Ginger's stomach?"

"Yeah, so what?"

"They were methamphetamines."

"Bullshit."

"Get one of your drug recognition experts to examine them. They will ID them as yaba, a type of meth that up until now has been a pretty uncommon find in Vancouver."

"How do you know all this?"

"Doesn't matter. What's important is that you start coordinating with your Gang Crime and Drug units ASAP. I'm willing to bet whoever took Ginger was in possession of a large quantity of yaba and that the snake accidentally ingested the meth and overdosed. That's why the kidnapper panicked and rushed the ransom exchange with Johnny."

Rya fiddled with her watchstrap while she considered what I had said. After a few moments, she responded. "How do you know that the kidnapper didn't intentionally kill the snake by feeding it the meth?"

"Because there are a hell of a lot more easy and cheap ways to bump off a reptile."

Rya leaned back in her chair as she absorbed the information. "Even if you're right, it doesn't change the fact that you're screwed. Cornish is absolutely livid and—"

The Inspector stormed into the room. "You're relieved, Detective Shepard." Rya gave me a warning look before disappearing into the hall. Cornish leaned against the two-way mirror and crossed his arms.

"Did you hear what I told Rya about the yaba?" I asked.

"I already heard it all from your little sidekick next door."

"How is Billy?"

"About ready to turn on your dumb ass."

I figured Cornish was playing me. But even if he wasn't, I could hardly blame Billy. First I get him beat up, then I get him arrested. He didn't owe me squat. "He's just a kid," I said. "He had nothing to do with this."

"Those surgical supplies suggest otherwise."

"He's a med student and I borrowed them from him. The kid was just my lookout while I cut up the snake."

Cornish chuckled and shook his head. "Do you know why I don't like you, Ounstead?"

"Because I have much better hair than you?"

"It's because you're an arrogant son-of-a-bitch. You think that your own personal sense of morality somehow entitles you to ignore proper conduct and act on your impulses. Even if it means leaving a giant fucking mess that other decent people have to clean up."

Cornish placed his hands on the table and glared down at me. "I guess I shouldn't be that surprised, though. Your old man was the same way."

"Are you sure you're not confusing a righteous sense of morality with having a set of balls, Inspector?"

Cornish slammed a fist down on the table and got in my face. "It's over, Ounstead. I've got you cold on obstruction, not to mention a handful of other charges. And I'm going to make it my personal mission to ensure you're convicted on each and every one."

"I don't give a shit. All I care about is that you follow up on the fact that whoever killed Johnny Mamba is connected to someone dealing a very rare type of narcotic."

"Oh, we'll follow up on your lead, Ace. Don't you worry about that. Unfortunately, the Drug Unit has a six-month backlog of cases. So I doubt they'll be examining those colourful tablets anytime soon, especially since they're probably nothing more than a bunch of fucking Skittles that were eaten by your friend's stupid snake."

"I identified those pills, Cornish. It's yaba meth."

"I'm afraid the VPD relies on actual evidence to build its cases, not the crackpot theories of burnout deadbeat civilians."

"Are you seriously telling me you're not going to investigate the yaba angle until six months from now?"

"I'll tell you what. When we finally do get around to it, I'll be sure to stop by your prison cell and let you know what we find out."

Cornish was gloating. I clenched my jaw, trying to summon the will to not do something stupid. I came awfully close to grabbing his tie and smashing his face into the table just as I had done at the strip club with Melvin. The only thing that stopped me was that the door to the interrogation room swung open and a towering figure stepped inside. It was my father.

Frank Ounstead was six-foot-five and had maintained his linebacker's physique all the way into his early sixties. Although I was a bit shorter than my old man, my build was more symmetrical and lacked some of my pop's more powerful features, like his barrel chest, Popeye-like forearms, and gorilla mitts. My pop's mouth was formed in a thin line beneath his salt and pepper mustache and it took him all but two seconds to size up the scenario before him.

"Get up, son. We're leaving."

"What do you think you're doing?" barked Cornish as he whirled around.

"What the hell does it look like, Cornish? I'm taking my boy home."

"He's under arrest."

"Not anymore," growled my father.

"Excuse me?" snapped Cornish.

"I just cleared it with the Chief Constable."

Cornish stood toe to toe with my pop, straining his neck as he looked upward. "You got some fucking nerve, old man."

My pop glowered at Cornish and exhaled through his nostrils like a snorting bull. "I could say the same about you for arresting my boy without my knowledge." My pop jerked a meaty thumb over shoulder.

"Let's go, son." I walked past Cornish and followed my father out of the room.

"I don't care what kind of pull you still might have with the brass," Cornish yelled after us. "This is my department, Frank. I'll run it whatever fucking way I see fit."

I caught up to my pop in the hallway. "I can't leave without Billy."

"Who?"

"The kid who was arrested with me."

"He's waiting with Rya."

I followed my father as he led the way out of the precinct, watching as the passing detectives and officers each acknowledged my old man with polite greetings or nods of respect. Billy hustled over to me when we reached the bullpen while my father went to Rya's desk to confer with his protégé.

"You okay, Jed?"

"I'm fine. You?"

"I'm all right. What's happening? Did your dad pay our bail or something?"

"They're dropping the charges."

"Thank God," exclaimed Billy. "I was already starting to worry about getting shanked if we got sent to the clink."

"Shanked in the clink?" I asked.

"Yeah, man."

I shook my head. "You watch way too much HBO, kid."

My pop shot me a look and nodded toward the exit. I caught Rya's eye as Billy and I followed my father out the door. She stared at me a moment, then looked away.

After dropping off Billy at his apartment I reminded my old man that my truck was still at Vancouver General. He grumbled something about not being a goddamn taxi service before turning up the country music in his Dodge Durango and driving toward the hospital. I knew better than to try and elicit a conversation from my father while he was humming along to Hank Williams Jr., so I spent the ride thinking over the potential ramifications of Ginger's cause of death.

Since yaba was such an unusual drug in Vancouver, trying to pinpoint its source was the logical next step. Whoever took Ginger had to be either a major customer or dealer due to the sheer volume of pills inside the snake. Obviously the VPD's Drug Unit had more resources than I did when it came to tracking down narcotics, but after the way Cornish scoffed at the validity of my discovery, I wasn't about to hold my breath that the police would make headway anytime soon. Which left me with two options: investigate the city's yaba distribution directly by attempting to scare up leads wherever I could find them, which seemed both unlikely and ineffective, or return to the root of the crime that had been committed and try and connect it to the yaba itself.

I looked at the facts. Someone associated with XCCW had kidnapped Johnny's snake. The snake was then held in a location where there were ample quantities of yaba. It then consumed the drugs and overdosed, causing the kidnapper to adjust the timeline and rush the ransom exchange. While I wasn't ready just yet to speculate on what went wrong at the exchange or why Johnny was murdered, I did have good reason to investigate a potential link between XCCW and yaba. And while I was certain that if meth was being distributed at XCCW then Bert Grasby would know about it, I doubted he would be very forthcoming with that information given our newly developed acrimony. But that didn't necessarily mean that no one from XCCW would talk to me.

My thoughts were interrupted when Hank Williams Jr. finished crooning about all the different ways in which a country boy can survive and my pop clicked off the Durango's CD player. I realized that we had left downtown behind us and were now cruising along Main Street. Once we passed through the intersection at Broadway I knew exactly where we were going.

"I don't know about you," he said, "but I sure as hell could go for a milkshake."

"You and me both, Pop."

"And you're buying, goddamn it."

The Dairy Queen on Main Street was perhaps my old man's favourite, but not because it necessarily served up better frosty treats. No, my father preferred this location due to the fact that it was small and quaint, perched on an unassuming street corner and surrounded by fewer commercial establishments and more heritage homes than your typical DQ. It also featured retro-style booths and a classic Dairy Queen red-bubble roof, which meant if there were no cars parked on the street then the malt shop pretty much looked like it had been undisturbed since the seventies.

We ordered two large milkshakes and took a seat in a brightly coloured booth. By the time we had nearly finished our drinks I had brought my pop up to speed on Johnny's case. He had spoken to Declan earlier that morning after his flight landed, and my cousin had done his best to summarize what had happened while he was at his security conference.

My pop took a sip of his shake and smacked his lips. "This is more like it. Can you believe that I couldn't find one Dairy Queen the entire time I was in LA? All they had down there were these Carl's Jr. places. Their shakes tasted like frosted piss." He took another sip of his root beer milkshake. My pop had always been one to like variety when it came to his shakes. But not me. I was a banana man through and through.

"Thanks for bailing my ass out," I said finally.

"Imagine my surprise," he chortled. "My son, the private detective."

Ever since I left pro wrestling my father had been on my case to go for my private investigator's licence and officially join the family business. I had never had much interest. It was the second time in my life that I had greatly disappointed my old man. The first was when I chose not to follow in his footsteps as a cop.

"This is kind of a one-time thing," I said.

"Maybe it shouldn't be."

"Come on, Pop. We've been over this."

"That was before you twice dug up evidence ahead of the police."

"The only reason I was able to do that was because I understand the wrestling world better than they do."

"Bullshit. You sniffed out those pictures Melvin took and were the first one to figure out that the ex-girlfriend wasn't a suspect. You also knew to examine the snake's guts for evidence. That didn't happen because you used to wrestle. It happened because you followed your instincts. Like it or not, you got a nose for this stuff, son. It's in your blood."

"Well maybe I don't want it to be," I snapped.

"So what then? You're just going to keep on wasting your life bouncing at clubs and living off what's left of your wrestling money? What the hell kind of life is that?"

"It's the one that I want right now."

"Goddamn it, John!" barked my father.

I had had enough. I was sick of having the same fight with my father over and over again. I also hated being called *John*, even though my full legal name was actually *John Edward Ounstead*. My old man stubbornly insisted upon calling me by my given name, despite the fact I'd gone by *Jed* ever since my mother gave me the nickname as a boy.

"I can't believe I'm saying this, but maybe stopping for a milkshake was a mistake. Thanks again, Pop. I'll find my way from here."

Heads turned in the Dairy Queen as a low guttural growl escaped my old man's throat. I had made it only a few steps from the table before I heard him grumble. "Get back here," he commanded.

"What?" I said, returning to his table.

"Sit." I did as I was told.

"You got your fancy i-gizmo with you?"

"You mean my iPhone?"

"Yeah."

"Right here," I said, withdrawing the device from my pocket.

"You get emails on that?"

"Yes."

"Check for a new one."

I activated my phone and opened the mail application. After a few seconds the phone chimed, indicating new mail. There was one unread message in my inbox from ktucker@vpd.ca. "Who's K. Tucker?" I asked.

"Old friend of mine who works in Criminal Records and Fingerprinting. After talking to your cousin I had Tuck run Bert Grasby's name and send you the results." I opened up the PDF attachment and saw the complete criminal records check on Grasby. I glanced up at my father, surprised. "Just be careful with this joker," he cautioned. "Declan told me how his boys jumped you the other night and Tuck mentioned that his rap sheet suggests he may be into some shady shit."

"Okay, Pop."

"And one more thing." He tossed me his badge, which had been confiscated by the cops upon my arrest.

"You might be needing that," he said with a wink. I pocketed the badge and we both took sips of our milkshakes.

"So what's your next move, detective?" he asked.

I proceeded to tell him about my intention to find the link between XCCW and the yaba. We each ordered another milkshake and continued to discuss potential leads and avenues of investigation that I could follow to find Johnny's killer. It was the happiest I had seen my old man in a long time.

TWENTY-ONE

I spent the next morning carefully going over Bert Grasby's criminal record. I scrambled some eggs and poured a glass of grapefruit juice, then spread out a printed copy of the PDF file I had received from my old man's police contact across my kitchen table. I opened the blinds and let a sudden burst of autumn sunshine light up my living room. Boats set sail in the Coal Harbour marina, and I could see the heated patio of the nearby posh restaurant Cardero's filling up with customers for brunch. Despite the action outside my front window, the only time I looked up from Grasby's file was when an attractive, blonde, female jogger who stepped in dog crap on the sidewalk proceeded to loudly berate an elderly man walking a terrier for not cleaning up after his pet.

Grasby's criminal career started off simply enough when he was arrested at age nineteen in his hometown of Hamilton for possession of marijuana. He followed up that charge with numerous minor summary offences. By the time he had reached his mid-twenties Grasby had graduated to more serious crimes, including theft and fraud. At thirty-one he was convicted of sexually molesting a teenage boy and sentenced to five years in prison, although he ended up only serving three years before being released on mandatory supervision.

Grasby's most noteworthy offense occurred in the late nineties while he was living in Montreal. He was arrested and charged for owning and operating a chain of massage parlours, which he was using as fronts for brothels. The case had garnered a lot of interest in the media because Grasby's businesses were part of a larger prostitution ring in the Greater Montreal area that was broken up by the Royal Canadian Mounted Police. More than fifty people were taken into custody during the sting, which was a multiple effort between the RCMP, the Canadian Border Services Agency, and the Integrated Border Enforcement Team, a joint task force comprised of both Canadian and US law enforcement agencies. The reason for the feds' involvement was that dozens of the people arrested were women and teenage boys whom the police believed could have been victims of human trafficking. Ultimately there was difficulty in making the human trafficking charges stick and they were dropped, but not before Grasby had traded intel on other Montreal brothels in exchange for a plea bargain. As a result, Grasby served six months in a minimum-security prison for procurement and keeping a common bawdy house before being released on parole.

I cross-referenced the criminal record with what I remembered from Grasby's background check and worked out that after serving time for his role in the Montreal prostitution ring he had made his way west, living for brief periods in Calgary and Edmonton before eventually arriving in Vancouver eight years ago. He kept his nose clean for a while until he was arrested again, this time on suspicion of aggravated assault.

The victim was Trevor Benton, a twenty-six-year-old gay male escort who had been known to advertise his services on Craigslist and other erotic websites. Benton was brutally beaten in his base-ment suite, which was then set ablaze in an arson attack. Benton managed to escape his burning home but wound up being hospi-talized for nearly a month. It turned out that Grasby was a regular client of Benton's, but after being brought in for questioning, the charges were dropped. Benton claimed to have no memory of his attacker and even though the cops liked Grasby for the crime there was a substantial lack of evidence.

A little red flag sprung up in the back of my brain. There was some previous connection between Grasby and arson. It took me a minute to connect the dots, and then I remembered what Stormy Daze had said about her fellow wrestler Chet Wilson while she was in police custody. Wilson had angered Grasby by attempting to leave XCCW for Edmonton's Monster Pro Wrestling, which resulted in his apartment suddenly going up in flames.

I put down Grasby's criminal record and went to my office. I did a web search for "*Chet Wilson Vancouver fire*" and found a story in *The Vancouver Sun* online archives. I skimmed the text until I found the detail that had made the story so newsworthy. Apparently the fire had started near several leaky propane cylinders stored inside the apartment. The resulting explosions caused tremendous damage to the small residence. A little jolt of electricity shot through my body.

I did a new web search for "*Trevor Benton Vancouver arson assault*" and came across numerous archived stories. Halfway through the second story I found the method by which Benton's basement suite was set on fire—several propane cylinders.

I leaned back in my chair and considered the facts. There was no doubt in my mind that Grasby was responsible. The coincidence of propane cylinders being the cause of both fires at Chet Wilson's apartment and Trevor Benton's basement suite was too unlikely. It also made me realize that Grasby was far more dangerous than I originally thought. I decided that if I was going to keep my plans for that evening, it might be a good idea to bring a little backup.

TWENTY-TWO

The XCCW Slam Academy was a professional wrestling camp that ran classes every Tuesday night at the Hyde Creek Recreation Centre in Port Coquitlam, a suburb about forty minutes outside of Vancouver. I drove past two trains as I neared the rec centre, which wasn't much of a surprise considering the city was known for being bisected by the Canadian Pacific Railway. The rec centre was located at the end of a semi-secluded street on a green belt, and lofty evergreen trees that hid a babbling brook surrounded the entire building.

Pocket and Tubbs had agreed to meet me at the Slam Academy after I contacted them through their email address that was listed on the XCCW website. They initially offered to stop by the pub on Wednesday but I had a lot of questions and wasn't about to wait around to ask them. Since this was the first time I was going to be on XCCW turf since the street fight with Grasby's goons, I wasn't about to take any chances. As a result Declan had agreed to accompany me, despite the fact he hadn't left downtown in years. I tried to prepare Declan for Pocket and Tubbs and their unusual appearance as we walked past the indoor swimming pool toward the gymnasium.

"You mean he's a wee little midget man?" Declan asked incredulously.

"I believe the appropriate term is dwarf," I replied.

"Do you think the tiny fella might know some lady dwarves?"

"I don't know, D, maybe. Why?"

"They're on me list."

"What list?"

"Me shagging bucket list. All the different types o'birds I want to have a go at before me arse starts pushing up clovers. And a wee little midget gal ranks surprisingly high, right in between a gymnast and an amputee."

"You've got some serious issues."

"Aye."

"Just stay sharp," I cautioned. "Grasby and his gang may be around."

We entered the gym to find dozens of teenage boys lining up to leap off of the second rope turnbuckle of a wrestling ring and practice their aerial moves on a dummy lying flat on the canvas mat. Pocket and Tubbs stood ringside coaching as a skinny blonde kid performed an uncoordinated flying elbow drop.

"C'mon, Kyle. You got to stick that shit," barked Pocket. Kyle nodded obediently before sliding out of the ring and hustling to the back of the line. When Pocket saw me he nudged Tubbs and clapped his hands. "Take five, guys," he announced.

The teenage wrestlers broke off into groups to hydrate and chat. Several of the boys gawked at me and I heard my former wrestling moniker repeatedly thrown around in hushed conversations.

"You feel like showing them a few pointers, bro?" asked Pocket. "I remember you had a sweet suplex back in the day and these kids are hurting when it comes to their fundamentals."

"I think my suplex days are behind me."

"Who be dis buggah, 'Hammerhead' Jed?" asked Tubbs as he eyed my cousin.

Declan stared at me in disbelief.

"Did this fat bastard just call me a bugger?"

Tubbs emitted a low growl and Pocket stepped forward. "It's Hawaiian pidgin, bro. '*Buggah*' means '*guy.*' Now apologize."

"For what?" asked Declan.

"Making fun of Ula," said Pocket, patting Tubbs' calf soothingly. "He's a little sensitive about his weight."

"Apparently not enough to cut back on the roasted pig."

"Declan," I said, in a scolding tone.

"Who the fuck is this Mick, Jed?" demanded Pocket.

"This is my cous—"

"*Mick?*" exclaimed Declan. "Why you poxy little bollocks. I take fuckin' shites bigger than you."

"Fuck you, bro!" shouted Pocket as he sprung forward and took a swing at Declan's groin.

Declan leapt back at the last moment and Pocket's small fist connected with the inside of his thigh. My cousin retaliated immediately. Before I could stop him Declan slammed a palm into Pocket's chest and shoved him backwards. The little man let out a loud "*oomph*" before sliding across the floor, his trajectory interrupted when he made impact with the side of the wrestling ring. Tubbs snarled and charged forward but fortunately the big man was slow. I leapt in between him and Declan as my cousin slipped into a *Dornálaíocht* Irish bare-knuckle boxing stance, his fists hovering dangerously in front of his face like twin cobras poised to strike.

"That's enough!" I shouted, shoving Declan backwards.

"Gobshite!"

"Damn it, Declan. Wait for me outside."

"Nah, nah!" snarled Tubbs. "Dis haole gots to pay, 'Hammerhead' Jed!"

All of the Slam Academy kids had stopped what they were doing and stood slack-jawed and staring in disbelief. I squeezed Tubbs' mammoth shoulder. "Let me handle this, okay?" Tubbs gave

Declan the Samoan stink-eye for what felt like an eternity before he lumbered off to check on Pocket. I glared at my cousin.

"The wee tosser took a swing at me love spuds!" he exclaimed.

"Outside," I said firmly. Declan snorted disapprovingly before lighting a cigarette and sauntering off. I approached Pocket and Tubbs just as the big Samoan was helping his partner to his feet. "Are you okay?" I asked.

"Who the fuck was that asshole?" demanded Pocket as he gingerly rubbed his elbow.

"He's my cousin. He's deadly in a fight so I brought him along in case Grasby or any of his boys took a run at me again."

I quickly filled Pocket and Tubbs in on how Grasby's goons had jumped me outside The Emerald Shillelagh. When I had finished they both started snickering.

"What's so funny?" I asked.

"Bro, Grasby or any of his boy brigade wouldn't be caught dead at Slam Academy. Me and Ula run the whole thing ourselves. Grasby just takes a cut for letting us use the XCCW brand name."

"Now I feel really bad about bringing my cousin along."

"Bygones, bro. It's not your fault he's a prick. And I don't blame you for watching your back. Grasby was talking some serious smack about you at the pay-per-view over the weekend."

"He is major huhu wit you, brah," warned Tubbs.

"Fuckin' rights," said Pocket. "Dude was fuming."

I wasn't terribly surprised to hear that. After all, because of me Grasby's prized stretching buddy had a crushed nose and the leader of his goon squad had one less thumb to style his spiky hair.

"I take it Dylan isn't able to wrestle with his nose all messed up?"

Pocket and Tubbs' faces broke into big smiles. "Bro, that was because of you? That's awesome! Grasby told us he took a bad fall at the gym."

"I can assure you that wasn't the case." They both had themselves a good laugh. "Listen, guys, what can you tell me about the drugs in XCCW?" I asked.

"Drugs?" said Pocket hesitantly.

"Look, you know I'm not a cop. But some evidence has come to light that suggests whoever killed Johnny was dealing. I know firsthand that every pro-wrestling promotion has at least one solid hookup so I was hoping you could point me in the right direction."

Pocket shot Tubbs a knowing look. The Samoan gave him a reassuring nod. "There's only one guy like that at xccw, bro. Anything you want, he can get. Pharmaceutical grade steroids, Vicodin, coke, weed—you name it."

"What about meth?" I asked.

"For sure, bro."

"Who is this guy?"

"Name's Remo. He swings by practice every couple weeks."

"How long has he been coming around?"

"Just a couple of months. The guy before him, Pavel, had a big falling out with Grasby or some shit. I don't know what happened. All of a sudden Grasby introduced Remo and said from now on he'd be hooking us up with whatever we needed."

Pavel. The name sent up another red flag in the recesses of my brain. Then I remembered what Grasby had said when he had held me at gunpoint. He thought I was working for someone named Nikolai and warned me that he had found another supplier. Was the pair of Russian names another 'coincidence' like the propane tanks? Or perhaps Grasby used to buy his narcotics from the Russian mafia, who happened to be well known in Vancouver for their drug trade.

"Do you know who this Remo worked for?" Pocket glanced at Tubbs. The Samoan shook his head.

"I only meet da kine a few time." I guess surprise registered on my face as Pocket immediately jumped to his partner's defense.

"Ula's got bad knees, bro. There's no way he could wrestle anymore without a little Oxy."

"I hear you, bub," I said, remembering all too well my reliance on painkillers after tearing my quadriceps early in my career. "Any chance you guys have a last name for this Remo character?"

"Willis, brah," said Tubbs.

"Ula, how the hell do you know that?" asked Pocket.

"We talk stories. Dis Remo, he date a wahine from Lahaina."

"What does he look like?"

"He's white, six feet, two bills or so. Pretty solid dude. Has short brown hair."

"Is there anything else distinctive about him?"

Pocket cocked his head while he considered the question. After a moment he snapped his fingers. "Actually, yeah. It's kind of weird. I mean, everywhere this dude goes he's always bouncing a ball."

"A ball?"

"Yeah."

"Like a small blue racquetball?"

"Exactly!" exclaimed Pocket. "How'd you know, bro?"

TWENTY-THREE

Tracking down Remo Willis' home address was surprisingly easy. Since my old man was so supportive of me working a case on my own, he not only agreed to let me use his PI software on his computer, but he also offered to do the search himself. I tried to reiterate over the phone that this investigation was a one-shot deal but he didn't want to hear it. Instead, my father chose to believe that I had finally embraced the family business and that one day soon he'd be changing the name on his office door to *Ounstead & Son Investigations*. I didn't have the heart to fight him on the issue so I simply thanked him for his help and hung up.

I exited the freeway and drove down Hastings until I hit a familiar Dairy Queen drive thru. I ordered a banana shake and parked my truck, hoping that a tasty treat might spark an idea as to how to articulate clearly to my father that I had no intention of ever becoming a private investigator. I guess I couldn't really blame him for not understanding why. To be honest, I'm not really sure I understood it myself. My pro-wrestling career was over. I didn't particularly like bouncing or doing the grunt work required when assisting my old man on his cases. Those were just a couple of quick ways for me to earn some income and slow the hemorrhaging from my once bountiful but now withering savings account. The truth was I actually liked working a case on my own and had even surprised myself with some of the leads I had managed to dig up while searching for Johnny's killer. Nevertheless, taking the necessary steps to become a licensed PI just felt wrong. Like I was turning my back on the guy I used to be. The guy I was before it all fell apart.

I heard Inspector Cornish's smug voice echo in my head: *"I know all about you, Ounstead. I know why you're wrestling career ended and I know what you did before resurfacing here in Vancouver."*

I felt bile rise in the back of my throat, as the memory that had haunted me for years broke free of the mental barriers I had worked so hard to construct. I saw myself with Max, just moments before it happened. I tried to scream out, to stop it from happening again, the singular, tragic incident that changed everything. Hank Williams Jr.'s song "Whiskey Bent and Hell Bound" snapped me out of my waking nightmare. I flushed my mind of its toxic thoughts and recognized my father's ringtone.

"Hey Pop," I said, holding the phone to my ear with a shaky hand. "What do you got?"

"Didn't find a Remo, but there are five different R. Willises in the Greater Vancouver area." I took down the addresses. "Are you going to take Declan along?" he asked.

"I can handle this on my own. Besides I don't want to have to worry about that dwarf-shoving hothead losing his temper again."

"Fair enough. Stay sharp, son."

"I will, Pop."

The first address I tried was a retirement community near Vancouver International Airport, and the second was an apartment across from the Fraser River in New Westminster that was home to a single mother and her two children. However, when I reached the third address in East Vancouver, I immediately got a strong vibe that it might be the place I was looking for. Unlike other more affluent Vancouver neighbourhoods, the East Side is known for being home to both the lower-income working class and an abundance of recent immigrants. The address I had was for a small, dilapidated, split-level, green house just a few blocks from a sketchy strip of Kingsway, a busy and diverse commercial street that was one of the longest roads in all of Greater Vancouver.

The rundown residence seemed like the type of place suited for a drug-dealing lowlife, and I circled the block and drove by the house twice before pulling my truck into an adjacent lot beside a small park. I opened the glove compartment and swapped out my old man's badge for my Colt revolver, then tucked the gun in between my waistband and the small of my back. I cut through the park and walked by two elderly Asian men in sweatsuits performing tai chi, but they were too engrossed in their *katas* to notice me. I approached the house and started down the lumpy and cracked asphalt driveway. The front door swung open when I got close, revealing a ten-year-old boy dressed in a UFC T-shirt.

"Who are you?" he asked boldly.

"My name's Jed."

"What happened to your face?"

"Got in a fight."

"Really?"

"Yeah."

"That's cool. Are you selling something?"

"Nope. Is your dad home?" The boy shook his head.

"How about your mom?" He started to shake his head again, then realized his mistake and tried to cover.

"She's taking a bath," he said urgently, and then started to close the door.

"Hold on a sec." The boy left the door slightly ajar, peering through the crack at me with suspicious eyes. I took a step backwards and raised my hands. "I'm just trying to find a friend of mine. I thought he lived here."

"What's his name?"

"Remo Willis."

"Oh. Yeah, he lives here. In the basement."

"Do you know if he's home?" The boy shrugged. "Where's the entrance to his suite?"

"Around back."

The boy closed the door, and I heard the deadbolt and security chain lock as I started around the side of the house. The downstairs side windows were all blackened and the one narrow window next to the rear door was heavily frosted, making it nearly impossible to see inside. I knocked. No answer. I knocked again, listening for any sound or movement inside. There was none. I tried the door. Locked. I walked around the house again, looking for any other potential access points. Once I had done a lap I made up my mind to try my hand at a little B&E.

Thanks to an eight-foot high wooden fence and several Douglas fir trees the backyard was quite private, which made it unlikely that I'd arouse suspicion from any neighbours. I unzipped my hoodie and wrapped it around my elbow. It took me a couple of tries before I was able to smash the frosted glass with enough force to break the window. I listened closely for any sounds coming from inside but again heard nothing. I carefully reached my hand through the shattered glass and reached around blindly until I found the lock. I quickly and furtively slipped inside the suite and closed the door behind me. My nose was immediately assaulted with the pungent stench of cat urine. After fumbling along the wall for a few seconds I found a light switch.

The basement suite was a grimy mess. Dressers were over-turned, ratty furniture was cut open, and clothes were strewn across the floor. Someone had definitely been here in search of something, and even more interestingly, had locked the door after they left. I had been on enough police ride-alongs growing up to know what a place looks like after it has been tossed by the cops. But there was nothing professional about the way Remo Willis' pad had been searched, as the one bedroom unit looked like it had been hit by a tornado. The kitchen was even more chaotic, its sticky countertops cluttered with countless coffee filters, measuring cups, and glass jars. I looked under the sink and found dozens of empty bottles of drain cleaner and turkey basters.

That's when I realized Remo Willis had been using his home as a makeshift meth lab. Yaba wasn't the only narcotic I had tried during the months I had bummed around Thailand and the Philippines, searching for ways to deaden the anguish that had plagued me since leaving professional wrestling. Suffice it to say that as a result of my travels the urine smell in Remo's home should have clued me in right away that his residence was being used to cook meth, especially when there was no evidence of kitty litter or cat food anywhere. Cooking meth produces a terrible odour, which is why the windows and door that connected to the upstairs of the house had all been sealed with duct tape, trapping the potent smell inside the basement suite. I used a crusty spatula I found in a drawer to inspect the garbage can under the sink, but all I found were fast food wrappers and more empty containers. I checked the refrigerator and found a paper bag containing three frozen dead mice. Kind of an odd thing to keep in your freezer, unless you happen to have a snake around.

A shrill ring caused my heart to skip a beat. I whirled around and zeroed in on the sound of a landline telephone partially obscured by a mound of dirty laundry in the corner of the living room. I used my foot to push aside denim and flannel and picked up the receiver.

"Hello?"

"Hi, may I speak to Remo Willis please?" chirped a young female voice.

"Speaking," I replied.

"This is Aurora from Scoff's Hockey Shop calling. How are you today?"

"Fine."

"Excited about the big game tomorrow?"

I had no idea what the hell she was talking about since the Vancouver Canucks weren't scheduled to play until the weekend. "You know it," I said finally.

"Well, have I got some good news for you. Your helmet came in early! It's here and all ready to be picked up." Now I clued in. Apparently Remo liked to hit the ice when he wasn't cooking meth in his shithole basement suite.

"Excellent."

"It's really nice. It's, like, the most totally badass helmet I've ever seen."

"Thanks, Aurora. I'll be by soon."

"See you then," the girl said in a singsong voice before hanging up the phone.

I had no idea why Willis had special ordered a hockey helmet and at the moment I didn't really care. I tossed the phone receiver onto the pile of clothes and continued my search. The medicine cabinet in the bathroom was stocked with an inordinate amount of prescription painkillers made out in several different names, none of which was Remo Willis. The toilet was gurgling, so I lifted the seat with my foot. The water was blue and there was something small and circular at the bottom of the bowl. I assumed it was one of those deodorizing toilet pucks until it occurred to me that it was a little odd that Willis would care enough to sanitize his john with every flush yet keep the rest of his suite in such a squalid state. I crouched down and used the toilet bowl brush to stir the water. It wasn't a deodorizing puck at the bottom of the toilet bowl after all. It was blue coloured yaba.

The coating of the pill probably seeped off the tablet and changed the colour of the water. Which meant that Willis had probably flushed his stash, making it likely that he knew his place would be searched. Clearly he didn't want to leave any evidence lying around. More importantly, between the link to the racquetball, the frozen mice, and the yaba in the toilet, I was now certain that Remo Willis had kidnapped Ginger and held her for ransom.

A shuffling sound behind me halted my train of thought like a crash test dummy hitting a wall. Before I could reach my gun and spin around a giant hand palmed the back of my skull like a basketball and smashed my head into the porcelain rim of the toilet. Black spots danced in front of my eyes before a searing pain enveloped my head. The world went dark.

TWENTY-FOUR

I was handcuffed to a Predator. The sci-fi alien, that is, just like the one Arnold Schwarzenegger battled to the death in the 1987 film. The cuffs were linked through the creature's forearm and around its long spear, which, like the Predator itself, was made completely out of metal. The sculpture was life-sized and depicted the creature roaring, its mask removed, revealing its sharp mandibles and hideous face. A two-pronged blade was mounted on the Predator's other arm while a laser cannon sat perched on the alien warrior's shoulder. I caught my reflection in the sheen of the Predator's lacquered body armour and saw the bewildered expression on my face. It's not every day you regain consciousness only to find yourself fastened to a hulking metal statue of an intergalactic trophy hunter.

As I adjusted to my predicament I noticed that the Predator wasn't just constructed out of any type of metal — its torso appeared to be some kind of contoured internal combustion engine, while its arms and legs were a fusion of hundreds of rods, pins, and chains. Welded spark plugs served as the Predator's fingers and the entire sculpture was smooth and gleaming with a dark silver and grayish lustre.

I squirmed and yanked as hard as I could in order to free my hands, but the surrounding metal where the handcuffs had been linked through the creature's forearm was too thick. I decided to try and tip over the statue in hopes of being able to better maneuver. I gripped my hands around the spear, jumped into a squat, and drove my heels into the ground with all my strength.

"You got some size pal, but unless you compete in strong man competitions there ain't no way you're moving that. It's over seven hundred pounds."

A mammoth of a man towered above me, his bulging arms crossed across his barrel chest. He was at least six-foot-eight and almost appeared wider than he did tall, his massive frame taut with layers of thick, beefy muscle.

"Any chance you want to move it for me? I asked. "Something tells me you may have rolled a few cars in your day."

The mammoth man chortled and stroked his thick Hulk Hogan-style horseshoe mustache. Behind him was an entire workshop filled with dozens of metal sculptures of varying size and weight. Terminators, Aliens, and other sci-fi and fantasy characters including Darth Vader, Iron Man, and Spider-Man were on display throughout the workshop. There were also numerous sculptures of vehicles and spaceships, including X-Wings, Imperial Walkers, the *Millennium Falcon*, and the USS *Enterprise*. Band saws, drills, and a variety of metalworking tools, in addition to an abundance of scrap metal, were scattered throughout the shop on worktables and benches. The workshop itself was very impressive but it was clear that Horseshoe Stache had no interest in my opinion.

"What were you doing at Remo's?" the hulking man asked.

As if on cue the side of my head began to throb and I remembered my sudden impact with the toilet rim. I bent my neck to try and touch the wound but the handcuffs made it difficult.

"I suppose I have you to thank for my headache." Horseshoe took an aggressive step forward.

"Why were you there?" he growled.

"Because I suffer from paruresis." Horseshoe gawked at me, clearly befuddled.

"Paru-what?"

"Paruresis. Otherwise known as shy bladder syndrome? I have a phobia of public toilets and had to go real bad so I broke into the nearest home I could find to take a piss."

"Really?" asked Horseshoe, his eyes widening.

"No, not really, you giant fucking retard. Now where the hell am I?"

Horseshoe seethed and cocked a ham-sized fist behind his ear. I braced myself for impact but the sound of a blowtorch sparking to life gave the massive man pause. A blue flame crackled as a man stepped out of the shadows of the workshop. He was dressed in blue jeans and a white tank top, although the colours of his clothes had been muted by oil and grease stains. He flipped up the facemask of his welding helmet to reveal his chiselled features. With his square jaw, dimpled chin, and flowing blonde hair he looked more like a Norse God than a metalsmith. He waved the blowtorch at Horseshoe.

"Leave us," he ordered. Horseshoe obediently exited the workshop through a door behind me, without giving me so much as a glance. I locked eyes with Thor the welder for several moments before the handsome man removed his helmet and turned off the blowtorch. I exhaled loudly, not realizing that I had been holding my breath.

"Do you know how long that Predator statue took me to make?" he asked.

"I want to say a couple of months, but that seems like an awful lot of time for a grown man to be playing around with a bunch of greasy auto parts. You could have saved yourself a big mess if you had just gotten yourself some Lego."

Thor placed his equipment on a bench and took off his gloves. "I'm being serious, John. What do you think of my work?"

"Honestly? It's impressive," I replied, wondering how he knew my name. "What are these things anyway? Coat racks for nerds?"

Thor smiled and pulled up a stool across from me. I shifted my weight and realized the familiar bulge of my wallet was missing from my back pocket. That's how he knew who I was and why he was calling me John instead of Jed.

"It's metal-art. I primarily use recycled motorcycle parts, although any type of scrap metal I manage to get my hands on usually finds its way into my work." Thor picked up a small Star Wars spaceship from a nearby workbench and held the sculpture gingerly in his hands.

"The secret is to let the metal speak to you. I knew I wanted to make a small vehicle, but I had no idea what kind. But when I started to polish this crankshaft here," he said, pointing to the middle of the spacecraft, "I saw the resemblance it had to the cockpit of a Tie Fighter." He began to proudly point to the different parts of the sculpture like a suburban dad showing pictures of his kids at a Christmas concert.

"So I ground down some gear parts and welded spokes on them for the wings, bonded some rods and chains alongside the command pod, and, as a finishing touch, fused the mesh from a cooking sieve between the winged spokes in order to give the starfighter a more aerodynamic feel."

Thor's passion for his craft was almost infectious, and despite the fact he was responsible for both my headache and my being handcuffed to an immovable object, I found myself getting a kick out of the eccentric son-of-a-bitch.

"What?" he asked, noticing my smirk.

"You're just awfully passionate for a guy holding me against my will."

"I'd rather you think of this as a friendly chat."

"With handcuffs."

"It's better than the alternative."

"You mean an unfriendly chat?" His pleasant demeanor vanished, instantly replaced by an ice-cold glare.

"If it were unfriendly there would be no chat at all," he said, his voice laden with gravitas. Just as quickly as it appeared, Thor's ominous attitude faded and the spirited metal-artist returned. He placed the Tie Fighter sculpture back on the workbench.

"Passion is the genesis of genius, John. Surely there's something in your life that lights a spark inside of you?"

"Banana milkshakes."

"Very funny."

"I'm not joking."

"Surely there must be something of more … substance."

I hesitated before answering. "Not anymore."

"Ah, but there was something," he said excitedly.

"Yes."

"What was it?"

"Wrestling."

"What's keeping you from doing it again?"

"A lot of things."

"Like what?"

"Shit happens. Things change." Thor eyed me curiously and crossed his arms.

"I came close to giving up on metal-art once. My sculptures were mediocre at best and my skills weren't improving. But then I decided that a life without doing what I loved wasn't a life worth living. So I went to Thailand and spent a year studying the craft from the people who invented it."

A shot of adrenaline coursed through my veins.

Thailand.

Whoever Thor and Horseshoe were, they sure as hell weren't cops, yet they had obviously had Remo Willis' place under surveillance. Now I was handcuffed to a seven-hundred-pound metal statue and surrounded by dozens more only to find out that my kidnapper had learned his trade while living in Thailand, the birthplace of yaba meth. It couldn't be a coincidence.

"Is that where you made the connections that allow you to smuggle and distribute yaba in Vancouver?" The shock was instantly evident on Thor's face and the creative artist façade that he worked so hard to maintain cracked faster than a can of cold beer in Declan's hand on a hot day.

"What do you know?" he asked solemnly.

"Let me out of these cuffs and I'll be happy to tell you."

Thor grabbed the blowtorch and sparked it to life. "If you don't start talking I'm going to scorch your testicles until they're blacker than rotten plums."

"You make an awfully convincing argument," I replied immediately.

I proceeded to tell Thor about Johnny's murder and the trail that led me to Remo Willis. His face betrayed little while I spoke, even when I explained how I found the yaba in Ginger's stomach. In fact, Thor's only response while listening to my story was to rotate his wrist back and forth, causing the blowtorch's blue flame to hiss as it arced through the air.

"What were you planning to do if you found Remo?" he asked.

"I'm not exactly sure."

"Would you turn him in to the police?"

"I don't know."

"Would you kill him?"

"I wouldn't be able to answer that question until I had gotten my fill of beating the hell out of the bastard first." Thor seemed to like that answer. He switched off the blowtorch.

"I like your style, John. You've managed to connect your friend's murder to Remo, which is something I know for a fact that the police have yet to do. You've also proven yourself a lot more adept than any of my boys, none of whom ever thought to try and locate Remo by any way other than staking out his residence. That's why I want to make you an offer."

"I'm listening."

"I'm going to let you go. I'm also going to ensure that none of my boys impedes your little investigation again. In exchange, if you do find Remo, you're going to turn him over to me instead of the cops."

"Say I was able to do that. What would you do to him?"

"Execute him," he said calmly.

"I'm confused. Why would a drug dealer like you want to take out one of your own guys?"

"I'm not some low-life peddler, John. I'm an artist and an entrepreneur. Distributing yaba just happens to be one of my many business ventures. And as for my reasons for wanting Remo Willis dead, well, let's just say it's something that is necessary, and, quite frankly, none of your goddamn business."

"If I find him I'm sure as hell not turning the son-of-a-bitch over to you unless I know why you want him dead."

"Isn't having retribution for your friend's murder enough?"

"I'm afraid not."

Thor walked to a workbench and placed the blowtorch in between a lathe and an unfinished metal bust of Optimus Prime. He also retrieved a large ring of keys, one of which he used to uncuff me from the Predator statue. I massaged my wrists while he took a seat back on the stool.

"Remo is a relatively new business associate of mine. Someone I trust vouched for him and I gave him a place in my organization. He was a modest earner at best but he was getting the job done. That was until recently, when his behaviour started to become peculiar and erratic. Turns out he got hooked on the meth he was dealing and was tweaking so bad he went broke. This must have been when he got the brilliant idea, which was completely unsanctioned by me, to steal your friend's snake and hold it for ransom. I guess the deal went bad and he killed your friend. No offense, John, but I couldn't give a shit. What I do care about is the fact that Remo Willis panicked and decided to abscond with over fifty thousand dollars worth of my product."

The conviction in his voice was stern. He clearly had a grudge against Remo Willis. Just like me. Normally in a situation like this I would take my time and weigh my options. I would get to know a person before I made a deal with them. Except I had already been bullied, beaten up, and bruised, and just the thought of Johnny being murdered by a hopped up meth head made my blood boil.

"I'll do it," I said.

"Excellent," said Thor, a big smile spreading across his face. He turned his back and walked briskly across the workshop to a refrigerator. He yanked open the door and grabbed a couple of bottles of Alexander Keith's Pale Ale.

"A toast to our arrangement," he said, as he popped the caps. I took the bottle and clinked it against his. I enjoyed a long sip and the cool beer felt wonderful as it washed down my dry throat.

"You know, John, if you're able to pull this off I might just have to custom make a sculpture for you."

"I probably wouldn't turn down a life-sized statue of Princess Leia in her gold bikini if you … whoa."

I heard buzzing in my ears and stumbled forward. My head started to spin and the workshop became a kaleidoscope of glinting silver and metal. I dropped my beer and the rattle of the bottle hitting the cement floor was deafening. I fell on my back and struggled to stay conscious while suds foamed around my ear. The last thing I remember was Thor standing over me.

"Nothing personal, John. But I figured you'd prefer a spiked drink instead of getting knocked unconscious again."

"Why?" I managed to croak.

"Because you have no idea who I am, where you are, or how you got here. And I intend to keep it that way."

TWENTY-FIVE

"Hey Mister." I felt something poke my side. "Mister, wake up."
I fought through the fogginess and opened my eyes. I was lying on the sidewalk across the street from Remo Willis' basement suite. Something poked me again. I sat up and saw the kid in the UFC shirt that I had spoken to before standing in front of me with a hockey stick in his hand.

"Are you okay?" the kid asked.

"Did you see how I got here?" I asked in a raspy voice.

"I heard some screeching tires and when I looked out the window you were just lying there." I cleared my throat, rubbed my face in my hands, and shakily climbed to my feet.

"You should go back inside, kid."

"Did you get in another fight?" he asked.

I checked myself and found that my wallet and gun had been returned to my person. I peeled off a ten-dollar bill and offered it to the kid if he took a hike. The kid snatched the bill and scurried back across the street. I noticed a glossy business card I didn't recognize sticking out of my wallet. I withdrew the card, which was blank except for a local 604 area code phone number. I flipped it over. There was a handwritten message scribbled in black ink. It read: *Call when you find him.*

I spent the drive home going over my encounter with Thor. The guy appeared to be involved in some pretty nefarious activities for a so-called artist, including the distribution of yaba. That also put him on a very short list of people in Vancouver who dealt in exotic narcotics. As a result, there was a strong possibility that Thor was already on the Vancouver Police Department's radar. Normally, I would ask my old man to call in a favour with one of his pals from the force but in this instance I already knew what he would say. There was only one person he was still in touch with who had a direct pipeline into the VPD's Drug Unit—his former protégé Detective Constable Rya Shepard. Rya had spent years earning a reputation as a tenacious investigator within the Drug Unit before transferring into the Homicide Squad and partnering with my father. If there were any mention of a guy fitting Thor's description in the VPD system, Rya would dig it up. The only problem with asking for her help was that she would be livid with me for not informing her about my lead on Remo Willis and investigating it on my own.

I glanced at the business card again. I could try and track the number myself but I had a feeling that Thor was smart enough to only give me the digits to an untraceable line or burner cell phone. I wasn't looking forward to it, but if I was going to have any chance of ascertaining Thor's identity then I needed to give Rya a call. I came to the conclusion that a little liquid courage could help me work up the nerve to pick up the phone so I decided a visit to the pub was definitely in order.

I drove home quickly, hoping that a hot shower and change of clothes would help shake the cloudiness lingering in my head as a result of the spiked beer. A light fog drifted in from the marina, turning the air into a misty haze that hovered throughout the ocean front cul-de-sac. I parked on the street in front of my townhouse, not bothering to pull the car into the garage as usual since I was just making a quick stop.

I had just gotten out of the vehicle and beeped the car alarm when my driver's side window exploded. I felt needles prick the side of my face as tiny shards of glass bit into my cheek. I spun around as I fell backwards and managed to get my hands out in front of me, bracing my fall as I dropped to the concrete. A metallic thwacking sound echoed but it wasn't until I saw the bullet holes in my Ford's crew cab that I realized someone was shooting at me. Squealing tires joined the cacophony of shattering glass and bullets piercing metal, and it was only then that I caught sight of the black SUV with tinted windows tearing down the street toward me. I launched myself up and out of plank position, took three quick powerful strides, then leapt through the air Bobby Orr style. I landed hard on the grass and rolled once before taking cover behind a transformer. Bullets hit the other side of the square metal box that housed the electrical device as I tucked my knees into my chest and desperately tried to shrink my bulk. An engine roared in the distance and just as quickly as it had begun, the shooting was over.

My ears were ringing and I couldn't hear a sound other than my hammering heartbeat and laboured breathing. I checked myself repeatedly and to my surprise found that aside from the glass in my cheek I was pretty much unscathed. I drew my Colt revolver and flipped out the swing cylinder—no bullets. Thor must have unloaded my gun while I was unconscious. I tucked the Colt into my waistband behind my back and peered around the transformer. The coast was clear. I made a beeline for my front door only to find it was slightly ajar, the wooden doorframe splintered from where a crowbar had pried the deadbolt free. It seemed as though the drive-by shooting was a contingency plan.

I slipped inside my place. It was dark and I wanted it to stay that way. I quietly opened the door to the garage and grabbed an aluminum baseball bat. I tiptoed up to the main floor, careful to avoid the creaky spots on my stairs. The house was silent as I crept around the corner into the living room, the bat cocked behind my ear and ready to swing.

My place had been trashed. The flat-screen TV had been ripped off the wall and smashed, my furniture was bleeding upholstery from where it had been cut open, and several bottles of Fess Parker's Frontier Red wine that I liked had been smashed against the walls and poured onto the carpet. My heart sank as I took in the damage. I picked up a half empty bottle of Frontier Red and looked at the smiling mug of Davy Crockett in his trademark coonskin cap staring back at me. I wondered what Davy would have done after getting beaten up, kidnapped, and nearly shot to death. I decided he probably would have gotten drunk and killed a bunch of Indians. But since I was out of bullets, far from a reservation, and not a racist, I figured I'd just stick with getting drunk. I took a swig of wine and licked my lips, certain that my day couldn't get any crappier. Then I heard the sound of a gun being cocked behind me.

"Drop the bat, asshole." I did as I was told. "On your knees, interlace your fingers behind your—"

"Rya?" I said, recognizing the familiar voice. The pistol's hammer uncocked and she let out an epic sigh.

"Jesus, Jed. I almost put one in your head." I turned around and watched as Rya stepped into the light, her face flushed.

"You okay?" I asked.

"Fine. You?" I nodded.

"What are you doing here?"

"I came to tell you that you were right about the yaba. One of our drug guys positively ID'ed it a couple of hours ago."

"Shocker," I said, my voice dripping with sarcasm.

Rya holstered her gun and braced herself against the kitchen counter. "You going to tell me what the hell just happened?"

"I'm still trying to figure that out myself."

"Did you get a look at the shooter?"

"Shooters. Plural. And no, I'm afraid I was too busy dodging a hailstorm of bullets to take a mental mugshot."

I took a swig of the wine. Rya groaned in disgust. "At least use a glass, for Christ's sake." I told her where to find the wine glasses and opened the last bottle of Frontier Red that my would-be murderers didn't smash. We both took sips while I explained the drive-by shooting in detail.

"They must have seen me enter the house," she said. "I only got here a few minutes before the shooting began."

"If it's the guys I'm thinking of then they probably know you're a cop and wouldn't be dumb enough to mess with you."

"You know who did this?" she asked, waving an arm wildly around my trashed living room.

"I'm pretty sure it was Grasby's crew."

"Grasby? But I thought he wasn't involved in Johnny's murder?"

"He's not. He just wants me dead because I slugged him and maimed one of his pretty-boy thugs." I quickly explained how Billy and I got jumped outside The Emerald Shillelagh. I left out the part where Declan blasted off Julian's thumb with his illegal and unlicensed hand cannon.

"Do you want me to look into police protection?" she asked when I had finished. "I might be able to leverage it if I claim that you're a key witness for the Crown." I shook my head.

"What I want is your help." I told Rya about my conversation with Pocket and Tubbs and how I tracked the lead to Remo Willis' basement suite.

"And of course you didn't think to call me before heading over there."

"I would have, except last I heard you geniuses over at the VPD had ruled out any yaba-related leads."

"Please tell me you didn't contaminate the scene at his residence."

"Relax, Detective. I'm not that obtuse. Besides, whatever your forensic nerds find inside of that basement suite won't be as revealing as what happened to me."

"Which was?"

"I got knocked out and taken to meet Remo Willis' drug-lord employer."

"You're screwing with me, right?" I filled Rya in on my meeting with Thor in his workshop. "Did you get a name or spot a licence plate? Anything that could help ID him?"

"Nothing. And that's exactly the way he wanted it. From what I gathered, this guy has solid overseas connections to some seriously exotic product. That's why I need your help. Someone has to access the Drug Unit's archive and see if there's anybody who matches Thor's description, and I doubt they'd be very receptive to the idea of letting me drop by and root through their files." Rya's eyes narrowed and she downed the rest of her wine. She was silent for a little while. I knew better than to speak.

"Okay, Jed. Under one condition. From now on, we're in this together. You get a lead, you fill me in immediately. I promise to do the same."

"I guess that makes us partners, eh? Just like T.J. Hooker and Heather Locklear. Except with better hair." Rya sighed and shook her head.

"The fourth graders at the elementary school where I give safety presentations are more mature than you." Rya placed her empty wine glass in the sink and headed toward the door. "And for the record, you're no T.J. Hooker," she said dryly.

"I know that, Rya," I replied matter-of-factly. "I was Heather Locklear in that scenario."

After Rya left I cleaned and bandaged the small cuts on my cheek, picking out a few pieces of driver's side window glass in the process. I phoned Declan and shared the details of my near-death experience. When he had finished cursing up a storm and threatening to do grievous bodily harm to Grasby and his goons in more creative ways than I can possibly describe, I asked him to keep word of the drive-by shooting from my pop. I saw no point in worrying the old man for the time being, plus, knowing my father, upon hearing the news he would immediately involve himself directly into my investigation and then I wouldn't even be able to check my email without his say so. We also agreed that while

Grasby had a bounty out on my head it would be best if I crashed at Declan's for a while. Declan called Sally, another bartender who worked at The Emerald Shillelagh, and had her cover his shift so he could come over and help me clean up my townhouse.

While I waited for Declan I went upstairs and retrieved some bullets from my closet. Then I sat on my ripped couch, reloaded my Colt revolver, and drank more Frontier Red wine. At some point my cell phone chirped and my heart skipped a beat. I was definitely rattled by the drive-by. I took a deep breath and let the phone ring a few times before answering.

"Hello?"

"Are you a fucking idiot?" barked an angry male voice. It was Russell, the manager of Tonix nightclub. I had completely forgotten about my shift that night.

"Damn, Russell, I'm sorry, bub—"

"Don't fucking 'bub' me, Ounstead! Explain to me why I've got no one here to cover the door."

I glanced around my trashed townhouse. I didn't even know where to begin.

"Look, I promise I'll make it up to you."

"Forget it. I need people I can rely on. You're done." *Click.*

And just like that, I was officially unemployed again. So I did the only thing I could think of. I poured more wine. Forty-five minutes later Declan was at my door dressed in an army green canvas jacket and carrying an arsenal of weapons that even John Rambo would find impressive.

"The only thing you're missing is a red headband," I said.

"Aye, and we're sure as shite going to get to win this time, you jammy bugger," he replied, before stepping inside and dropping a large unzipped canvas bag onto the floor from which numerous gun stocks sprouted like the stuffing of a twice-baked potato.

"Jesus Christ, D," I said staring at the bag of weapons. "I know you don't like to talk about your time in the IRA but what the hell? Were you some kind of Irish commando or something?"

"Or something," replied Declan, as he surveyed the damage to my townhouse. He scratched his head and let out an audible sigh. "Bloody hell, what a pisshole."

"Tell me what you really think."

"I think if I'm going to get me drink on tonight we better get our arses to work."

We spent the next two hours cleaning like a couple of coked-up Molly Maids. We boarded up broken windows, picked up glass, and scrubbed the walls and carpets as best we could. We moved the ruined furniture to the centre of the room and propped the broken plasma television up against a wall. I then proceeded to place Post-it notes on any areas or items that had been damaged or vandalized for the insurance company, which I would call first thing in the morning. Finally I filled a backpack with some clothes and my most valuable possessions, including my passport, photos of my mother, a scrapbook of my wrestling career, and a wrestling DVD that featured me in a spotlight segment. With my personal belongings slung over my shoulder, I bid adieu to my home, hopped in my truck, and followed Declan in his 1974 Pontiac GTO.

We crisscrossed through the city, making our way toward the heart of Yaletown. We reached the posh neighbourhood and cruised down Hamilton Street. Traffic jammed up in front of Rodney's Oyster House, due to a bachelorette party consisting of dolled-up women in matching pink T-shirts and feathered boas spilling out of the restaurant into the tight one-way street. I waited patiently as Declan rolled down his car window and struck up a conversation with a couple girls, but after thirty seconds I had enough and laid into the horn. He flipped me the bird before flooring his GTO and tearing into his condo's underground parking less than a block away.

I grabbed a bottle of Steam Whistle Pilsner out of Declan's fridge and headed to the guest room. As I unpacked my bag I dropped the scrapbook and it serendipitously fell open to a clipping from *The Advocate*, a newspaper in Baton Rouge, Louisiana.

A sports writer that had been in attendance the night of the fateful Indian Strap match had done a follow-up piece on the wrestling show and decided to do a profile on me and Johnny and how we unexpectedly dazzled the live audience with our untelevised dark-match. The clipping featured a photograph of the both of us standing back-to-back in front of the ring the day after the match. Although his arm was in a sling, Johnny was beaming, as was I. We had gambled and it had paid off, as we proved to both our peers and ourselves that we had what it took to thrill a crowd. I don't think I had ever been happier than I was at that moment. I stared at the clipping for a long time and wondered if I would ever feel that way again. Eventually I closed the scrapbook and stuffed it back into the bowels of my backpack.

I joined Declan on the living room couch, and he had already placed a fresh bottle of Steam Whistle Pilsner for me in one of the armrest cup-holders. We hadn't said a word since arriving at his place and proceeded to drink in silence while watching some crappy sitcom with the volume down low. I hadn't really had a chance to process the day's events and with each sip of beer my mind jumped from thoughts of Remo Willis' meth-lab basement suite to Thor and his formidable metal-art sculptures to the feeling of bullets whizzing by my body. Eventually, I spoke.

"Grasby isn't going to stop coming after me until I'm dead, is he?"

"Nope," replied Declan.

We knocked off a few more Steam Whistles before I decided to turn in, the bluntness of Declan's answer lingering in my head.

TWENTY-SIX

The last time I was in a sporting goods store a Vancouver hockey riot was an isolated incident and Tiger Woods was still considered a faithful husband. Scoff's Hockey Shop on Hastings Street was a no-frills, warehouse-like retail store that seemed less concerned with curb appeal and more concerned with providing the best selection of hockey gear in the greater Vancouver area. Although I promised to keep Rya in the loop regarding my every lead, I saw no need to update her on what could turn out to be a wasted trip, especially since, at the moment, all I had to go on was a phone call from a perky sales girl. Still, there was an outside chance that some of the information that Remo Willis left on file with Scoff's could conflict with what I had already obtained and give me a new direction in which I could pursue the son-of-a-bitch.

I strolled through endless aisles of helmets and shin pads until I spotted a dilapidated Customer Service sign. I headed toward the desk, the narrow walkway leading there lined on both sides with rows of glossy wooden and composite hockey sticks that made me feel as if I was walking the highway to hockey heaven. I reached Customer Service but before I could ding the little bell on the counter a short brunette girl popped up from behind the desk like a submerged buoy.

"Welcome to Scoff's, how may I help you today?" Hearing her voice confirmed that this was the same bubbly gal I had spoken to on the phone while at Remo Willis' place.

"I'm here to pick up a helmet," I said.

"Name?" she asked, flipping open a ledger.

"Remo Willis." Her jaw dropped open and she stared at me with googly eyes.

"You're Remo Willis?" she asked excitedly. "Oh my God. I'm Aurora. It's so cool to meet you."

"Actually, Remo's a friend of mine. He's pretty swamped right now so he asked me to pick up his helmet for him."

"Oh. Okay," she said, the pep fading from her voice.

"How do you know of Remo?" I asked.

"My brother's in the same hockey league. I've seen Remo play. He's, like, amazing."

"Really?"

"Dude, he's like a frickin' brick wall. Are you going to the game tonight?"

"What game?"

"Uh, the big ASHL Div 1 game between the Ice-Holes and Masterbladers?" The ASHL, or Adult Safe Hockey League, was one of the most prominent amateur hockey leagues in the province.

"Is Remo playing?" I asked. She looked at me like I was an idiot.

"He's the starting goalie for the Ice-Holes, man. Of course he'll be there."

"Right." I finally had a bead on Willis. It was all I could do to keep from pumping my fist in celebration.

"Geez, for his buddy, you sure don't know much about him," said Aurora.

"Remo and I are kind of new friends," I said, trying to recover and maintain my impromptu alias. "So where's this game being played, anyway?" Aurora sighed and seemed irritated. She scribbled a web address down on a Post-it note and slid it across the counter.

"It's all on the site," she said.

"Remo didn't happen to leave an address or a cell number with you guys, did he?"

"I don't know. Why?"

"It's kind of a long story." Aurora shrugged and twirled her hair with her finger.

"I've got time."

"Of course you do," I muttered sardonically.

"What's that supposed to mean?" she snapped.

"Nothing," I said in an apologetic tone. "Look would you mind checking for me? It's really important." Aurora glared at me skeptically. After a moment, she cracked open the ledger and rifled through its pages.

"Here," she said, thwacking an index finger down at the bottom of a page. "No address, just one phone number. Six oh four, seven two three—"

"That's okay," I said, knowing that the digits had to be for the landline at Remo's basement suite. "I already have that number." She sighed dramatically and half-rolled her eyes.

"I'll grab the helmet," she said.

Aurora disappeared into the back room while I opened the web browser on my phone and punched in the address. The Adult Safe Hockey League website appeared and I clicked on the link that had all the information about that evening's game, including the rosters. Both Remo's team and the Masterbladers were undefeated, so the winner of tonight's league game would move into first place. I clicked on Remo Willis' name and was taken to his player profile page, which included a picture. With his stocky build and close cropped hair, Willis closely fit the description that Pocket and Tubbs had given me. I saved his picture to my phone but before I had a chance to read his profile in detail Aurora returned with a cardboard box.

She carefully removed a helmet from inside and unwrapped a soft cloth in which it was swathed. A Bauer goalie's mask shimmered under the florescent light and I realized instantly why the item was a special order. The artwork that had been airbrushed onto the helmet was stunning, and the entire mask was engulfed in blue lightning bolts and charcoal storm clouds. At the top of the helmet, just above where the facemask's cage began, was a hyper-stylized, muscular, and ferocious looking crab. The crab was silver and had the number *20* painted on the back of its shell, and its razor sharp pinchers reached down the side of the mask while its remaining legs wrapped around the back of the helmet down to its base.

A crab. What the hell was it about a crab that seemed so familiar? After a moment I remembered, and quickly brought up the ransom email that Johnny had forwarded me on my phone. The email address was thesteelcrab@gmail.com. "Son-of-a-bitch," I muttered under my breath.

"Frickin' sweet, eh?" chirped Aurora, admiring the artwork.

I thanked Aurora for her time and she wrapped the helmet back in its cloth. I tucked the box under my arm and headed toward my truck, wondering the whole way what the hell steroid-enhanced crustaceans meant to the man who had murdered my friend.

TWENTY-SEVEN

I was reading Remo Willis' hockey stats on the ASHL's web site and cursing Declan's home computer's sluggish Internet connection when my phone rang.

"We need to meet," said Rya, by way of a greeting.

"The Shillelagh?"

"No. This needs to be on the down low."

"I'd extend an offer to my place but something tells me you would prefer to not cop a squat on wine-stained carpet."

"Foo's Ho Ho. One hour."

Forty-five minutes later I was driving underneath the golden tiles of the Millennium Gate, the historic and ornamental landmark that serves as the official entranceway to Chinatown. Nestled in between Gastown, the Downtown Eastside, and the Financial and Business districts, the area is renowned for not only being one of the largest Chinatowns in North America, but for also being a cultural hotspot and showcase for Vancouver's incredible diversity and distinctiveness.

I tried to park on the street at the corner of Pender and Columbia outside the restaurant, but it was too crowded. Instead

I doubled back and found a spot a block south of Pender in Shanghai Alley. I zipped up my vest and buried my hands in my pockets, trying to keep myself insulated from the cold snap that had hit the city that afternoon. I made my way past a serene Zen courtyard and down Shanghai Alley's centuries old cobblestone road until it fed into Pender Street. I zigzagged my way between red street lamps and no-frills storefront displays, which were cluttered with everything from clusters of spiny scarlet rambutans to dried seahorses to gutted and flayed geckos impaled on sticks. The main drag of Chinatown was crackling with the spicy smells of exotic herbs and cooked meats, and after walking past a window filled with dangling Cantonese roasted ducks, I had a pretty good idea of one of the dishes I was going to order for lunch.

Foo's Ho Ho was not only the oldest restaurant in Chinatown, but it was also the best. The eatery was situated on the ground floor of a weathered four-story building, and the levels above had originally served as lodgings for Chinese labourers who helped build the Canadian Pacific Railway. I selected a wobbly table in the back of the restaurant, and had to dip my head underneath a string of hanging paper lanterns in order to take a seat on a dated, maroon vinyl chair.

I was blowing on a spoonful of wonton soup when Rya strode into the restaurant a few minutes later with a slender, meticulously groomed, and well-dressed man. He carried a light-brown briefcase, which stood out against the backdrop of his crisp black slacks and blazer. The two slid into the empty seats at the table across from me without a word. Moments passed until I realized they were both waiting for me to speak.

"Potsticker?" I asked, pointing with my chopsticks to the appetizer next to my soup. The man shot Rya a vexed look before she made introductions.

"Jed Ounstead, this is Sergeant Dwayne Sankey of the GCU."

The GCU was the Vancouver Police force's Gang Crime Unit, an outfit that functioned not only as a resource to the department, but also to other law enforcement and intelligence agencies.

Sankey gave me a curt nod before slipping a file out of his briefcase. I moved the appies out of his way but almost spilled the soup when I saw the photos he began laying out on the table. Most of the snapshots were of Horseshoe Mustache and other rough-looking characters I didn't recognize. The last photo Sankey placed on the table had been taken from a great distance. Still, there was no mistaking the person in the picture. *Thor.*

"That's him," I said. "That's the guy." Sankey and Rya exchanged a knowing glance.

"The man you met is Damian Kendricks," said Sankey. "He is a high-priority target within the GCU and we've been tracking his criminal activities for several years."

"So these guys are doing more than just dealing drugs, I take it?"

"Kendricks and his crew's illegal enterprises go a lot deeper than narcotics," said Sankey. "His biker gang is one of the most prominent independent pockets of organized crime currently operating in all of Western Canada. We also have Intel that suggests Kendricks and his gang are close to being absorbed into the Hells Angels."

The Hells Angels Motorcycle Club was the single most powerful syndicate of organized crime in Canada, and had been for decades. If they wanted Kendricks, then that made him a major player.

"I guess that explains where all the motorcycle parts he uses in his statues come from," I said.

Sankey ignored me and continued. "If and when they join the Angels, the case we've been building against them, and our chances of taking them down, are going to be significantly hindered."

I speared a dumpling with my chopstick. "Why are you telling me all this?"

"Because as far as we can tell, you are the only person to have had an audience with Kendricks and lived to talk about it." Sankey tapped the black and white pix with his index finger. "This photo was taken three years ago. It's one of the only pictures of Kendricks that exists within any law enforcement databank. He conducts all of his business through subordinates. Every now and then we get wind of a sighting, usually in relation to his metal-art. Other than that, Kendricks doesn't exist. He's a fucking ghost."

"A ghost who learned of my investigation and introduced himself to me."

"That's the only reason I'm here, Ounstead. I don't like it one bit, but you're suddenly the GCU's best shot at cementing a case against this guy."

I glanced at Rya and caught her in a smirk. "What?" I asked.

"I'm just amazed at how you manage to keep inserting yourself into the eye of one shitstorm after another."

"It's a gift," I said wryly.

Sankey produced some more files from his briefcase. "You're going to need to familiarize yourself with the rest of the Steel Gods."

"Is that an eighties' hair band?"

"It's the name of Kendricks' biker gang. The Steel Gods of Asgard. It's a reference to Norse mythology."

"No, I get it, Sergeant. You don't spend six months with 'Baldur the Badass' as a tag-team partner without learning that Asgard is the region in the centre of the universe inhabited by Norse Gods. I'm just a little surprised Kendricks didn't name his little gang The Transformers or something."

"Why would he do that?" asked Rya.

"Because the guy's a huge nerd. There weren't any sculptures of Odin or Loki in his workshop. It was all comic book characters and sci-fi stuff."

"I don't see how any of this is relevant," said Sankey tersely.

"It's relevant because it tells you that Kendricks is a poser. His self-image is a potential weakness."

"You're basing all this upon the name of his biker gang?"

"That and the fact I had a conversation with the guy while handcuffed to a seven-foot statue of a space alien."

Sankey shuffled some papers, clearly irritated. "Are you going to let me brief you or not?" he asked.

"Shouldn't we be more focused on finding Remo Willis?"

"That's up to you and Constable Shepard. But if you do manage to locate Willis, things will happen fast and you need to be prepared. Kendricks is extremely cautious and very dangerous, so if you want to stay alive, then you damn well better know just what it is you're getting yourself into."

I popped the last dumpling in my mouth. "Have at it, bub."

Half-an-hour later I was still hungry and Sankey was getting peeved.

"Anybody want to go halfsies on some egg foo yung?" I asked.

"Christ, Jed. You eat like a sumo wrestler, not a pro wrestler," said Rya, motioning to the smorgasbord of empty plates scattered across our table.

"I'm burning calories just listening to him yammer on," I replied, nodding at Sankey.

"Am I wasting my time here, Shepard?" he huffed.

Rya played peacekeeper and tried to ease the tension that had been mounting between the tight-assed Sergeant and me.

"Relax, both of you. Jed, you got this by now, right?"

"Pretty much, but I still don't see why he just can't make me some copies."

"Because it doesn't work like that," snapped Sankey. "This is classified information."

I sighed and sifted through the GCU dossiers on the table that I had spent the last thirty minutes committing to memory. I picked up a photograph of Horseshoe Stache. "This beast with the Hulk Hogan mustache is Kendricks' right-hand man."

"His name is Lance Dennings," said Sankey.

"I don't care if it's Mahatma Gandhi, Sankey, this is how I'm going to remember him, all right? So Hulkamania here is essentially Kendricks' proxy and the main buffer between him and the bulk of the Steel Gods' criminal activities."

"Correct," said Sankey.

I put down the photo and picked up another one of a heavy man with an enormous beer gut. The paunchy biker also appeared to suffer from a significant case of gynomastia. "Bitch Tits here is an ex-con who has done time for second-degree murder and other violent crimes. He typically serves as one of the gang's primary enforcers."

"We also believe he handles gun and other weapons smuggling for the organization," said Sankey.

"For Christ's sake, Sankey, I was getting to that," I snapped. "How am I supposed to demonstrate that I got this stuff down if you keep beaking off and interrupting me?"

"Moving on," he said, before picking up several photos off the table and proceeding to present them in succession.

"Ponyboy is their numbers guy," I said, referring to a picture of a baby-faced man with slicked blonde hair. "He handles the books and launders the money."

Sankey flipped to another photograph of two muscular punks. One was tall and beefy, the other short and stocky. Both had matching shaved heads and bushy goatees.

"Those are the Zeppelin boys," I said. "They're the muscle and gophers of the group. They're also the most visible, and like to Get The Led Out while tearing around town on their bikes, which are decorated with spray paintings of Vikings."

Sankey nodded and thumbed through the pix until he came to one of pasty thin man with long greasy hair.

"That's, uh, the wheelman. He's done time for large scale auto theft and is very good at boosting cars."

"What's the matter, Ounstead? Run out of clever nicknames?" taunted Sankey.

I scratched the stubble on my chin as I searched for the appropriate moniker. "How about Shitrat? His little ratfink ass kind of reminds me of you," I said, pointing to the picture.

"Goddamn it!" shouted Sankey, before slapping the photos down on the table. Chopsticks throughout the restaurant froze in place as other patrons stared.

"Easy, Dwayne," cautioned Rya.

"I've had it with this wiseass. I've put my ass on the line here, Shepard."

Rya kicked me under the table. Hard. I sighed and swallowed my pride. "I'm sorry, Sankey, all right? My bad."

Sankey exhaled slowly, trying to regain his composure by pulling the shirt cuffs out from under the sleeves of his blazer.

"I think we're about done here, anyway," said Rya. She snapped her fingers at me. "The card, Jed." I plucked the glossy business card Kendricks had given me from my wallet and handed it to Rya. She copied the phone number onto the back of one of Sankey's photos.

"This is the cell number Jed is supposed to use to contact Kendricks when he finds Willis. It's probably a pre-paid burner that's next to impossible to trace, but it's worth a shot."

Sankey nodded and scooped up the photos and other papers on the table. "We'll talk soon, Shepard," Sankey said, before ignoring me and exiting the restaurant.

"I think I hurt his feelings," I said, after he was gone.

"You can be a real jerk, you know that?"

"Come on, that guy is a tool."

"A tool who is doing me a favour."

"I promise I'll play nice next time. So how about that egg foo yung?"

"I should really get back to the station," she said, rising to her feet.

"Are you sure?"

"I got a lot on the go, Jed. Your friend's murder is not the only case I'm working."

"That's too bad. Especially since I was about to invite you to Remo Willis' hockey game tonight." Rya sat back down. We ordered the egg foo yung. It was delicious.

TWENTY-EIGHT

The Canlan Ice Sports Centre, better known as 8 Rinks for its number of sheets of ice, was the premier ice sports facility in all of Metro Vancouver. As a result, the place was a veritable Mecca for hockey lovers, advanced and amateur alike. The actual rinks themselves were split into two adjoining, warehouse-sized buildings, each housing four playing surfaces. Remo's team, the Ice-Holes, was scheduled to play on Rink 1, the nicest of the facility's six regulation-sized rinks.

A Zamboni engine whined in the distance and the smell of cold sweat and beer wafted by as we passed open doors to locker rooms. I spotted Willis' team huddled around the gate to the rink, waiting for the ice to finish being cleaned. They wore retro Hartford Whalers-style, green and white jerseys with blue trim, and the team crest of a cartoonish hockey player squeezing a bikini-clad babe in one arm and a mug of beer in the other made the Ice-Holes pretty easy to identify. I nodded at Rya and she fell in line behind me, having agreed on the drive there to let me take the lead. The goalie for the Ice-Holes was facing away from me, crouched down in a deep groin stretch. My heart skipped a beat before I saw the number 11 and read the placard on the back of his jersey. It read *Connell*.

"Shit," grumbled Rya.

"Yeah," I said, thinking the same thing.

Either Remo Willis was wearing someone else's jersey or he wasn't here. I glanced back at a nearby locker room and saw the Ice-Holes team captain fiddling with a padlock on the door. I approached him just as he snapped the lock shut and turned around.

"Love the team name," I said.

"Thanks. My backup was the Fog Duckers."

"We're looking for Remo Willis." The captain snorted and popped in a mouth guard.

"You and me both, pal."

"So he's not here?" The captain looked me over.

"No, he's not. Who's asking, anyway?"

I flipped the lid on the box I had been carrying under my arm and showed him the goalie mask with the lightning bolts and roid-raging crab. "Delivery from Scoff's Hockey Shop," I said, patting the helmet.

"Damn," said the captain, his eyes twinkling at the sight of the airbrushed design. "That is pretty fucking sweet."

"Do you have any idea where Remo may be?" Rya asked impatiently, apparently having forgotten our earlier agreement. The captain glanced at her curiously as if suddenly realizing she was present.

"No, but if you see him feel free to tell the prick that he's off of my team," he snarled.

"I don't understand," I said. "I heard he was quite the hotshot in this league."

The captain popped out his mouth guard and leaned on his graphite hockey sticks.

"A hotshot who left his team high and dry five days ago. Do you know we had to play an entire period without a goalie? Bastard didn't even call to let me know we needed a sub."

Rya shot me a knowing look. Between his old gang staking out his basement suite and bailing on his hockey team, it was looking more and more like Remo Willis was on the run.

"I guess we'll just keep the helmet at the store then," said Rya. "Thanks for your time." The captain nodded and popped in his mouth guard again. Rya turned to leave, but I hesitated.

"Why crabs?" I asked.

"Excuse me?" replied the captain. I pointed at the helmet. "Oh, right," he said. "Remo likes to call himself 'the crab.' You know, like Tretiak."

"The Russian goalie from the Summit Series?"

"Yeah. Why do you think he carries that goddamn racquetball with him everywhere he goes? He constantly throws it off walls and catches it in order to improve his reflexes, just like Tretiak used to."

The Zamboni finished its last lap and the players took to the ice. The captain lumbered past me on his blades while a better understanding of the man who killed my friend was slowly taking shape in my mind.

"One last thing," I said, catching up to the captain just before he stepped on the ice.

"What?" he asked, exasperatingly.

"Was Remo having any money problems that you know of? Did he ever mention anything in the locker room?"

"That's a pretty weird question for a delivery guy," said the captain, eyeing me suspiciously.

"Long story."

"Whatever."

"Come on, bub. Help me out."

"Hey, I'd tell you if I knew. I don't owe Remo shit after the way he screwed us over. But this is a beer league, man. We only talk about hockey, tits, and ass."

The captain stepped onto the rink, the blades of his skates crunching loudly into the ice as he took a few quick choppy strides. After a moment, he circled back and came to a sharp stop, spraying my shoes with ice shavings.

"He was actually a pretty generous guy. Always bringing beer for the locker room or picking up the tab at the pub upstairs. Not sure if that helps but it's all I can tell you."

"Thanks," I said. "Good luck out there." The captain nodded and skated off down the ice.

"What was that about?" asked Rya, as I joined her by the locker room door.

"I just learned some valuable information."

"What?"

"There's a pub upstairs. Come on, I'm buying."

TWENTY-NINE

The Thirsty Penguin Grillhouse was a popular post-game watering hole that overlooked the numerous ice rinks on each side of 8 Rinks. We snagged a booth in the corner, away from a rowdy bunch of twenty-something hockey players who were in the midst of celebrating a victory. I topped off Rya's pint glass before doing the same to mine with a pitcher of beer while she stared out the window and watched the Ice-Holes score a goal against their opponents below.

"Don't you find it odd," I said, "that Remo Willis was always so generous with his money and springing for beer with his team and yet he tried to squeeze a measly ten grand out of Johnny?"

"You don't know that he wasn't hurting financially," she replied. "He could have just seen your friend as an easy mark."

"I just don't understand why he would hatch a plot to hold a snake for ransom if he wasn't hard up for cash."

"People do stupid shit, Jed. I see it all the time."

"It just bothers me, I guess."

"I think you're reaching."

"My instincts have been serving me pretty well up until now."

"You're right, they have. But they can only take you so far. You have a good nose for sniffing things out, I'll give you that. But you've got to start using that big melon you call a brain."

"Stop, you're going to make me blush."

"I just think if you looked before you leapt a little more you might not have a vindictive, lunatic, wrestling promoter out to kill you."

"Fair enough," I said, before taking a big sip of beer.

Rya leaned back in her chair and sighed. "Well, at least the mystery of the racquetball has been solved," she said.

"I'm assuming that Remo Willis' fingerprints weren't in the system?"

"No, but we have several clean prints on the ball. If we find him, it'll be a slam dunk placing him at the scene." I nodded. We both enjoyed our beer for a while.

"Are you seeing anyone?" I asked out of the blue. Rya's eyelids fluttered for an instant, but then she recovered.

"What's it to you?"

"Just curious." I shrugged. Moments passed. More sips of beer. Finally, she spoke.

"There's a guy," she said cautiously, "that's sort of in the picture."

"Another cop?"

"God, no. He works for the city."

"How did you meet?"

"None of your business."

"It's like pulling teeth trying to have a personal conversation with you, do you realize that?"

"All right, I'm sorry. It's a little embarrassing."

"Is he a Chippendale or something?"

"No, asshole, he's not. He's a nice guy. A really nice guy. It's just, well … I met him online," she said, in a hushed tone.

"What's wrong with that?"

"I don't know. Isn't that something I should be embarrassed about?"

"It's not 2005, Rya. The stigma of online dating is no more."

"Well, good then."

"Is it serious?"

"It's … comfortable."

"Move over Kimye."

"Shut up," she snapped. "And it's not like I see you tearing it up with the ladies. What's your story, anyway?"

Pleasant memories of Connie flashed in my head, but they were soon replaced with the awkwardness of our recent phone call. "I was with this girl for awhile. She was great, you know? Genuine. But I guess I kind of screwed it up."

"How?"

"She wanted more."

"Like marriage?"

I shook my head. "She wanted *me* to be more. But I never bothered to try."

"You mean she didn't see your bouncing career as a building block for domestic bliss?" Rya said dryly.

"I like you better when you dish it out, Detective."

"I'll bet. So why did you let her go?"

"I didn't mean to. I guess she just got fed up waiting for me to get my shit together."

I felt my phone vibrate in my pocket. I dug it out of my jeans and saw that I had one missed call and a voicemail.

"Go ahead," Rya said, before excusing herself and going to the restroom. I played the voicemail from a number I didn't recognize.

"Yo, what up, bro?" chirped a familiar voice. "This here is Pocket, you know, of Pocket and Tubbs? Anyway, I just wanted to drop you a line and make sure you had the 411 on Johnny's funeral. It's going down at Forest Lawn tomorrow at two o'clock. Maybe me and Ula will see you there. Peace."

I felt like an ass. The thought of Johnny having a funeral service hadn't even occurred to me, and if it weren't for the consideration of a loquacious dwarf I would have missed it altogether.

I killed the pitcher of beer and silently chastised myself. I was so caught up in running around town trying to honour my friend's memory by catching his killer that I forgot there was an even more important way for me to pay my respects.

Rya returned with a fresh pitcher of Sleeman Original Draught and two shots of whisky. "What the hell is this?" I asked.

"Boilermakers," she said, before downing her whisky shot and chasing it with a sip of beer.

"Are we celebrating something?"

"Yeah, the first ever meeting of the not-having-your-shit-together club."

I smiled and hoisted my whisky in the air. "I'll drink to that, darlin," I said, clinking her glass.

"Glad to hear it. But call me 'darlin' again and I'll shoot you in the kneecaps."

We drank more beer.

I told Rya about Johnny's funeral but refused any type of police escort despite the fact Bert Grasby and company were likely to be there. Rya agreed that there was probably a pretty low risk of either Grasby or his boys taking another run at me in such a public venue. We talked about Rya's work and how even though it wore on her from time to time she still loved the job. Her passion for justice and strong moral compass were clearly evident by the way she spoke, and a couple of times she sounded just like my old man. She told me about the current political bullshit going on within the department as well as a couple of humourous anecdotes that made Inspector Cornish seem like an even bigger dick than I had originally thought.

At some point the Ice-Holes finished their game and the Zamboni performed its laps before two new teams took to the ice. Rya and I continued talking and drinking, and eventually the conversation circled its way around to me again.

"Remember back when you were still wrestling, and coming and going from Vancouver all the time?" she asked.

"You would not believe the amount of Air Miles I have."

"You and I ... well, we were pretty good friends back then, weren't we?"

"Rya, my pop had just taken you under his wing as his protégé. I'd been waiting decades for someone else to come along and shoulder the burden." Rya smiled, but kept pressing forward. She was driving at something.

"When I heard you had retired from pro wrestling and were moving home ... I was excited. I figured we'd sort of pick up where we had left off."

Where we had left off was a point where there was a palpable romantic tension between the two of us. Rya had known I was interested in her, but due to the fact she was my pop's partner and I was never in town for more than a few days at a time before flying off to my next big time wrestling show, it wasn't exactly practical, or respectful, for me to make a move.

"It's not that I didn't want to," I replied.

"You could have fooled me. I tried reconnecting with you several times after you moved home. You ignored me."

"I know."

"You weren't the same guy, Jed."

She was right. And I realized she needed to know why. I don't know if it was Johnny's case, the guilt over having distanced myself from Rya, the boilermakers and beers, or the combination of all of the above, but I slowly felt a chink widen in the emotional armour I had fashioned ever since my pro-wrestling career ended so abruptly and in such disgrace.

"It wasn't you," I said, by way of apology. "I was in a pretty bad place after I left wrestling."

"Frank mentioned that you took getting let go pretty hard."

"I wasn't fired. I quit. And you have no idea."

"Enlighten me."

"Do you remember when my pop and my cousin took that trip to Thailand a couple of years back?"

"Sure," she replied. "Didn't you meet up with them over there and all go backpacking or something?"

"Oh, I was there, all right. But it wasn't a vacation." I signaled the waitress and pointed at the empty shot glasses. If I was going to tell this story, I was going to need some more whisky.

"So what was it then?" she asked.

"An intervention. My pop and Declan put an end to my tropical alcohol and drug-fuelled pursuit of a perpetual high, and probably saved my life in the process," I replied.

"I don't understand. Why the bender?" The waitress arrived with the shots and I downed one before she could lift it off her tray. She gave me a funny look before returning to the safety of the bar.

"Because I couldn't live with the guilt of what I had done." Rya looked at me curiously and waited for me to continue. "Two and a half years ago, a couple months before I was regularly getting obliterated in Thailand, I was in the midst of the biggest push of my wrestling career."

"Push?"

"It's when a wrestler gains popularity with wins and positive exposure. The higher-ups had me pegged as having superstar potential and wanted to try and turn me into the next Stone Cold Steve Austin. At the time I had just broken up with my tag-team partner and our resulting feud was supposed to be our springboard into solo careers. My partner, Mad Max Conkin, was also tasked with helping to put me over as a main event talent before beginning his own campaign for the Intercontinental Championship. Max and I had been working on some edgy routines, as the pay-per-view event that would finally pay off our feud was a month away. We knew the more we could dazzle at the pay-per-view the better our chances would be of becoming top draws within the company. It was a lot of pressure, but also the opportunity we had both been waiting for."

I took a long sip of beer before continuing.

"It was my idea to use our pay-per-view match to introduce a brand new finishing move. Max loved the idea. After weeks of racking my brain, I finally came up with a spectacular move — a modified jackhammer slam. Basically, I'd grab my opponent by his trunks with one hand and wrap my arm around the back of his neck with the other. The other wrestler had to play along, of course, and jump into the move as I lifted him up above my head. He then helped balance himself as I kept him hoisted vertically for a second or two, before rolling my shoulder and using our collective bodyweight to forcefully slam him to the mat. All in all, it was a pretty sweet move, and aside from pro-wrestling legend Bill Goldberg, nobody else had ever really used a version of this move as a finisher because it requires excellent balance and upper body strength.

"Anyway, about three weeks before our big match we were at this little Podunk arena in Binghamton, in upstate New York. It was just another non-televised house show, so while the lighting and pyrotechnics guys were setting up, Max and I were in the ring working on the jackhammer slam."

I downed another shot but this time I didn't chase it with beer. I wanted to feel the whisky burn as it slowly trickled down my throat.

"To this day, I still don't know what went wrong. I performed that move hundreds of times before I began to slowly increase the velocity with which Max would hit the canvas. But on that day, for whatever reason, Max's head wasn't tucked when I slammed him to the mat. The doctors think his cervical vertebrae snapped the moment I came down on him with the full force of my bodyweight. If I had eased off a bit, or lessened the momentum just a little, Max might not have been paralyzed. Instead, because of me, a married father of three is now a quadriplegic who spends his days hooked up to a breathing machine, crapping into diapers, and desperately trying to wiggle his right index finger."

I killed the rest of my beer. My confession hung in the air for what felt like ages. I couldn't bring myself to look at Rya until she reached across the table and gently held my hand. Her deep green eyes sparkled with sympathy. She opened her mouth to speak, but no words came out. There was nothing left to say.

THIRTY

The rich aroma of roasted coffee beans gently lured me from my slumber. I found myself naked and enveloped in satin sheets on a queen-size bed, my head resting on the fluffiest, most comfortable pillow it had ever known. I snorted and scratched as per my usual morning routine, but for the life of me I couldn't recollect where I was or how I had gotten there. Fortunately for me, and more unfortunately for my liver, I had a significant amount of experience in such situations.

"Morning," Rya said, before padding into the bedroom barefoot. She was wrapped in a slim velvet robe that accentuated her curves, carrying two steaming mugs.

"You take your coffee black, right?" she asked.

"Uh, right," I said, taking the mug she offered me.

Rya perched herself on the edge of the bed and sipped her coffee. My pulse was already racing, even without the caffeine kick. "Listen, Jed," she said. "I want you to know that last night, well, it meant a lot."

I desperately sifted through the fogginess in my head, but it was no use. My memory went blank after us drinking our faces off at the pub. "Which part of last night, exactly?" I asked.

Rya smiled radiantly. Seeing her like that — no pant suit, her tousled raven hair down, and without her usual crusty cop demeanor — it revealed what a knockout she really was, and how hard she worked to mask that beauty with an air of professionalism. She placed her mug of coffee on the nightstand before leaning in to give me the softest, most tender kiss. Her lips tasted like strawberries and her hair smelled of vanilla, which combined with Mother Nature and the morning, contributed to an unintended activation of a launch sequence in my loins. I withdrew from the kiss and subtly moved a pillow onto my lap before a tent could appear in the sheets, but I'm pretty sure Rya knew what I was trying to hide. She slid off the bed, grabbed her coffee and padded back toward the door.

"Rya, wait."

"Yes?" she said, turning her head and flipping her hair over her shoulder like a model in a Vidal Sassoon shampoo commercial.

"Last night, did we, uh …"

"What?"

"You know," I said, motioning to the bed.

"You don't remember?"

"I was a little drunk."

"I noticed."

"So did we?"

"No, Jed. We didn't."

"But … the satin sheets?" I said, hearing the disappointment in my voice as I held up a lacy throw pillow.

"Are for my guest bed, dumbass. My bedroom is across the hall. I guess those detective instincts of yours don't kick in until the afternoon."

"Then why did you just kiss me?"

"Why did you decide to finally tell me about your past?" Rya smiled. "And for the record," she said, "if we had slept together, your world would have been so epically rocked there's no amount of alcohol that could impair your ability to remember it, *bub*."

I chuckled heartily. For a guy planning to attend a funeral, my day was suddenly looking pretty bright.

THIRTY-ONE

The gravestone was covered with weeds. It had only been a couple of months since I had last visited, but with the frequent autumn rainfall it was enough time for dandelions and crabgrass to sprout up and shroud the engraved bronze plaque that adorned the granite memorial.

I emptied dead flowers and dirty water out of the cremation plot's vase, then unwrapped a bouquet of pink and white ger-bera daisies and placed them on display. I caught a whiff of the freshly cut flowers and was swept away to a Sunday afternoon decades earlier, where I saw my ten-year-old self holding my mother's hand as we strolled up and down the aisles of Art Knapp Plantland & Florist garden centre. The floral scent faded. The memory slipped away.

I removed the weeds surrounding Linda Annalise Ounstead's memorial and wiped down the plaque with a handful of water from the nearby Koi pond. A crisp breeze brushed my hair to the side, and I watched as a lily pad floated across the water and underneath an arched redwood bridge. A black and orange fish swam by my feet, and I stood still while I listened to the soft sound of swaying branches.

I was with my mother the day she had picked the spot where she wanted to be interred, and remembered fondly the numerous times she spoke about the Koi pond's serenity during her final days. I knelt down on one knee and kissed the bronze plaque, then headed off down the winding road that led to the chapel at Forest Lawn cemetery. Emerald grass shimmered with dewdrops as far as the eye could see, and the vibrant green landscape was peppered with black as a murder of crows cawed and hopped over graves.

I shifted uncomfortably in my navy suit and plunged a thumb into my waistband to relieve some of the pressure on my abdomen. Despite being a made-to-measure Coppley suit, the high-quality fabric was having difficulty adapting to the extra pounds that had taken up residence around my midsection since my wrestling days.

I entered the chapel and found it was at about one-third of its capacity, the long oak pews filled with what had to be a more eclectic congregation than what the Forest Lawn funeral director was used to. Muscle-bound meatheads, cleavage bombs, and numerous people with multi-coloured and extreme hair styles were crammed into the first few rows, whereas the handful of attendees with a more mundane appearance had sought refuge from the outcasts in the pews behind them.

"Yo, Jed!" I turned to my left but couldn't see the person calling my name.

"Over here, bro!" I scanned the pews again until I saw a tiny hand breach the surrounding shoulders and heads and wave frantically. I walked toward Pocket as he climbed on top of Ula's thigh and continued to motion me over.

"We saved you a seat," Pocket said proudly.

I excused myself as I made my way down the pew. I scanned the crowd but didn't see Grasby or any of his goons. I did, however, make eye contact with Stormy Daze, who was dressed elegantly in a black dress that covered her usual buxomness. She smiled sadly and nodded her head. I returned the gesture.

"It's good you made it, bro," declared Pocket as I sat down beside him. "Mamba would like it that we're here together."

"I think you're right," I said, shaking hands with them both. "Grasby's a no-show, eh?"

"Fuckin' spiteful prick," griped Pocket, shaking his head.

A few minutes later a well-groomed and dapper man in his mid-forties walked to the podium, which was beside a large, dated portrait picture of Johnny in a suit and tie. The man introduced himself as Rick Schumacher, Johnny's older brother. He launched into a spiel about his childhood memories of growing up with Johnny. I leaned over to Pocket and whispered.

"I didn't know Johnny had a brother."

"They weren't very close. Hadn't seen each other since Mamba's mama passed." I remembered that Johnny had been extremely close with his mom and was devastated when she had died, about six months before our fateful Indian strap match.

"Did he have any other family?" I asked. Pocket shook his head. Johnny's brother prattled on about how he and Johnny used to make paper sail boats and float them down a stream. He made no mention of Johnny's passions in life, no mention of his fervent love for his pet snake or professional wrestling.

A beanpole with a red Mohawk went up to the podium next to talk about what an inspiration Johnny had been for the younger aspiring pro wrestlers in XCCW. His words were earnest and heart-felt and by the time he finished speaking there was hardly a dry eye in the chapel.

Next Johnny's contractor boss, for whom Johnny had worked part time when not wrestling, took to the podium and told a funny story about how he took his employees to see Johnny perform one night. The construction workers were blown away by Johnny's skill and panache, and upon returning to work the following week Johnny quickly became the most popular guy on the crew.

The floor was then opened up to anyone who wanted to say a few words about Johnny. Several more wrestlers stood up to speak about my friend, and they all said more of the same — Johnny was a good and kind man, he had a big heart, he truly loved what he did.

Pocket nudged me. "Aren't you going to say something, bro?"

"I wasn't planning on it." There was no mistaking the disappointment on the faces of Pocket and Tubbs.

"You should geev'um, brah," said Tubbs. "'Tis what Johnny boy would want." Pocket followed that up with a firm nod.

A few moments later I was behind the walnut and cherry oak podium looking out into a sea of faces made up of Johnny Mamba's closest family and friends.

"As a lot of you know, Johnny Mamba had a signature wrestling move. The Cobra Clutch. It's a solid submission hold. Nothing too flashy, maybe a bit dated, but it gets the job done. While other wrestlers would experiment with new moves and try out different finishers over the course of their careers, Johnny never did. He loved using that damn Cobra Clutch, and there was no coach or co-worker anywhere that could convince him otherwise." There was soft laughter throughout the room, as many of Johnny's peers knew all too well what I was talking about.

"I always assumed that Johnny preferred the Cobra Clutch because of its name and natural affiliation with snakes and his in-ring persona. It turns out that wasn't the case. One time, back when Johnny and I were both working as tag-team partners out of a developmental territory in La Belle, Florida, the city was in the midst of hosting its annual Swamp Cabbage Festival. Never one to miss a good party, Johnny dragged me out for a night on the town, and before I knew it we were doing everything from judging the Miss Swamp Cabbage Pageant to tossing back tequila shots while placing bets on armadillo races.

"Needless to say, by the end of the night we were pretty loaded. Johnny, ever the animal lover, convinced me to sneak into the rodeo bullpen with him so we could feed the bulls some swamp cabbage. We did, and I had a particularly muscular bovine eating right out of the palm of my hand when suddenly some idiot security guard spotted Johnny and started screaming bloody murder.

The guard ran toward us, waving his flashlight, not realizing that he was spooking the hell out of the bulls. Johnny yelled at him to calm down, but the guard kept raising hell. The bulls were quickly growing more and more agitated. Unlike Johnny, who was near the gate, I was trapped in the middle of the bullpen, surrounded by a herd of anxious horned beasts. That's when Johnny sprung over the fence, swept the guard's feet, and applied an actual Cobra Clutch hold around the man's neck that rendered him unconscious in seconds.

"Within moments, all of the bulls settled down. I was able to exit the pen safely, and only after we had run half a mile did we stop to catch our breath and laugh over the absurdity of how I had nearly been trampled to death. As we walked home I remember teasing Johnny that even in life-or-death situations he still insisted upon using the Cobra Clutch. That's when he told me why he used it.

"Johnny said that to him, the Cobra Clutch was much more than just a move. It was a metaphor. One that applied not just to his wrestling career, but also to how he lived his life. He said that there are two types of people in this world—those who grab life by the throat and apply a Cobra Clutch, and those who sit back, take it, and wind up stuck with nowhere to go.

"There have been times in my past when I've gone for it and really grabbed life by the throat. But there have also been times when I've been stagnant and in a rut. Johnny Mamba never made that mistake. He was a brave and kind soul who lived life to the fullest. He made the world a better place and I can't think of a better way to honour him than to try and live my life like he did his."

Before I could step down from the podium the crowd broke into a rousing applause. I tried to shun the attention and slip quietly back into my seat, but it was difficult considering that Pocket had gotten so emotional he started pumping his tiny fist and whooping. A minister closed out the service with a prayer. I noticed Wendy Steffen, the realtor whom Johnny had fallen for, quickly exit out the rear door of the chapel. I felt a tinge of sadness that she and Johnny never got a fair shot. The fact that she came to his funeral at all spoke volumes about the type of connection, however brief, they must have had.

We made our way to the reception hall and I quickly discovered that my presence was attracting many of the XCCW rookies whom Johnny had mentored. I dutifully glad-handed them and answered their questions, although it amazed me that Johnny had been able to be so patient with these kids when I found most of their eagerness and enthusiasm to be nettlesome and draining. Pocket and Tubbs set up shop beside me, acting as my de facto gatekeepers and essentially regulating the order in which I would meet the XCCW folk. More than a few wrestlers seemed to get a mischievous thrill each time I confirmed that I had indeed slugged Bert Grasby for disrespecting Johnny.

After half-an-hour I needed a break from the non-stop socializing so I excused myself to go to the washroom. Instead, I slipped outside into the parking lot, climbed behind the wheel of my truck and dug the flask of Crown Royal I had brought out of the glove compartment. I spun off the sterling silver top but before I could take a sip a chill tap danced down my spine as cold metal pressed against the base of my skull. I chanced a glance in the rear-view mirror and saw a revolver held against my head. But that wasn't nearly as disconcerting as the revelation of who was holding the gun. Remo Willis was seated in the extended cab behind me. He looked heavier and more haggard than in his ASHL hockey profile picture, and I felt his breath on the back of my neck when he spoke.

"Drive."

"Where?"

"Metrotown."

"You like to do a little shopping in between murders?"

"Go," he said, pressing the gun into my head.

We drove in silence as we wound our way through the cemetery. We reached the front gates and I pulled out into traffic, stealing a quick look at the glove compartment. If I could just find a way to distract him I could make a move for my revolver.

"Looking for this?" he said, tossing the Colt onto my lap. "I already unloaded it." I drove us away from the cemetery and down a hill toward Metrotown, the massive shopping complex in Burnaby that was the second largest in Canada.

I reached up with my right hand and started loosening my tie.

"No sudden movements," cautioned Willis, before tapping the the gun barrel to the back of my head again.

"If I'm going out, I'm sure as hell not going out wearing a damn necktie," I replied. I yanked the tie over my head, threw it on the passenger seat, then loosened the top two buttons of my dress shirt. "What do you want, Willis?"

"To talk."

"About what?"

"About Johnny."

I shot daggers at him with my eyes through the rear-view mirror. "Don't you dare say his name you piece of shit," I growled. "You don't get to talk about him. You want to shoot me? Fine. But I swear to Christ I'll drive this truck into oncoming traffic before I let you say another word about my friend."

"Even if I told you that I wasn't the one who killed him?"

"What?"

"You heard me."

"Bullshit. Your prints are on the racquetball. You were there."

"I never said I wasn't there. I said I didn't kill him."

I glared at Remo Willis in the rear-view. His eyes were wide and pleading. "Even if you didn't kill him yourself you were still complicit in his murder."

"No, I wasn't. Johnny was never supposed to get hurt."

"Then why is he dead?"

"Because my boss ordered the hit."

"Kendricks?"

"Yes."

"Why would he do that?"

"He was furious when he found out about my kidnapping plot. Accused me of putting his entire operation at risk for a meagre ten grand, even though if he paid me more I wouldn't have been so hard up for cash in the first place. You have to understand, nobody was ever supposed to get hurt, not even the fucking snake. But I was strapped and Johnny wouldn't stop yapping about the twenty Gs he'd just inherited. I mean, I wasn't greedy, I only asked for half—"

"Save it. I don't want to hear your excuses."

"It's the truth."

The truck rolled to a stop at an intersection. I looked back over my shoulder. "Why come to me?" I asked.

"Where else am I going to go, the cops?"

"They would have cut you a sweet deal for turning on Kendricks."

"Do you even know who you're talking about, man? I'd be dead long before the case ever got to trial. The only chance I've got now is to run."

The light turned green. I followed the road as it curved around Deer Lake Park. The nature reserve was an urban oasis of forests, trails and marshlands, and the Metrotown area skyline stood tall in the horizon. A skein of geese flew overhead, honking loudly as they soared above in a V-shaped formation. Remo glanced furtively out the window and shifted nervously in the back seat. I needed to keep him talking.

"So if you're not a murderer, then why are you sitting in the back of my truck with a gun to my head?"

"Because you don't believe me yet. And because I know Damian hired you to find me."

"He said you're a tweaker who stole fifty thousand dollars worth of product."

Remo laughed heartily. "Just because I smoke and peddle a little rock on the side doesn't mean I'm a junkie. You saw my place. Why do you think I cook my own meth? Damian's shit is expensive and he doesn't exactly offer employee discounts. Not to mention the fact that the man keeps records so meticulous they'd put a Jew accountant to shame. I never had more than a couple grand's worth of Damian's shit to sell at any given time."

Willis made sense—his crappy basement suite seemed more likely to be the residence of a low-level dealer, not a professional with access to tens of thousands of dollars worth of product. I also took note of his appearance, and with his muscular build and white teeth, he hardly looked like a person who was battling a meth addiction.

"The only thing I ever stole was this," he said.

Willis handed me a large plastic Ziplock bag. Inside was a six-inch bloody knife. The weapon had clearly been custom made. Several skulls and crossbones made out of familiar looking engine parts were mounted along the handle in between engravings of swirling Celtic designs and studded red rubies. At the base of the blade where it met with the hilt there was a spiralling sea serpent wrapped around the T-shaped dagger. The knife looked like a gaudy prop from a *Pirates of the Caribbean* film. I realized that if this was the weapon used to murder Johnny, then a knife that had a coiled snake on its handle killed him. The sickening irony made me want to vomit.

"What is this?" I finally managed to ask.

"Lance's knife. He's the one who killed Johnny."

Lance. Why did I know that name? I recalled my briefing with Dwayne Sankey of the VPD's Gang Crime Unit. Lance Dennings AKA Hulkster Mustache. The massive muscle-bound monster who had knocked me unconscious and handcuffed me to the Predator statue.

"Tell me exactly what happened at the volleyball courts," I commanded.

"By then the snake was already dead," he said. "It ate some drugs that I forgot were stashed in the closet where I was keeping it. Damian had found out about my scheme and sent Lance along with me to ensure that everything went smoothly and that we got our money. We wore ski masks ... at least, at first we did.

"Johnny had the ten Gs in a paper bag as he approached us and looked relieved when he saw the sack that held the snake. Lance ordered him to stop when he got close. Johnny obeyed and tossed the bag of money onto the sand in front of us. Lance motioned for me to pick it up. I did as I was told and bent over to grab the bag. But by the time I stood up again Lance had pulled his knife and was charging Johnny. I tried screaming but it was too late. Lance slit Johnny's throat before he was even able to get his hands up in self-defense. I dropped the money and ran to Johnny. His throat was spewing blood and, uh—Christ, are you sure you want to hear this?"

"Every detail," I said solemnly. Willis nodded and continued.

"His throat was spewing blood and he was trying to talk but all that came out were these gurgling sounds. I pulled off my mask and used it to apply pressure but it was no use. Lance yanked me to my feet. I took a few swings at the son-of-a-bitch but he dropped me pretty quick with a kidney shot. I laid there gasping for breath while he told me I was an asshole for putting the Steel Gods in jeopardy with my extortion plan and that I should be thanking him and Damian for cleaning up my mess. He placed his mask and knife on the bag of money and started dragging Johnny toward a portable toilet.

"That's when I decided to make a run for it. I wrapped the knife in my ski mask and was careful not to touch it. Then I grabbed the money and bolted." Remo Willis pointed at the blood-crusted blade. "This knife is all you need to put them away. It's covered with Lance's prints and Johnny's blood, and it was custom made by Damian himself."

We cruised by a couple of high-rise apartment buildings before turning right onto Kingsway. We passed a skate park on the right and I watched as skater after skater kept bobbing up and out of the concrete pit, each time executing different flip tricks or aerials. The sprawling shopping complex that was Metrotown was now visible in the distance. I realized that I no longer felt the cold metal of a gun barrel against my neck. I looked in the rear-view and saw that Willis had lowered his weapon. If I was going to make a play for it then this was the time. The only thing was that I no longer saw the need. I wasn't afraid. I didn't feel like my life was in danger. And most importantly, I believed everything Remo Willis was saying.

"Do you think Lance would turn on Kendricks if the cops offered a deal?" I asked.

"I think he'd probably give up the entire crew," replied Willis. "Why?"

"Because underneath all that muscle is a selfish prick. Lance would do everything in his power to avoid hard time. The drug trade, the weapons smuggling, even the prostitution—he's dialed into it all. He's the lynchpin of every single operation because he's Damian's number one guy."

"Aren't you worried about doing time if this comes out?"

"They can't arrest me if I'm in Mexico, man."

Willis raised his weapon again and motioned toward the Metrotown SkyTrain station creeping up on the left. "Drop me off over there," he said. I headed in the direction of the station.

"There's one thing I don't get," I said. "Why take the knife and run? Why not just go along with the murder after the fact rather than turn on your friends?"

Remo Willis chewed on his bottom lip as he searched for an answer. "I've done some bad things," he finally said. "But never to anybody that didn't deserve it. What happened to Johnny—that shit was straight up cold-blooded. And I'll never forget the way he looked at me when I took off my mask. He was lying there with his throat slashed, blood gushing everywhere, and he didn't even seem scared. He just looked so confused. He didn't understand what was happening to him and died without ever knowing why. I see his face every time I close my eyes, man. It haunts me. I may not be able to take back my part in getting him killed, but maybe by giving you this evidence I'll be able to unburden myself enough to get some fucking sleep."

I pulled up to the sidewalk that led to the SkyTrain station. I put the truck in park, switched off the ignition, and turned around. Willis leaned back, raising the gun.

"You don't need to keep waving that gun at me," I said. "I believe you."

"I'm not taking any chances. But even if you don't believe me you will once the cops run the DNA and prints on that knife." Remo Willis started to get out of the truck.

"Willis, wait." He hesitated.

"I understand why you didn't go to the cops. But I don't get why you brought this to me," I said, motioning to the bagged knife. "How did you even know I was looking into Johnny's murder?"

"I've still got friends in XCCW. And from the way they tell it, you stormed in there looking for answers about Johnny's death and sucker-punched Grasby so hard the douchebag shit his velvet pants. Wish I could have seen that." Remo Willis hopped out of the king cab. He kept his gun pointed on me, but hid it underneath his coat. "For what it's worth, I'm sorry," he said earnestly.

Remo walked backwards to the sidewalk before turning and starting up the stairs to the SkyTrain station. I exhaled loudly and took another look at the knife. My gut told me there was sincerity to Remo Willis' plea. Besides, if he was lying and did kill Johnny, why would he take such a huge risk by coming to see me just to give me a fake murder weapon? No, I was certain Remo Willis was telling the truth.

I tucked the bagged knife under my seat just as I heard the rumbling of a couple of Harley-Davidson engines behind me. I bolted upright in time to see the Zeppelin boys, the bald headed enforcers for the Steel Gods, leap off their bikes and charge toward the stairs. Remo Willis was almost at the top and had his back turned to the thugs below. I fumbled with my seatbelt before jumping out of my truck.

"Remo!" Willis spun around and saw his former gang members barrelling toward him. His face went chalk white and he started scrambling up the stairs. I gave chase. Halfway up the stairs I heard gunshots.

A young mother clutching a toddler to her chest led a stampede of civilians desperate to get away from the SkyTrain platform. I pushed and shoved my way past them and up the stairs, wondering how in the hell the Zeppelin boys had tracked us. They couldn't have been following Remo, as they would have certainly jumped him while he was waiting for me in my truck. The only explanation that made sense was that they had been tailing me already. But why? To check up on my progress? To deliver a message for Kendricks? It didn't matter now. I could only imagine the looks on their faces when they saw their old pal step out of my truck.

I reached the platform. Damaged CCTV cameras dangled from their overhead perches, crackling with electricity while shooting off sparks. I realized the gunshots I had heard were the Zeppelins ensuring there would be no record of the murder they were about to commit. Remo and the Zeppelin boys were by the eastbound track. The bigger Zeppelin was holding Remo's arms behind him while his smaller and stockier buddy laid into him with vicious punches to the gut.

"Where is it?" screamed the smaller biker, before striking Remo Willis again.

Big Zeppelin had his back to me, and due to his small stature, Little Z couldn't see me over the combined bulk of Remo and his partner. Even though I had not run a forty-yard dash since high school, I all but channelled my sophomoric speed as I sprinted across the platform and closed the gap.

I neared Big Z from behind and leapt through the air, extending my legs and executing a textbook dropkick. My feet connected with the backside of his rib cage and the big man folded like a cheap accordion. Remo fell to the concrete and was knocked free of the bigger biker's grip. I hit the ground as well, but before I could jump to my feet Little Z pounced on me. The diminutive biker shrieked and threw wild haymakers, scoring some solid blows to my neck and face. I grabbed Little Z by his throat but he countered by boxing my ears and punching me square in the nose. I heard a crack and knew it was broken, but that was the least of my problems. Remo made a break for it. Clutching his side, Big Z lumbered after him, pulling a gun out of a holster attached to the back of his leather chaps.

"Gun!" I yelled, just as Little Z pulled an eight-inch blade, which looked like another knife that had been custom made by Damian Kendricks. He stabbed downwards. My hands shot up and gripped his wrists, stopping the blade's decent just six inches above my heart.

A gunshot boomed. I had no idea if Remo Willis had been hit as it was taking everything I had to keep Little Z from plunging his knife into my chest. My arms burned like they were on fire as I pushed against his wrists. He leaned forward, using his bodyweight as an edge to tip the scales in his favour. It was working. Despite my best efforts, the stainless steel blade inched closer and closer to my chest. I tried to squirm but had nowhere to go as Little Z had pinned my legs down with his shins. Light glinted off the side of the blade and I heard an approaching SkyTrain's brakes whine in the distance.

I steadied myself, knowing I had only one chance. I stopped pushing against his wrists for a split second and the blade dropped. The tip sliced through my shirt and I felt it pierce my pectorals. Little Z sensed the kill was close and put even more of his body-weight behind the knife. It was an instinctive move, the only caveat being that he was no longer able to pin down my legs with his shins. I threw my weight to the side and drove my knee into his groin. He yelped and jerked upward, involuntarily lessening the pressure he was putting behind the knife. I tucked my knees to my chest and shoved the balls of my feet into his waist. I summoned all the strength I had left and pulled his wrists apart and downwards as hard as I could.

The muscular little man fell into me as I rolled backwards and launched him with my feet like a springboard. Little Z released his grip on the knife as he soared through the air. I rolled over just in time to see his stocky body land on the tracks before getting creamed by the oncoming train. The impact knocked Little Z backwards, and he flopped around on the tracks before getting crunched beneath the tremendous force of the slowing monorail. The train ground to a halt, leaving a splattering of blood across the track. Most of Little Z was under the front car of the train, with the exception of a bloodied stubby arm and a broken leg that were both sticking out at gruesome angles. I struggled to my feet and saw Big Z staring at the train in disbelief. Remo Willis laid at his feet. Big Z quickly composed himself, glared at me and opened fire. I dove behind a cement pillar as bullets whizzed by.

"Police!" shouted a transit cop as he came charging up the opposite stairs.

I peeked around the pillar. Big Z fired two into the cop's chest, who dropped to the platform, dead. The doors to the train opened. Passengers on board screamed and hid inside the car. Sirens wailed in the distance. Big Z made a run for it.

I hurried over to Remo. He was wheezing and bleeding out badly from a gunshot to the chest. He tried to speak but the only thing his lips were able to form was a bloody spit bubble. He reached a hand out toward me. It hovered there, just for a moment, before dropping to the ground.

THIRTY-TWO

I was three blocks away before I was certain that no police cars were in pursuit. Although I had bolted from the scene immediately after Remo had died and was careful to ensure that no suspicious do-gooder wrote down my licence plate, the potent combination of shock and paranoia in my system caused me to assume that being chased down by the cops was inevitable. Especially since I had just killed a man.

Sure, it was self-defense. But it didn't change the fact that at that moment a SkyTrain railway was slicked with biker blood. The weird thing was I didn't feel any different. My old man had killed several criminals in the line of duty. And I had no idea how many UVF paramilitary loyalists had died at the hands of my cousin. I had asked them both many times before about what it felt like to take a life. Neither one said much other than that I should consider myself lucky for not being in the club. I guess my membership status had just changed.

I didn't have time to brood over killing a punk like Little Z anyway. If it were up to him his custom Hobbit dagger would have left me deader than the Orc army at the end of *Lord of the Rings*.

Besides, after the incident at the SkyTrain, it was clear that both of the Zeppelin boys were murderous scum who clearly had no issue taking a life. Johnny could have just as easily been killed by their hands had Damian Kendricks given the order. The only one of the Steel Gods who had shown a modicum of morality was Remo Willis, and he had paid the price for that with his life.

I unbuttoned my shirt and used the rear-view mirror to take look at my chest. It was bleeding pretty badly. I pulled into a drugstore, grabbed some items to dress the wound, and was back on the road before the clerk had finished ringing up her next customer. I was still a good twenty minutes away from the pub or Declan's condo so I put my geographic knowledge of Dairy Queens to work. I got off of Kingsway and cut down Boundary Road, the heavy traffic corridor that divided the cities of Burnaby and Vancouver. I turned right on East 49th, purposely taking a back roads route to the DQ location I had in mind. I hit Fraser and drove north until I saw the comforting red-and-white oval beckoning me.

After parking I went directly to the bathroom and locked the door, where I proceeded to reset my broken nose. Thanks to my years in professional wrestling I was pretty much an expert on the matter, although the shooting pain that spider-webbed throughout my head when the cartilage popped back into place was something you never got used to. I moved onto disinfecting and bandaging my chest wound. Upon second look it didn't seem as bad, although I probably needed a couple of stitches. But now was hardly the time for a visit to an ER.

For all I knew Big Zeppelin had gotten Remo Willis to confess that he had given me the bloody knife. I had to operate under the assumption that he did, which meant the Steel Gods would be coming for me with a vengeance. And after the way I had turned one of their gang members into public-transit mush, I think it was safe to say that Kendricks and his pals wouldn't come looking for me in order to have a friendly chat.

Kendricks. That smug son-of-a-bitch. I had bought into his bullshit about Remo Willis. Part of me had even liked the guy and gotten a kick out of his eccentricity. I had been face-to-face with the man who gave the order to have Johnny killed and didn't even know it. It made me so livid I wanted to snap off the bike-chain tail of one of his Alien metal statues and use it to gouge out his eyes.

I put my savage fantasies on hold and called Rya. Straight to voicemail. I hung up, left the bathroom and ordered a banana milkshake. I took a seat in a booth and tried to calm myself, as my entire body was flush with anger and adrenaline. A few deep breaths and a couple of sips of my milkshake helped settle me down. I tried Rya again. Voicemail. I left a message for her to call me ASAP, hung up, and then dialed my cousin.

"Aye," piped Declan, answering on the first ring.

"It's me," I said.

"How's she cuttin'?"

"Bad."

"Need me help?"

"Not yet. Where's Pop?"

"In his office."

"Something happened, D. Some bad people are going to be gunning for me."

"Grasby again?"

"Worse. Bikers."

"Now we're talking."

"Just let the old man know and promise me you'll stay sharp. They might come looking for me at the pub."

"Not unless they want a bullet to the barse, they won't."

"Barse?"

"Aye, the wee patch o'skin between your balls and your arse." I shook my head for asking.

"I need to figure out my next move. You mind if I lay low at your place?"

"Have at it, mate."

I hung up and sucked back my shake so fast I felt the sharp tickle of an oncoming brain freeze. I pressed my fingers to my temple and closed my eyes, immediately seeing the image of the diminutive biker getting squashed by the SkyTrain over and over again. I ordered another banana shake to go.

Despite changing out of my suit into a comfortable pair of jeans and a Henley shirt, nearly half-an-hour later I was still shifting restlessly on Declan's couch while surfing TV channels and obsessively checking my phone to make sure I hadn't missed an incoming call from Rya. I finished my milkshake and cracked a Bavarian lager. I sunk into the couch and tried to push the anxiety out of my head. I flipped past pro wrestling but eventually returned to the channel and tossed the remote onto the couch beside me.

It had been years since I had watched my former profession, mostly because just the sight of a wrestling ring was enough to trigger images of Max lying paralyzed at my feet. Of course that was before I had started killing people so my usual pangs of guilt seemed to be more or less absent for the time being. I sipped the lager and watched as a couple of B-list jobbers went through the motions in the ring. The bigger man sported a lion's mane of blonde hair that flowed like windswept silk with each faux punch he threw against his Mohawked opponent. The golden-haired giant slung the punk wrestler into the turnbuckles with an Irish whip, then delivered a running clothesline that knocked the other man out of the ring.

My eyelids drooped as the wrestlers took their fight ringside, and a wave of fatigue suddenly hit me like I had an anesthesia needle in my arm and was midway through counting backwards from ten. I knew the adrenaline I had been running on since the incident at the SkyTrain was fading fast. I tried valiantly to stay awake, but my will couldn't overcome the combination of Declan's comfy couch and the smoothness of the wrestling announcer's hyperbolic voice, which all but lulled me to sleep. The last thing I remember was the Mohawked wrestler slowly climbing to his feet, only to get smashed over the head with a metal folding chair. He never even saw it coming.

THIRTY-THREE

I jolted awake in darkness. The only light in Declan's condo came from the flickering images of a poker tournament on the television. I checked my watch. Six o'clock. I had been asleep for over two hours. I fumbled with my phone and saw that I had one missed call from Rya. She didn't leave a message. I called her back but it went straight to voicemail. I cursed to myself and dialed Declan. No answer. I called the pub. No answer there, either. My pulse quickened. The landline to The Emerald Shillelagh had no answering machine or voicemail. Someone always picked up the phone during business hours. By the time the phone rang for the twenty-second time I was in my truck and speeding through a red light.

The fire was ravenous. Smoke billowed along Hastings Street in all directions. A group of destitute street people had migrated a couple of blocks northeast from the squalor of Pigeon Park and lined the sidewalk in front of The Emerald Shillelagh, laughing and getting drunk on Listerine while watching the inferno destroy the establishment. I pushed my way past them toward the pub, but the heat from the blaze was so searing my skin hurt when I got within twenty feet of the flames.

"Get back," ordered a firefighter. I ignored him and charged toward the entrance. The flames were so high I couldn't see through the windows or doorway.

"I said get back," barked the firefighter, as he grabbed me on the shoulder. I snapped his arm down and twisted it, putting pressure on his elbow joint with my palm. The firefighter yelped and dropped to his knees. I pushed him aside and started screaming for Declan and my pop while trudging through the unbearable heat toward the pub's front door.

Three firefighters converged on me and pulled me back. I was about to start swinging when I heard someone call my name. Billy was wrapped in a blanket and sitting on the bumper of an ambulance, waving frantically from across the street. Beside him were two paramedics loading an occupied gurney into the back of an ambulance. I broke free of the firefighters and raced over, my heart sinking when I saw the person on the stretcher. *Declan.* He was shirtless and unconscious, with an oxygen mask strapped to his soot covered face. Blood-soaked gauze covered wounds on his upper chest.

"Are you family?" asked a paramedic.

"Yes. What happened?"

"Gunshot wound."

"Will he live?"

"He's lost a lot of blood but is stable now. We won't know more until we get him to the ER."

"St. Paul's?"

"Yes." The paramedics slammed the rear door shut, blipped the siren, and drove off.

"Jed?" Billy said softly. I took a long look at the kid. His eyes were puffy and red and his cheeks were streaked with tears.

"Are you okay?" I asked.

"I think so," he replied, wrapping himself tighter in the blanket.

"Where's my pop?"

"They took him." My stomach knotted up and I tasted bile rising in the back of my throat.

"Describe them to me."

"I didn't get a real good look. It all happened so fast. But they weren't like those punks who jumped us the other day. These guys were hardcore."

"Let me guess. They were wearing leather jackets and vests."

"How'd you know?"

"They're a biker gang. And they were after me."

A Coroner's van arrived on scene and only then did I notice the two, blanket-covered bodies that had been placed on the ground in between two fire trucks. The street was a swirling cacophony of emergency sirens, spraying fire hoses, and excited chatter, and even more lookie-loos had come out of the woodwork since I had arrived.

"I need you to tell me exactly what happened."

"Like I said, it all happened so fast," he replied. "One minute I was reading about the lymphatic system, then the next thing I know these guys come storming in shooting up the place. I, uh, hid under a table. I'm sorry, Jed. I didn't know what else to do."

"You don't have to apologize, kid. You did the right thing." Billy nodded and continued.

"So then this one huge guy, I mean, he must have been almost seven feet or something, he runs upstairs to your dad's office with a shotgun."

That had to have been Lance Dennings. As tough as my old man was, even he would have had a hard time going toe-to-toe with a guy that size. Nevertheless, my pop kept a revolver locked in a safe in his office, and if there were shots fired he would have gone for his weapon immediately.

"Did you hear any gunshots come from my pop's office?" Billy shrugged.

"I don't know, Jed. As soon as that huge guy went up the stairs everything went crazy."

"Declan," I said, knowing there's no way my cousin would not have pulled his Browning 9mm and returned fire.

"He was unreal, man! All of a sudden he leapt up from behind the bar and shot this one guy, like, three times square in the chest before the rest of the bikers even knew what was going on. Declan ducked back down again just as those guys turned and shot up the bar for like a minute straight."

"How many were there, not counting the big guy upstairs?"

"Three, I think. I don't know for sure."

"What happened next?"

"I thought Declan was dead. I mean, he had to have been after the way they had blasted the bar to hell. So while one of the bikers started to douse the place with gasoline this fat guy walked over to the bar with his gun drawn. He pointed it downwards as he peered over, when all of a sudden his fucking head exploded! The guy's brains splattered everywhere and suddenly Declan slid out from behind the other end of the bar. The rest of the bikers were still watching their fat buddy tip over and didn't even see him. Declan was about to shoot them all when the huge guy blasted him from behind with the shotgun. Declan collapsed on the floor and your dad started screaming until the huge guy cracked him over the head with the butt of the shotgun and threw him over his shoulder. Next thing I knew they were all gone and the pub was on fire."

I brooded silently as I imagined the scene in my mind.

"What are you going to do?" Billy finally asked.

I didn't have an answer. I put my arm around Billy to give him a squeeze, but he turned into me and wrapped me up in a hug. It caught me off guard, but after a moment, I hugged him back. I promised Billy that I'd check in with him later then marched back across the street toward the dying fire, which had finally been contained. A sharp looking businessman in a three-piece suit asked me a question as I walked by, but I ignored him. He muttered something under his breath before striking up a conversation about the blaze with a jazz hippie in a beret holding an armful of vinyl records and a one-legged vagrant in a wheelchair. Only in Vancouver.

I approached the Coroner from behind as he uncovered the two bodies and began his inspection. The skull of the dead, obese biker had a hole in it the size of a toonie. The Coroner did his best to maneuver the corpse into a body bag while minimizing the amount of brain matter and bloody goop that slopped out of the cranium, but it was a losing battle. The blubbery remains jiggled with each movement, particularly the dead man's enormous man-boobs. No wonder I had nicknamed him Bitch Tits during my meeting with Sankey. I noticed the extensive jailhouse tats on his arms, and they reminded me that Bitch Tits had done hard time before serving as a weapons smuggling enforcer for the Steel Gods. Declan didn't just take down some punk—this guy had been a serious badass.

I didn't recognize the other dead man beside Bitch Tits. I ran through a mental checklist of Damian Kendricks' associates that Sankey had briefed me on, but none of them resembled the deceased young man before me. I made him for early-to-mid-twenties, with smooth, tattoo-free skin and milky white hands that were anything but calloused. The guy looked more like a preppy dressing the part than an authentic biker. A new recruit maybe? Not that it mattered. Damian Kendricks himself could be lying dead at my feet and it still wouldn't make me feel any better about the fact that my cousin was in the hospital and my old man had been taken hostage.

Some uniformed cops tried to remove me from loitering around the crime scene, but as soon as I explained that I was Frank Ounstead's son they let me be. The last of the flames that had ravaged The Emerald Shillelagh were finally extinguished and the firefighters diligently went about their clean up. I was still staring at the charred remains of the quaint Irish pub that had been the lifelong dream of my parents when Rya and Inspector Cornish arrived.

Rya immediately embraced me, and Cornish awkwardly looked the other way before grumbling his condolences. I recapped for them my experience and what I had heard from Billy, but was careful to leave out the parts where I obtained Johnny Mamba's murder weapon and facilitated the mangled death of one of the members of the Steel Gods biker gang.

"Do you have any idea why they would come after your father?" asked Cornish.

"No," I lied.

"They took him alive, so it must have been for a reason," said Rya. "That gives us hope."

"Hope?" I snapped. "Are you kidding me? Look at what they did, Rya. Why should we have any hope at all?"

"I fucking warned you about this," growled Cornish. "I told you to stay out of the pool but you just had to go and take a piss in it."

"Just tell me what you're going to do to get my father back," I pleaded.

"Everything we can," said Cornish. "Shepard, I want you to bring Sankey and the GCU in on this right away. Ensure somebody takes Ounstead here back to the station for an official debriefing. We need to piece together every last detail in order to figure out what the Steel Gods are after. Kendricks really screwed up this time. Nobody fucks with one of our own. We've got him now."

Cornish and his bravado strutted off to take control of the scene, leaving Rya and me alone. A cold gust of wind blew down Hastings, and a light stream of smoke funnelled out of the pub and in between us.

"Where were you?" I asked, batting at the smokey air with my hand. "I've been calling you all afternoon."

"I'm sorry, I was in a meeting so my phone was off."

I stared through the pub's shattered front window at a smouldering pile of wood that used to be a bar stool.

"Jed?"

"This is all my fault."

"You can't blame yourself."

"Yes, Rya, I can."

"You lied to Sankey. You know why Kendricks targeted you, don't you?"

"Yes."

"Why?"

"Because I found Remo Willis."

"Shepard!" bellowed Cornish, waving her over to a group of cops huddled by a squad car.

"Shit. Just wait right here, okay?" I shook my head.

"I have to get to the hospital. You can debrief me there."

"Five minutes, Jed."

"I'll be with my cousin," I said, before leaving the scorched and blackened remnants of my family's business behind.

THIRTY-FOUR

I ignored the text message at first. Declan had just gotten out of surgery and the nurses had finally let me visit him in the ICU. His upper torso was bandaged with gauze that was seeping with spots of blood. He had a tube inserted down his throat and was much paler than usual, which was saying something. I sat silently beside him and held his hand for I don't know how long. My cell phone chimed again with a text message alert. It was inside the pocket of my jacket, which I had taken off and slung over one of the chairs. I didn't move to get it. I just kept squeezing my cousin's hand.

I still don't know how to explain what I felt in that moment. The closest I can come to describing it is to say that something inside of me was slipping away. It was like I could feel myself being hollowed out, leaving me empty except for the gnawing, pulsing pain of my stomach being twisted into knots. I tried to convince myself that Declan would pull through. I tried to reassure myself that I'd get my pop back safe and sound. It didn't work.

If Declan's surgeon hadn't come into the room to talk to me at that minute, and if she hadn't distracted me from my despondent thoughts by updating me on my cousin's condition, then I'm not sure I would have been able to keep the crippling panic of what might happen to my family at bay any longer.

"Mr. Ounstead?" asked a stout, female doctor with an Eastern European accent.

"Yes."

"It looks like your cousin is going to pull through." My eyes became wet and blurry. When I tried to speak it took me a moment to find my voice.

"Really?" She nodded.

"Mr. St. James is quite a fighter. One of the lead shots from the shotgun nicked an artery and he lost a great deal of blood. But he responded extremely well to the transfusions and he stabilized very quickly."

I nodded and cleared my throat. "That's good," I mumbled dumbly.

"Has your cousin seen military combat?"

"Uh … yeah."

"I thought so. He has quite a bit of shrapnel inside him."

"You should see him go through a metal detector at the airport."

"He might want to consider having surgery to try and remove it in the future. For now, I'm positive that we were able to get all of the lead shots from the wound out."

"Thank you, doctor."

By the time she was gone the crushing weight that had been pressing against my chest had lightened. Declan was going to be all right. The world didn't seem as grim as it had moments before. My phone chimed again, and this time I left my seat to retrieve it. I opened a text message from an unknown number. The crushing weight returned, and with greater force. The text message was a photo, one that showed my father beaten and gagged. His arms were handcuffed behind him around a gleaming life-sized metal-art statue of RoboCop. I zoomed in on his face. My pop's eyes and nose were swollen and bruised, and his cheeks were streaked with blood.

I screamed. My body coursed with rage and I felt like I was about to explode. Before I realized what I was doing I had punched three holes in the wall. The only thing that snapped me out of my fury was the combination of my throbbing fist and ringing phone. Powdered drywall floated around my head like fairy dust so I stepped into the hallway in order to see my phone's display. I accepted the incoming call.

"Hello, John," said Damian Kendricks.

I took a deep breath and tried to compose myself. "Let me speak to him."

"No."

"I need to know he's alive."

"You saw the photo."

"Either I talk to him or I give the cops the knife."

"You seem to be confused about who has more leverage because—"

I hung up. Was it a risky move? Maybe. But it was exactly what my pop would have wanted me to do.

At one point in his storied career my old man served on the Emergency Response Team, the Canadian version of SWAT. He participated in hundreds of ERT operations, including hostage negotiations and rescues. He used to tell me how in every negotiation there were always two types of criminals: those who needed a calm voice to reason with them and talk them through the stand-off, and those who only responded to bold and aggressive action. I had just bet my old man's life on Damian Kendricks fitting into the latter category. I knew the only reason he would hold off on executing my old man would be if he thought he needed my pop alive as a bargaining chip. My refusal to deal without definitive proof of life showed Kendricks that. I also wanted him to think I was dangerous and unpredictable. The more uncertainty Kendricks had about what I was capable of, the more likely it was my old man would make it through this ordeal. I had held my breath for exactly nineteen seconds when the phone rang again. I exhaled forcefully and answered the call.

"Hang up again and I put a bullet in his fucking head," threatened Kendricks.

"Let me speak to him." I heard rattling then muffled voices.

"Son?" croaked my father.

"Are you okay?"

"I'm fine," he declared, the bluster returning to his voice.

"I'm so sorry, Pop."

"Not your fault. Don't ever think this is your fault."

"I will get you out of this. I swear on Mom's soul."

"Listen to me, son."

"Yes, sir?"

"Give the evidence you have to my boys in blue. I want each one of these pussies locked up so they can all get the multiple butt-fuckings they deserve."

Kendricks bellowed in the background.

"Son-of-a-bitch!" I heard the phone clatter to the ground followed by distant thuds and grunts of what could only have been biker fists striking my old man.

"Stop it!" I screamed. "Kendricks, I'll deal! Do you hear me? Kendricks? I'll deal!"

A frightened elderly woman picked up her pace as she wheeled her IV pole past me. I clutched the phone to my ear, desperate for a response. More muffled voices and sounds.

"We meet tonight," said Kendricks finally. "Two AM."

"Where?"

"You'll receive a text. Follow the instructions exactly. If you breathe a word of this to the cops I will know, and the old man dies. Try anything cute and I swear to God I'll cut his heart out of his chest and send you the video."

"If I don't see him alive there will be no exchange. Understand?" Kendricks was silent for several moments.

"Two AM," he said again, before ending the call.

THIRTY-FIVE

Kendricks warned me that if I went to the cops he would know. Maybe he was bluffing. But it also wasn't out of the realm of possibility that he had strategically placed contacts within the VPD. No police department was immune to corruption and Damian Kendricks had managed to remain invisible despite a full-blown investigation into his criminal network by the Gang Crime Unit. It certainly reasoned that a little inside information could go a long way in helping him stay one step ahead of some of the city's finest investigators.

I simply couldn't take the chance of involving the VPD. I desperately wanted to call Rya but wasn't sure that I could convince her to help me without police knowledge. Although I knew she would do anything for my pop, her loyalty to the badge was such that it was difficult to imagine her not wanting to strategize with the GCU. Their involvement would lead to the use of the Emergency Response Team during the exchange, in which the VPD's joint objectives would be to recover my father and take down the illusive criminal organization that they had been trying unsuccessfully to build a case against for years. That was the difference between the police and me — my only concern was getting my father back. I was going to have to do this on my own. Even worse, I had to do it without the help of Declan and his lethal skills and combat experience.

Kendricks and his gang outnumbered me greatly. They had until two AM to plan the exchange and ensure that the location they selected worked to their advantage. And as soon as they got their hands on the knife that killed Johnny my pop and I would be as good as dead. Even though taking out a legendary ex-cop like my father would bring a lot of heat down on the Steel Gods, I had no doubt Kendricks would do it. My pop could ID both him and his gang, and Kendricks had to know that if he let my old man go it would only be a matter of time until Frank Ounstead and the Vancouver Police came after them in full force with the evidence and testimony needed to put them away.

I left the hospital in a state of despair. I didn't know where to go. I didn't know what to do. I floored the gas pedal and tried to speed away from the pain. My mind raced faster than my truck, and I sifted through ideas quickly. I drove aimlessly until I found myself in Gastown. That's when a plan started to take shape in my head. I flew past red brick buildings and weaved in and out of traffic, the heavy-duty suspension of my F-150 absorbing the bumpiness of the cobblestone street. The steam-powered clock struck ten as I neared the intersection at Cambie and Water Street, and the grill of my pickup sliced through the thick vapour released by the famous landmark as it drifted into the road. I took a hard left off of the one-way street and shot up a block to Cordova, before cranking the wheel again and heading back in the other direction. Once I passed the crusty, green-hued statue of old Gassy Jack a few blocks later, I was as confident in my next move as Vancouver's founding father was when he set sail down the Fraser River with nothing but a barrel of whisky and dream of a saloon.

THIRTY-SIX

The strip club was rocking. A giant disco ball spun overhead, reflecting a dizzying array of coloured light off of tabletops, glasses, watches, jewelry, glittery, naked breasts, and g-strings. I shoved my way through a bachelor party and even though several rowdy guys shot me dirty looks, they all had the good sense to not make an issue of it.

Melvin Van Lowe was halfway through his steak dinner when I interrupted him, and he seemed less than pleased. "You ratfink bastard," he snapped.

"I need your help."

"Fuck you, Ounstead. My nose still hurts and you gave me up to the cops even though I did you a favour."

"Look, I'm sorry about your nose. I was upset over Johnny's murder and shouldn't have taken it out on you. But I had to tell the cops that Stormy Daze hired you. Besides, I knew for a fact they were preoccupied with other leads so I doubt they gave you much of a hassle."

"Yeah, well, they still called me. I almost had a fucking anxiety attack, man."

"You know what's good for treating anxiety?"

"Pussy?"

"I was going to say a round of beers on me, but hey, whatever works."

"Can you just hurry up and tell me what you want? I'm trying to enjoy my dinner."

I pulled up a chair next to Melvin and pleaded my case. "I'm in some serious trouble."

"Not my problem."

"Just hear me out. Believe it or not, you're the only person who can help."

Melvin eyed me curiously as he sliced off a chunk of baked potato and plunged it into a tiny cup of sour cream. "Go on," he said.

I quickly summarized my encounter with Remo Willis and how I obtained the knife that had killed Johnny. Again, I skipped over the part where I made a fleshy-biker scramble out of one of the Steel Gods, but I did inform Melvin of the shoot-out and fire at the pub and my pop's subsequent kidnapping. Melvin was so stunned a piece of potato fell out of his mouth.

"They got Frank?" he asked incredulously.

"Yeah. But I know how to get him back."

"How?" I laid out my plan. "Look, Jed, you know I got a lot respect for Frank and all, but this is some hardcore shit. I mean, yeah, I'm pretty good at snapping photos of slutty housewives and stuff, but I'm not exactly a surveillance expert. I'm sorry. I really think you need to bring in the cops."

"I can't risk it. I can do this, Melvin."

"Maybe you can. But I can't risk a bloodthirsty biker gang discovering that I helped you and then coming after me."

"They'll never know. Even if things go bad, I'll leave your name out of it. I give you my word." Melvin took another bite of his steak.

"If I were to help you do this, I'd like something in return."

"Name it."

"I want Frank to float me some business. It doesn't have to be his top-tier clients or anything. Just some jobs here and there that don't require me to squat in the bushes and wait for some horny buffalos to start knob-gobbling. If he did that, I could really start to grow my agency and attract a broader clientele."

"Done," I said. "Although if you really want to accomplish that goal, you might want to think about painting over the big-breasted, warrior women who adorn your office walls."

"Are you fucking crazy? Those chicks are awesome."

A flexible stripper laid down on the stage directly in front of us and proceeded to bend her legs in all directions. Melvin was so deep in thought he didn't even look.

"What do you say, bub?" I finally asked.

"Okay," he said, before paying his bill and following me out of the club.

We spent the next half-hour next door in Melvin's office carefully filling a duffel bag with all types of surveillance equipment, including parabolic microphones, audio recorders, GPS trackers, and LCD digital camera binoculars.

"I thought you said you weren't a surveillance expert?"

"Just because I own it doesn't mean I know how to use it yet."

"Where did you get all this stuff anyway?"

"The Spy Store. That place is awesome. It's like every cheater's worst nightmare."

Melvin zipped up the duffel bag then outfitted both of our cell phones with Bluetooth headsets. When we were finished and ready to leave he went around the office, kissing his fingertips and tapping the cleavage of each of the bosomy fantasy women that were spread throughout the room on the walls.

"What the hell are you doing?" I asked.

"I do this before every job. For luck." Melvin walked over to a mural of a winged vampiress with a battle-axe. "I call this babe Solita. She's my favourite."

"I'm just going to wait for you by the car," I replied.

Melvin nodded and leaned his forehead against Solita's enormous rack, and I think the little freak may have started to motorboat her two-dimensional boobs as I left. But considering he was about to help me try and rescue my father from a pack of homicidal bikers, I decided to cut the guy some slack.

Melvin followed me in his cherry-red Dodge Viper as I drove my truck through the downtown streets of Vancouver. I checked my watch. 10:45 PM. I only had about three hours until the exchange. When we arrived at our destination I instructed Melvin to wait in his car.

"How long you going to be?" he asked.

"Depends," I replied.

"On what?"

"On how convincing I am."

"Can you ballpark it for me?"

"No, Melvin, I can't."

"Well, what the hell am I supposed to do in the meantime?"

"Wait."

"Fine. But I'm going to pull my car around to the other side."

"Why?"

"Because I think I saw a couple of MILFs drinking wine on the patio of one of those houses we drove by," he said, before digging a pair of LCD digital camera binoculars out of the duffel bag.

"Just stay sharp, okay? And keep your phone close."

"I'm not a fucking idiot, Ounstead."

I left Melvin to his Peeping Tom preparations and entered the building. I double-checked that my snub-nosed .38 Colt Cobra revolver was tucked behind my back and under my shirt in my waistband, and my fingers lingered momentarily on the reassuring comfort of the pistol's cold steel.

It didn't take long for people to stare. Conversations turned to hushed whispers. The room grew smaller as bodies slowly circled me. I could feel the cumulative gazes like the growing heat from an increasing number of spotlights. When I got close the people around him parted like I had just waved the staff of Moses. I climbed up and under, and then walked until we were standing toe-to-toe. The expression on his face was a mixture of shock and vexation. He crossed his arms and waited for me to speak.

"We need to talk," I said.

Bert Grasby burned holes into me with his eyes, before glancing outside of the wrestling ring and taking note of the dozens of XCCW wrestlers who had stopped packing up after the evening's show and were instead transfixed by the scene playing out in front of them. Even Pocket was silent, standing slack-jawed next to Tubbs. Grasby took a step forward and got in my face.

"And then some," he replied.

THIRTY-SEVEN

"Do you know what my favourite animal is, Ounstead?"

"I don't really care."

"Take a guess."

"No."

"Take a fucking guess."

"A monkey."

"A monkey?"

"That's right."

"Why a monkey?"

"They have pudgy bellies, can't keep their hands off their dicks, and have been known to hump other members of the same sex. Reminds me of you."

I didn't see the punch coming. The fist came from behind and clocked me pretty good on my left cheekbone, but I instinctively rolled with it in hopes of limiting the damage. Bert Grasby's face was extremely flushed, and combined with the snow-white, velour tracksuit he was wearing, his chubby head looked like a cherry tomato that was balanced atop an egg.

"There's more where that came from, cockbucket," snapped Dylan, as he individually flexed his pecs in what I assumed was intended to be an intimidating gesture. I'm pretty sure the combination of what I said next and my use of air quotes made it clear to Dylan I was far from rattled.

"I think the only 'cockbucket' around here is your asshole, kid." Dylan snapped and lunged toward me.

"Enough!" barked Grasby, and Dylan responded with the promptness of a well-trained attack dog.

The room was silent for a moment as Grasby, Dylan, and two skinhead, muscle-bound wrestlers I didn't recognize glared at me venomously. We were in the same community centre arts and crafts room where I had first encountered Grasby. Dylan was again dressed in a Lycra Speedo, although I noticed he had heeded my advice and forgone the neon tassels around his biceps. Dylan's nose was heavily taped and he wore a protective clear plastic mask over top of it. Remembering how he had squealed after I had shattered his nose during our street fight made the pain in my cheekbone lessen. Having regained his composure, Grasby leaned against a desk and continued with the point he had tried to make earlier.

"Leopards are my favourite animal. They're amazing predators. The thing about leopards though, what really makes them special, is the way they treat their prey. You see, after a leopard makes a kill it doesn't just eat and go on its way. No, a leopard eats a little, then clenches its prey between its teeth, climbs up a tree, and places its kill in the branches so no other predator in the jungle can have it. The leopard will then continue to return to that tree and devour its prey until there's nothing left but bones." Grasby pushed himself off the desk and sauntered toward me until I could smell his spicy foul breath.

"You're all mine, Ounstead. And I'm going to keep coming after you. Because of what you did."

"You mean hitting you for disrespecting my friend?"

"It's not just that. Hell, I probably could have let that go, especially after Mamba got killed. But you started sniffing around my past. You messed up Dylan's handsome face and now he looks like Hannibal Lecter. And because of you my cousin only has nine fucking fingers. He even had to quit his fucking bowling team."

"There's no shame in having a big toe for a thumb."

"Why the fuck are you here? If you think I won't end you just because dozens of people saw you walk in then you really don't know shit about Bert Grasby."

. I sighed and shook my head. The jerk referred to himself in the third person more than Mr. Miyagi.

"I'm here because I want to settle things between us."

"You want to call a truce?" he said, scoffingly.

"I want to make you an offer." Grasby eyed me curiously.

"I'm listening," he said, a few moments later.

"I don't care that your goons jumped me. Insurance will cover my trashed house and I'll even look the other way on the fact that you tried to kill me in a drive-by shooting. I'm willing to wipe the slate clean between us so that we can move forward and help each other out in a way that is mutually beneficial."

"Help each other out how exactly?"

"I need you to make a phone call."

"To who?"

"Whichever member of the Steel Gods biker gang it was who set you up with Remo Willis."

"Don't do it, boss," said Dylan. "This is some kind of trap. He's probably wearing a wire." I lifted the front of my shirt, revealing that there was nothing attached to my chest except for the bandage covering my knife wound and an abundance of chest hair.

"Remo Willis was the person who stole Johnny Mamba's snake. When his boss Damian Kendricks found out, he was furious that Remo had jeopardized their operation over such a small-time score. So he ordered a hit on Johnny. I found Remo and learned that while he was guilty of extortion, he wasn't complicit in the murder. After Johnny was killed, Remo felt so guilty he swiped the murder weapon and gave it to me. But before I could do anything with it, the Steel Gods killed Remo, shot my cousin, and kidnapped my father. They want to make an exchange in a few hours and we're both smart enough to know that my old man and I wouldn't make it back from that meeting alive. That's why I need you to call your contact in the Steel Gods and lure them here."

Grasby stared at me in disbelief. He glanced around at Dylan and the muscle heads, but they looked utterly confused.

"Wait, Remo took Johnny's snake?" Dylan asked, scratching his head. "The guy who hooks us up with our Oxy and juice?" Grasby rolled his eyes at Dylan's slow-wittedness. He snapped his fingers and pointed at the door.

"Outside, all of you."

"But boss—"

"Go." Dylan and the meatheads left without another word. Grasby sat on a desk and rubbed the bridge of his nose.

"You still haven't told me what I'd get out of this," he said tiredly. I made Grasby my offer. His eyes nearly popped out of his head.

"How do I know you'll be able to deliver?" he asked.

"I'm a man of my word, Grasby. And I'd be in your debt." Grasby stewed over the proposition for almost a minute.

"Deal," he said finally. "But I still don't know how I'm supposed to lure the guy here."

"What's the name of the person who set you up with Remo?"

"Lance. I don't know his last name."

"It's Dennings. He's the same sasquatch son-of-a-bitch who slit Johnny's throat."

"Jesus Christ," muttered Grasby.

"All you have to do is call him and tell him that I just paid you a visit. When he asks for details tell him you're not comfortable talking about it over the phone. Trust me, he'll come running."

"And when he arrives? What do I say then?"

"Tell him I came storming in here, all crazed and upset. Mention that I demanded to know where I could find the Steel Gods but you told me you didn't know."

"I don't know!" said Grasby emphatically.

"Good. That will make it an easier sell."

"What are you going to do while he's in here talking to me?"

"You don't need to worry about that. Just try and stall him for as long as possible." Grasby nodded and ran his fingers through his wispy hair.

"And that's all I have to do?"

"That's it."

"Whatever it is you got planned, something tells me it's not going to be good for the Steel Gods' business."

"So what if it isn't?"

"They're the best supplier in the province and literally hook my wrestlers up with any drug they want. Not to mention the fact I just went through a lot of trouble in order to switch my business from the Russians over to them."

"The Steel Gods and the Russians aren't the only dealers in town. Surely a man as resourceful as you can find what you need elsewhere."

"I suppose, but it's a fucking headache I could do without."

"Remember what I'm offering you." Grasby chewed his bottom lip for a few moments.

"Fine. But what about my safety? How do I know these guys won't find out I helped you and come looking for blood?"

"If you do this for me, then you're also saving my old man's life. I would die before ratting you out." Grasby nodded, his jowls jiggling with trepidation.

"One more thing," I said.

"What?"

"I need a vehicle. Untraceable. Preferably a large pickup or SUV and it has to be at least a 1998 model or later."

"What the hell for?"

"It's better you don't know. Can you make it happen or not?"

"Okay," he grumbled. Grasby whipped out his mobile phone and dialed a number, staring at me while he waited for it to ring. "You know, I think I liked you better when I just wanted you dead."

THIRTY-
EIGHT

The roar of the Harley-Davidson Fat Boy's engine was deaf-ening. Lance Dennings cut a path through the haphazardly parked vehicles outside the Russian community centre with such ease that even Wyatt from *Easy Rider* would have been impressed.

"There he is!" chirped Melvin's voice excitedly through the Bluetooth headset in my ear.

"Way to be on the ball, Melvin."

"Uh-oh."

"What?"

"He's parking right in front of the main entrance," he said, in a hushed whisper.

"I see that," I said, peeking out from behind the Honda CR-V that I was hiding behind.

"What now?" asked Melvin.

"Stick to the plan. Keep eyes on that door." Slouched in his parked Dodge Viper over a hundred feet away, Melvin had his LCD digital camera binoculars trained on the entrance to the community centre.

"I'm not going to be able to give you much of a warning when he comes back out," said Melvin. "And you're going to be exposed."

"Nothing we can do about that now."

The Harley's rumbling sputtered then slowly died as Dennings turned off the bike's ignition and used a big boot to extend the kickstand. He removed his black half-shell helmet, which was emblazoned with a pair of silver Viking wings. Dennings tucked his helmet under his arm and strode through the front doors of the home of XCCW with more authority than a prison warden.

I made a break for it. With Melvin's duffel bag slung over my shoulder, I crouch-ran and zigzagged between cars as I made the fifty-foot dash to the motorcycle. I knelt beside the bike's back tire and unzipped the bag, using the Fat Boy's large custom frame to shield myself as best as I could from the view from the front entrance doors. I activated the GPS tracker like Melvin had shown me, then peeled the plastic covers off of the adhesive strips on the back of the device.

"It's on," I said into my Bluetooth headset.

"Okay, sit tight," replied Melvin. The seconds that ticked by felt like minutes.

"Come on," I said impatiently.

"Five more seconds." I glanced around and saw there was still no one around in the parking lot.

"All right, we're good to—Jed, the door!" I sprung to my feet like Usain Bolt out of the starting blocks and took three big strides before leaping over the hood of a nearby Toyota Corolla.

"Shit!" I exclaimed in a hushed voice.

"What?"

"I forgot the bag."

I dropped into a low plank position and looked under the Corolla to see the community centre door slowly open. The duffel bag was on the ground next to the motorcycle, and its unzipped wide mouth revealed a treasure trove of surveillance equipment within. I silently cursed myself for beings so careless. How the hell was I going to track Dennings now? Following him by car was risky and it would be easy for him to shake us on his bike if he got wise. Even worse, there was no way he'd miss the duffel bag. Seeing the surveillance equipment on the ground next to his bike would make him awfully suspicious, and Dennings and Kendricks would likely assume I was up to something—which meant my old man was as good as dead. I closed my eyes tight and tried to think of a solution, but my thoughts were interrupted when I heard the clip-clop sound of high-heeled boots on pavement.

"Nice," cooed Melvin, in my ear.

I stole a look through the Corolla's windows and saw a muscular, broad-shouldered Amazon woman dressed in pink latex wrestling gear strut through the community centre's front doors. Relief swept over me. Dennings was still inside.

"What's she doing?" asked Melvin.

"Who cares," I said, looking at the surveillance device still clutched in my hand. "Is the GPS working?"

"Yep. Got your location right here on my laptop."

The woman strutted over to a nearby Nissan Sentra, leaned in the driver's side and retrieved a makeup bag. "She's going back in," I said.

"How the fuck do you know that?" snapped Melvin.

"Because lady wrestlers tend to sweat off a lot of makeup during their matches and need to constantly reapply it." The woman wrestler popped open a compact and added an abundance of lip liner and eye shadow while walking briskly past the motorcycle and the duffel bag without a second glance.

"Look at the guns on her, Jed."

"Stay focused, bub."

"I am, man. But come on. Just think of the hand jobs she could give with arms like that."

"You really are a skeevy little douche, you know that?"

"Yeah, well you're just an axe and a flannel shirt away from being a real-life Paul Bunyan you overgrown son-of-a-bitch." I silently promised myself that if I made it out of this mess alive I'd get a haircut and a shave.

"All clear," said Melvin.

I hurried back to the Harley and proceeded to plant the GPS receiver underneath one of the saddlebags, in the narrow space between the bottom of the leather pouch and the bike's twin chrome exhaust pipes. I zipped up the duffel bag, slung it back over my shoulder, and worked my way through the maze of parked cars until I reached Melvin's Dodge Viper.

"So what now?" he asked.

I grabbed the extra pair of LCD digital camera binoculars from the backseat and collimated them on the entrance.

"We wait."

"What do you think this Grasby cat is telling him?"

"Whatever it is, it's working."

Three minutes later the door swung violently open and Lance Dennings stormed out of the community centre. His barrel chest was heaving and he looked out of breath.

"Why's he sucking wind so bad?" asked Melvin.

Dennings was clutching his motorcycle helmet in his right hand. I looked through the binoculars and grimaced when I saw the stains on the Viking wings.

"Probably for the same reason that his helmet is covered in blood."

THIRTY-NINE

I raced through the halls of the community centre until I reached the arts and crafts room. The place looked like a tornado had ripped through it. Dennings had left a path of destruction littered with overturned desks, crushed paper-mache masks and broken and bloodied bodies on the floor.

I found Dylan first. He was unconscious and looked like he had taken a hit from the motorcycle helmet square in the face. His clear plastic face shield had split in two, and the impact had re-broken his nose and turned it into a bloody and pulpy mess. I took the mask off of the kid and made sure that he was breathing through his mouth before moving onto the others.

Both of Grasby's muscle head enforcers were writhing on the ground. The bigger meathead had his right arm bent at an unnatural angle while his partner was rocking back and forth in the fetal position clutching his ribs. They were both conscious and there wasn't much I could do for them, so I kept searching the room until I found Bert Grasby underneath a rolling chalkboard that had been cracked and overturned.

"Grasby," I said, pulling the chalkboard off of him. "You okay?" Grasby spit out some blood. A tooth came with it.

"Do I fucking look okay?"

"What happened?" I helped Grasby to his feet and he steadied himself against a wall.

"The guy fucking snapped."

"Why?"

"I don't know. I told him exactly what you said to. He asked me if I had any idea where you were headed and I told him no. Then he just flew into a fucking psycho rage and started kicking the shit out of all of us."

"I'm sorry."

"You're sorry? Look at me. Look at my boys. Fuck you, Ounstead. You can take your apology and shove it up your goddamn ass."

"The plan worked, Grasby. I was able to plant a tracer on his bike. Now I can track Dennings back to the rest of the Steel Gods and my father."

Grasby glared at me, his eyes still burning with anger. "I want to amend our agreement," he hissed.

"How?"

"First, promise me you'll kill each and every one of those motherfuckers."

"They'll get what's coming to them."

"Second, I want to renegotiate the specific terms we set."

"What do you have in mind?" Grasby told me what he wanted. I didn't like it. Not one bit. However, the guy had kept his part of the bargain and taken a brutal and undeserved beating for it.

"Deal," I said finally. "Now what about that vehicle?"

FORTY

I called Melvin on my way to the impound lot. He left the Russian community centre a couple of minutes after Lance Dennings had, with instructions to follow the Harley-Davidson motorcycle from an out-of-sight distance using only the GPS tracker.

"What happened back there?" asked Melvin.

"Dennings went postal. Beat the hell out of Grasby and his entourage."

"Why?"

"I guess I've really gotten under their skin."

"I can relate."

"Where is Dennings now?"

"Looks like he's headed to North Van."

That gave me pause. The city of North Vancouver was an upscale and urban waterfront municipality. Not exactly the kind of place I had in mind when I considered possible locations the Steel Gods were keeping my old man captive. Then again, maybe Dennings wasn't rendezvousing with the rest of his crew just yet. I felt a stab of fear in my chest as I considered the possibility that

Dennings might not lead me to the rest of the Steel Gods and my father at all, but it was fleeting. Dennings was not only Kendricks' right-hand man, he was also the one who killed Johnny and would be facing a lifetime jail sentence if the cops got their hands on the murder weapon. There was no way he would miss the meet.

"Stay on him, but remain out-of-sight," I said. "If and when he enters a building, see if you can get close enough to pick something up with one of those parabolic microphones."

"That's one of the gadgets I don't know how to work yet," whined Melvin.

"Then it's a good thing you packed the instructions, isn't it?"

I hung up and exited the Burrard Street Bridge. I followed Pacific Boulevard as it wrapped around False Creek, the short inlet that separated downtown from the rest of the city. I drove past the colossal geodesic dome that was home to Science World, and the structure's evening lights enveloped the silver sphere in a golden spider-webbed pattern. The illuminated downtown skyline shimmered in the distance, and I could see the city's brilliant colours dancing across the dark waterway until I turned onto Industrial Avenue and followed the road to the impound lot.

Buster's Towing had been an institution around Vancouver for over fifty years. The company had long been contracted by the city, and was so efficient that I didn't know anyone who hadn't had to pay a visit to their impound lot after parking illegally. I drove past the lot, and although I knew it was open twenty-four hours, it looked as if it had closed up shop for the night.

I parked a block away on a nearby side street. I grabbed a pair of thin leather gloves and the Ziplock bag containing the knife Dennings used to kill Johnny out of the glove box and hoofed it back to the lot. I let myself in through the front gate, which had been left unchained. The SUV was waiting for me by the portable office, just like Grasby said it would be. I didn't know who he had contacted or why I was picking it up from an impound lot, but Grasby assured me that the vehicle couldn't be traced back to either of us and that was good enough for me. I slipped on the gloves and approached my new ride. The vehicle's bulky frame and rusted, dark green paint showed its age, and I made the Jeep Grand Cherokee for mid-aughts, as per my request. The keys were on the right front tire and when I started it up the rumbling of the old-school engine reverberated through the quiet lot like a subwoofer blasting a rap song in church.

I pulled into traffic and checked my watch. 12:47 AM. I had to move fast. I drove back the way I came then turned onto Pacific Boulevard and followed it straight into Yaletown. The stylish street in front of Declan's condo was teeming with nightlife, and I had to give the Cherokee's horn several blasts and receive even more flipped middle fingers before I was able to get close enough to the building to park. I left the Jeep in a handicapped spot and hurried inside, tearing through the residence until I found the canvas bag of munitions that Declan had brought to my house after the drive-by shooting.

I sorted through the bag until I found what I was looking for: a Smith & Wesson .22 caliber J-frame handgun with ankle holster, a Ruger .44 Magnum Super Redhawk Alaskan double-action revolver with a fluted cylinder, and an all black 12 gauge Mossberg 500 shotgun with a synthetic stock. I didn't pick these guns by coincidence — they were the ones Declan had shown me how to use over the years on camping trips. Unlike my old man, my cousin was not a fan of gun ranges, especially since most of his weapons were unregistered and had not exactly been procured in a legal manner. I knew for certain that the three guns I had selected were clean pieces that could not be traced back to Declan in any way. I cinched my leather gloves on my hands, then took the small bottle of firearms lubricant and the clean cloth that were in the bottom of the bag and proceeded to spray and wipe down all three guns, removing any oil and fingerprints that may have been on them.

My phone chimed. I had one new text. My heart pounded in my chest. They were early. I wasn't ready yet. I needed more time. I held my breath as I checked the message. I exhaled forcefully when I saw it was from Melvin. The text message read:

"He drove to remote residence on Burrard Inlet in N. Van. House with HUGE detached garage. Very isolated. Driveway filled with motorcycles. No visual on Frank. Will keep you posted. Don't call. Can't talk cuz I'm in bushes. Again! Asshole."

I texted back *"Roger"* and stopped for a moment to think. Dennings had to have regrouped with the Steel Gods. And the conspicuously large detached garage sounded exactly like the type of building that could house a metal-art workshop. Which meant my father had to be somewhere at that location.

A wave of doubt suddenly swept over me. Was I doing the right thing by excluding the cops? I didn't have a choice at first—I simply couldn't risk calling Kendricks' bluff in case he actually had sources inside the department. But that was before I knew exactly where to find the man who killed Johnny Mamba and had a probable location of my father's whereabouts.

I brought up the redial list on my phone. My thumb hovered over Rya's number. And hovered. And hovered some more. I couldn't do it. Although it seemed likely, I was not one-hundred percent sure that my pop was being held at that location. If the VPD ERT team burst in there and took down only some of the Steel Gods and found no hostage, then my old man was history. Besides, I had a plan. And I still thought it could work.

I took the remaining guns, ammunition, knives, and Kevlar vests out of the canvas bag and placed them on Declan's coffee table. I took off my jacket and strapped on a Kevlar vest, then covered it with one of the black windbreakers that Declan had left in the bag. I quickly inspected and then loaded the .22, the .44 Magnum, and Mossberg shotgun. Satisfied, I double-checked that the safeties on each of the guns were on, then strapped the holstered .22 to my ankle and placed the Magnum and shotgun back in the canvas bag. I wrapped the Ziplocked-bagged murder weapon that had killed Johnny in the gun cleaning cloth and put it inside the bag as well. Finally, I tossed extra ammo and a ten-inch hunting knife with a sheathed blade inside, marvelling at the miniature arsenal, and realizing there was a hell of a lot about my cousin I still didn't know. I decided that if I got through this nightmare he was going to start sharing some IRA stories whether he wanted to or not.

I slung the bag over my shoulder and ran back to the Jeep. I ignored some drunken yuppies across the street yelling at me for parking in a handicapped spot, loaded my gear into the truck, then slid behind the wheel of the Jeep Cherokee, and peeled out down the road. I crisscrossed through the downtown streets, making my way toward the North Vancouver location where the GPS had tracked Lance Dennings. My phone rang. I tapped the Bluetooth headset in my ear. It was Melvin.

"They're on the move," he said.

"Where?"

"South."

"Toward the city?"

"Looks that way."

"Where are you?"

"Near their clubhouse. I just made it back to my car. I'm still tracking them."

"Did you see my pop?"

"Yes! They loaded him into a black van and took off."

He was still alive. Unfortunately, I didn't have a chance to revel in the good news. "How did he look?"

"Roughed up. But that didn't stop him from kicking one of those bikers in the balls while they were moving him from the house. He took a pretty good beating for it."

"Where are they now?"

"Approaching the Lions Gate Bridge."

"Good."

"Why?"

"Because I'm right by Stanley Park," I said, as I left the distant silhouettes of treetops and totem poles behind me in the thousand-acre park that bordered the city.

"You're driving toward them?"

"Yes."

"Have they texted you yet?"

"No."

"What's your plan exactly?"

"I don't have time to get into it. I just need you to keep feeding me their location until I get a visual."

"Okay, hold on."

I pressed the pedal to the floor. The Cherokee's outdated transmission chugged momentarily before responding and allowing the vehicle to pick up speed.

"They're just about on the bridge now," said Melvin. "Jed, there's a lot of them."

"How many?"

"Five. Two in the van, three on bikes. They were riding in formation when they left — two bikes behind the van and one out in front."

"What about Dennings?"

"That big bastard was leading the pack."

I reached the bridge and slingshotted between the two concrete sculptures of magnificent lions that guard its entrance. The bridge was empty as I drove across it, standing almost as still as the pitch-black water of the first narrows of the Burrard Inlet underneath. I squinted my eyes and looked in the distance but didn't see any motorcycles coming the other way.

"Hey, Melvin?"

"What?"

"Thank you. For everything."

"Just don't forget to tell Frank about sending me referrals."

"I won't."

"And Jed?"

"Yeah?"

"Whatever you're doing — good luck."

I touched the Bluetooth earpiece and clicked it off.

A moment later Lance Dennings appeared on the concrete horizon, leading a motorcade consisting of a van and two motorcycles, just as Melvin had described. I glanced over at the passenger seat floor at the canvas bag of weapons, and then looked back at the roadway in front of me. The motorcade was only a few hundred feet away now. The collective roar of the Harley-Davidson motorcycles grew louder as the distance between us shrank. I gripped the steering wheel and backed off the gas. Dennings was looking straight ahead, paying no attention to oncoming traffic. I checked my rear-view mirror and confirmed there were no cars behind me. Then I cranked the wheel, swerved into the other lane, and crashed the Jeep Cherokee into Lance Dennings and his motorcycle.

FORTY-ONE

Time seemed to slow down in the split second it took for the vehicles to crash into each other. The screeching of metal on metal went on forever. I heard a hissing sound as my airbag deployed, and the safety device cushioned me as the violent collision caused my entire body to thrust forward with more force than a dozen body-slams combined. The Jeep had hit the motorcycle on an angle before plowing into the van behind it. All three vehicles slid toward the edge of the bridge together, and the guardrailing bent as it took the brunt of the sudden impact and kept us all from going over. My head was tingling and I felt dizzy. My thigh throbbed from having slammed into the underside of the steering wheel, but the adrenaline was pumping and helping to numb the pain. I grabbed the canvas bag off the floor and unsheathed the hunting knife and used it to pop the airbag. As it deflated I looked through the cracked windshield and rear window to see the carnage.

The Jeep Cherokee's entire front end had collapsed inwards, hemorrhaging steam and twisted steel. It was also entwined with the motorcycle, which had been so completely wrecked by the crash it was hard to tell where the Cherokee ended and the

Harley-Davidson Fat Boy began. There was no sign of Dennings. I had seen sheer panic materialize on his face in the instant after I had swerved, however, the next thing I remembered was my vision being enveloped by the deploying airbag. Since I didn't see a hulking, lacerated body coiled around the Cherokee's crumpled engine parts I assumed he must have been thrown clear by the impact.

One of the bikers from behind the van had managed to avoid the collision altogether and appeared to have gone into a controlled slide, which placed him about twenty feet behind the scene of the crash. I couldn't make out which Steel God it was through the windows. I tucked the .44 Magnum revolver in my belt and grabbed the Mossberg 500 shotgun. I kicked open the passenger side door and slid out, flicking off the safety and racking a round in the chamber of the 12 gauge. I planted the stock of the shotgun into my shoulder and limped toward the biker who had wiped out behind the site of the crash. As I got closer I recognized him—it was the baby-faced guy with slicked blonde hair I had nicknamed Ponyboy. He was grunting as he struggled to free his left leg, which was pinned underneath his motorcycle.

A car whizzed by on the other side of the bridge, using one of the lanes that was not blocked by the wreckage. Another vehicle followed and slowed, until the driver saw me holding a shotgun. I glanced around for any sign of Lance Dennings but before I could locate him Ponyboy sprung his leg free and jumped to his feet. His eyes widened and brimmed with rage upon seeing me. He pulled a high-calibre handgun from a hip holster despite looking down the barrel of my shotgun.

Ka-boom! The pellets ripped Ponyboy's torso to shreds and he collapsed backwards onto his bike. The sound of the ear-splitting blast thundered over the bridge and carried on, echoing across the inlet. A moment later the bridge was silent, and the only movement came from a red cloud of bloody mist that floated in the night air underneath the glow of a street lamp.

I spun on my heel, racked the Mossberg, then hurried back toward the scene of the accident, and cautiously approached the van. Hunched over in the driver's seat was the greasy-haired wheelman Sankey had shown me pictures of at Foo's Ho Ho. Unfortunately for him, he didn't have an airbag that activated upon impact. The greasy biker's head hung limply over the steering wheel, bone protruding from his neck. Two down. Three if you counted Dennings, whom I now assumed had been thrown over the side of the bridge. That left Kendricks, my old man, and Big Z, the Zeppelin boy who had executed Remo Willis on the SkyTrain platform.

Another car sped by in one of the bridge's unblocked lanes but it barely slowed. Holding the shotgun tight, I came around to the back of the van at a wide angle, in case one of the Steel Gods tried to surprise me by jumping out of the back of the van.

Big mistake. Apparently Ponyboy wasn't the only one who was able to put his bike into a controlled slide, as Big Z sat crouched behind his motorcycle with a hand cannon drawn and at the ready. Before I could even turn the Mossberg in his direction he fired. The shot hit me like a sledgehammer to the chest and knocked me clean off my feet. I dropped the shotgun. Searing pain slashed across my ribs. I tried to move. It was no use. Had the Kevlar vest even worked? I had broken ribs in the past while wrestling but the pain had never been so immobilizing.

As I lay on my back struggling to breathe my mind suddenly filled with random images: the photograph of Johnny and Ginger ringside, Rya with her hair down wearing a robe and sipping coffee, Declan hooked up to a ventilator clinging to life, my old man beaten and bound to a metal-art statue. Then I saw Max, his muscular body lying broken and paralyzed at my feet, looking up at me with a terror so pure that it had forever marked my soul.

No. I refused to go out like this. My father needed me. Johnny deserved justice. And I still had to atone. I summoned a force of will I didn't know I had and reached for the .44 Magnum revolver in my belt. Big Z pounced on me and stomped on my hand, pinning both it and the revolver to the asphalt. He crouched over me and jammed the barrel of his gun against my forehead.

"Rot in hell, motherfuck—"

His parting words were cut short when I snatched the .22 from my ankle holster with my other hand, shoved the pistol into his stomach, and pulled the trigger twice. He stumbled sideways, still clutching his gun. Before he could raise it again I sat up and put a third bullet in his head.

My ribs screamed in pain as I picked up the shotgun and stepped over Big Z's corpse. I stumbled over toward the back of the van, which had started rocking back and forth. I yanked open the door and the first thing I saw was the face of Damian Kendricks, which was swollen and beet red. My father was behind him, using the chain in between his cuffed hands to choke out one of the most elusive and dangerous criminals in the city.

"Son!" he exclaimed upon seeing me.

My old man swung his wrists to the side, smashing Kendricks' head into the metal hinges on which one of the van's rear doors hung. Kendricks crumpled to the ground, gasping for air.

"The rest of them?" my old man asked.

"Dead."

"Where's Declan?"

"Hospital. He's okay."

My father glanced at the wreckage from the crash and noted the dead bodies of his former captors. "You did this all by yourself?" I nodded.

My father pulled me into a fierce hug, which was cut short by sirens wailing in the distance. He nodded at the mangled remains of the Jeep Cherokee.

"Stolen?"

"Yeah."

"Guns clean?"

"Yes, sir."

He took the shotgun out of my gloved hands. "Hand them over. You were never here."

"How are you going to explain—"

"Go, son."

I handed over the .22 but left the Magnum in my belt. "I didn't fire this one," I said, patting the revolver. "There's a bag in the front seat of the Cherokee. Inside is some ammo and the knife that killed Johnny Mamba."

"Take that knife and get the hell out of here," said my father.

"What about him," I asked, motioning to Kendricks. My father used his foot to roll him over onto his back.

"Fuckers!" Kendricks spat venomously, in between laboured breaths. In one fluid motion, my old man grabbed the .44 Magnum out of my waistband, pulled back the hammer, and shot Damian Kendricks centre mass in the chest.

"Jesus Christ!" I exclaimed, completely startled. "What the hell, Pop?" My old man glared at the lifeless body of Damian Kendricks.

"Needed to be done."

"He was unarmed."

"It was either him or us. This piece of shit was the kind of man who would have kept coming after us until we were all dead. And he was resourceful enough to do it whether he was behind bars or not."

"But—"

"Enough! Leave now, while you still can!"

The sirens were getting louder. In the distance flashing red and white lights from a fire truck lit up the night as the vehicle barrelled toward the bridge. I grabbed Johnny's murder weapon out of the Jeep and ran over to Ponyboy's Harley-Davidson, which was still idling despite its deceased owner being flopped over on the vehicle. I pulled off the corpse, mounted the bike, and took off down the bridge, silently thanking my former, rebellious, teenage self for insisting upon buying a motorcycle rather than a car after I turned sixteen.

Fifty feet later I squeezed the front brake lever hard and skidded the bike to a stop. Strewn across the middle of the asphalt was Lance Dennings, his fractured and massive leather-clad frame looking as if an eighteen-wheeler big rig had flattened it. I was about to crank the throttle grip and take off, when I noticed something. He was still breathing.

I climbed off the bike and approached him. As I got closer I saw that he was bleeding badly, and that the asphalt behind him was streaked with bloody skid marks. His femurs and tibias had been shattered, and his long legs were flopped on the ground in opposite directions like wet noodles. His leather jacket bulged in different places from the broken and dislodged ribs underneath. One arm appeared to be undamaged, but the other was twisted under his body at a sickening angle. But the worst injury by far had happened to his face, as half of Lance Dennings' jaw had been completely crushed. Blood dripped from what was left of his mandible, the bottom corner of his face reduced to a squishy blob of tissue, tongue, and teeth. His eyelids fluttered when he noticed my movement, and after a moment Dennings opened his eyes. They were glazed over but slowly began to focus and make their way upward toward me. There was a spark of recognition when our eyes met, and his shredded tongue flopped like a fish out of water as he tried to speak. All that came out was a gurgling sound.

I took my phone out of my pocket. I brought up the picture I had taken of Johnny's prized photograph, the one of him beaming while standing ringside with Ginger draped over his shoulders. I held the screen in front of Dennings and waited until his eyes slowly registered what was being shown to him. I walked back to the motorcycle. I slid into the deep softail seat, gunned the engine, and sped past the approaching fire truck and into the night.

FORTY-TWO

"Interesting piece of fiction in the paper," I said, before slid-ing a copy of *The Vancouver Sun* across the table.

"The important thing is that they bought it," replied my old man, before slipping on his reading glasses and examining the story. The headline *"IRON COP CRUSHES STEEL GODS: Hero Survives Bridge Shootout With Biker Gang"* was splashed across the broadsheet newspaper's front page. Underneath the print was a crime scene photograph of the wreckage I had caused on the Lions Gate Bridge a couple of days earlier. Next to the picture of the mangled vehicles was a several-years-old portrait of my father in his full-dress police uniform.

"I forgot how nicely you clean up," I said. "You should really post that pic on an online dating site. You'd be replacement hip-deep in postmenopausal GILFs."

"What in the blue hell is a GILF?" snapped my father.

"Ask Declan sometime."

"Fine. Now quit it with the Rodney Dangerfield routine and listen up."

"Rodney Dangerfield?"

"The stand-up comic."

"Yeah, I know who he is, Pop. You do realize we're not living in the seventies?"

"Enough jokes, wiseass."

He tapped a thick finger on the newspaper. "I'll get to this in a minute. First, tell me how you're holding up."

"I'm fine."

"Your nose looks better."

"Yeah," I said, gently touching the bandage. "And I got that knife wound on my chest stitched up when I went back to the hospital to see Declan."

"How's he doing? I feel terrible I haven't been by yet."

"I filled him in on what went down. He knows you have your hands full. And he's doing great."

"Define great."

"Well, there's a good chance he may be facing some sexual harassment charges for repeatedly groping an Asian nurse. And he got in a fistfight with a security guard after he was caught drinking the beer he made me smuggle into the hospital for him."

"That son-of-a-bitch," said my father, chuckling.

"I have a feeling they might be releasing him earlier than expected."

"All right, then," he said, cracking open the newspaper. "Pipe down for a bit and let me read."

I smirked and stirred my banana milkshake. We were back at the retro, red-bubble roofed Dairy Queen on Main Street, and the quaint environment seemed to be helping to soothe my father's nerves. The old man had definitely been on edge since the show-down on the bridge. He'd also been keeping me at a distance while he dealt with the fallout from the armed assault I led that saved his life but left five people dead.

"Did you get to the part about Dennings?" I asked after a while.

"Not yet. Why?"

"He died last night in the hospital."

"Good," said my pop gruffly, before folding the newspaper in half and scooping up a spoonful of Oreo Blizzard.

"Since when do you eat Blizzards?"

"I figured it was about time I tried something new."

We enjoyed our frozen treats in silence. After a while, I asked the question that had been gnawing at me since the moment I had left my father behind on that bridge.

"Are you sure this was the right call? You taking the heat like this?"

"Yes. And there isn't much of it."

"I still don't see why we had to lie. Kendricks and the Steel Gods were scum. They murdered Johnny and would have killed you too. I did the VPD a favour."

"You're damn right you did," said my father proudly.

"Not to mention the fact that all the killings that night were in self-defense. Well, almost all of them."

"Come on, son. You know why I had to do what I did."

"I know, Pop. But it doesn't change the fact that it was kind of …"

"Kind of what?"

"Cold-blooded."

"Watch your mouth, boy."

"I just didn't realize you were capable of something like that."

"Damn it, John. Quit being so goddamn naïve. This isn't about morality. It's about mathematics. It was Kendricks or us. It's that simple." I stirred my shake some more and considered my father's words. "It's the same reason why I put all this shit on me," he continued. "You haven't thought about the logistics of what would happen if we told the truth."

"What do you mean?"

"You're just a civilian. I'm a highly-decorated former cop and a licenced PI. Your actions would be viewed as calculated and premeditated. Mine are seen as justified self-defense against violent criminals. You withheld information and evidence from the police. I'm an innocent victim who got caught in the crossfire. And let's not forget that you took down this biker gang with a stockpile of illicit arms. I simply used their own weapons against them."

"Okay, Pop. I see your point."

"What do you think Cornish would do? Even if you were cleared in the shootings he'd come after you for obstruction and illegal firearms possession." I nodded slowly.

"Mathematics," I said.

"Exactly."

"So what's the excuse you're pushing for the accident on the bridge?"

"Hit and run."

"So they just think it was dumb luck?"

"It's good enough for the VPD. Believe me, they like neat and tidy. Besides, guys like Cornish and Sankey are too busy trying to take credit for the huge bust at the Steel Gods' clubhouse to bother looking for holes in my statement."

"You gave them the address?" He nodded.

"The second you gave it to me."

"What was your explanation for knowing the location? You were blindfolded."

"They don't know that."

"So nobody finds it odd that a reclusive criminal like Kendricks just flaunted his secret hideout in front of you?"

"Nobody cares, son. This is the biggest bust the department has had in years. That clubhouse wasn't just loaded with narcotics. It also had evidence linking them to dozens of organized crimes and criminal networks." I slurped the last of my shake. My father was making a lot of sense.

"Okay, but there's still one thing I don't understand," I said.

"What's that?"

"How do you explain what happened at the Shillelagh?"

"First thing I did was to make sure Declan was cleared. The gun he used was registered. Text book self-defense."

"No, I mean how are you explaining the fact that the Steel Gods targeted you?"

"Ah," said my father, taking another bite of Oreo Blizzard. "That one's easy. My son is a meathead."

"Excuse me?"

"You planned on handing over that murder weapon to Cornish and Rya the second you got your hands on it. But you were so traumatized by seeing your cousin shot and the family business burn down that you completely blanked. You were contacted by Kendricks about an exchange and were told if you talked to the police I was a dead man. You did what you were told and kept your mouth shut, but before they contacted you with a location they got into an accident on the Lions Gate while transporting me."

"So, basically what you're saying is that the entire Vancouver Police Department thinks I'm a dimwit chickenshit."

"Pretty much."

"I don't even care about everyone else. But there's no way I'm letting Rya think that's the truth."

"She does and you damn well will. This is not up for negotiation."

"Come on, Pop. You know better than anyone that we can trust her."

"This isn't about trust, son. As long as she doesn't know the truth, when asked, she doesn't have to lie. I'm protecting her too."

"She hasn't been returning my calls."

"Just lay off for now. You'll hear from her when things settle." I sighed begrudgingly.

"I need another milkshake." My father scooped the last of his Oreo Blizzard out of its cup and smacked his lips. "I'll try a Peanut Buster Parfait," he said with a smile.

FORTY- THREE

The skeletons were everywhere. Crawling through piles of golden orange leaves on the ground, hanging from mossy gnarled branches of age-old cedar and hemlock trees, even draped over the tombstones that were scattered throughout the forest. A pair of dancing skeletons emerged from the shadows, and began to waltz around the train and across the tracks.

"You know, when you asked me out for a night on the town in order to blow off a little steam, this isn't exactly what I had in mind," I said.

"Ah, dry your arse, you big baby," said Declan. "This is a fuckin' gas and you know it."

A chubby kid in the train car ahead of us turned around and gave us the stink-eye. "You said a swear," he said solemnly, before wiping his runny nose on his sleeve.

"Aye, and I'll sure as shite say some more if I goddamn feel like it."

"He's just a kid, D."

"And a bloody nosey one at that." Declan snapped his fingers at the kid. "Turn back around you wee bucket o'snots." The kid did as he was told. I breathed in the crisp and biting forest air as we chugged past a rickety log cabin that had a front porch full of flickering jack-o'-lanterns.

The Stanley Park Miniature Railway is known for being one of Vancouver's more popular attractions. After a disastrous storm tore through the park in the sixties, a horseshoe-shaped miniature railway was built along the path of destruction that was left behind. The diminutive train is also a replica of the historic Canadian Pacific Railway Engine #374, which was made famous for pulling Canada's first transcontinental passenger train into Vancouver in the late eighteen-hundreds.

All year round the little locomotive takes passengers on a winding route over trestles and through tunnels in Stanley Park's dense and lush forest. However, every October the miniature railway transforms into a Halloween ghost train, and the area surrounding the tracks in the woods comes alive with spooky lights and decorations, live-action dioramas, and all kinds of creatures of the night. Declan and I were in the train's caboose, and I was immediately grateful for our secluded seating when I saw my cousin pull a couple of cans of Red Racer Pumpkin Ale out of his jacket pockets.

"Trick or treat, mate."

"For God's sake, D. It's a kid's ride."

"So what? Just because this teeny choo-choo appeals to a bunch o'manky muzzies doesn't mean we can't have a grand time."

I popped the top of my beer and took a swig, enjoying the spicy flavour of the rich and creamy brew. "What is it with you and Halloween, anyway? I didn't know you even celebrated it in Ireland."

"We don't. We celebrate Samhain."

"Samhain?"

"The Gaelic harvest festival o'the dead."

"Do you dress up in scary costumes?"

"Aye."

"Give out candy to kids?"

"Aye."

"Bob for apples?"

"Like a motherfucker."

"So it's exactly like Halloween."

"Except with more carnivals, parades, and piss-ups. This ghost train is about as close as you Canuckleheads get."

The conductor sounded the horn as the tracks curved ahead. The miniature train crossed over a lagoon filled with floating candles and buoys disguised as ghosts. Declan downed the rest of his beer in a single gulp, belched, then tossed his can in the water.

"What's the matter with you?" I said. "This is a world-class park."

"Keep your alans on. It's decorative."

"How's that?"

"The can is orange and its got pumpkins on it."

"You don't give a shit about anything, do you?"

"Not true. I give a shite about those nightmares you've been having." I took a big swig of my pumpkin ale before responding.

"I told you I don't want to talk about it."

"Unless you want a kick in the bollocks you better start to jabber on. Here, this will help loosen those lips," he said, before pulling more pumpkin ales from his jacket. I pounded back what I had left of my beer and cracked open the next one. Declan held his pumpkin ale up in a toast.

"To Jimmy Mimbo."

"Johnny Mamba."

"Whatever. All I know is he had to o'been a good lad to have had a mate like you. May he rest in peace." We tapped our cans and took big sips. We were silent for a while. I didn't speak until the train chugged past a bloodied dummy hanging by a noose from a railway signal.

"The dream is always the same," I said. "I'm back on the bridge. Everything happens like it did. I smash the Jeep into the motorcycle. I take out Dennings and the others. But when I open the back door of the van, Kendricks is standing over Frank's dead body.

He's soaked in the old man's blood and is grinning from ear to ear." Declan nodded knowingly.

"Your mind is showing you what could o'been."

"Why?"

He shrugged. "Lord knows I've had me own share o'haunted sleeps. I used to dream regularly about the first UVF arsehole I ever killed, even though the sadistic bastard was beating a pregnant lass to death with a cricket bat when I put a bullet in the back o'his head."

"What stopped it?"

"Time. Taking a life changes you. What went down with those biker gits could be weighing on your arse in ways you don't even know yet."

"That's the thing, D. I don't think it does. And I'm pretty sure it never will. I killed five men in one day and I don't feel the slightest bit bad about it. When I wake up in the middle of the night, I'm not upset. I'm furious. All I want to do is fall back asleep so I can dream about killing each and every one of those sons-of-bitches all over again."

"I understand, mate."

"That rage over how they wronged Johnny, and you, and Pop—it's still inside of me. And it's not going away. How am I supposed to get rid of it?"

"Simple," Declan said. You use it."

The miniature locomotive slowed as it neared an elaborate backdrop of a Transylvanian castle. Dracula appeared with Mina Harker in tow, and the passengers on the train squealed in delight as the actor playing the count pretended to bite the damsel's neck and drink her blood. A moment later Van Helsing leapt out from behind a tree and confronted the vampire with a cross and wooden stake. The train picked up speed again as Mina Harker sought refuge at Van Helsing's side. I looked back over my shoulder as we left Bram Stoker's climactic scene behind us. The hunter stood tall over the monster, battling the wickedness before him with nothing but his will and a piece of wood.

FORTY-FOUR

The renovations were not going smoothly. My old man had hired a contractor who was a retired police officer well-known for his craftsmanship and woodworking, and although he did a great job gutting the charred remains of The Emerald Shillelagh and beginning construction on an improved layout for the pub, he had also recently taken on two, inexperienced, twenty-something apprentices. As a result the contractor was doing a lot of on-the-job training, which was slowing down the renos. The fact that his apprentices were idiots didn't help much either. Declan and I were eating a couple of submarine sandwiches at the pub's new mahogany bar when one of the apprentices made an error and my cousin lost his temper.

"Put that hammer down you plonker!"

"What?" said, Tony, the simpler of the two apprentices.

"What do you mean, 'what'? You're about to bugger up the Irish wall o'fame."

"How?"

Declan pointed to a wooden shelf in Tony's hands. "What were you about to do with that?"

"Anchor it to the wall."

Declan threw half of his sandwich at Tony, who used the shelf to shield himself from the projectile cold cuts. "I should anchor your fuckin' scrote to the wall, you stupid little shite."

"Settle down, D," I said, mediating yet another one of my cousin's spats. "I'm assuming that's supposed to go somewhere else?"

"Aye, you're goddamn right it is. The shelves are for vintage Guinness ads. The wall o'fame is for photos."

"Got that, Tony?" I said.

"Yeah, fine, but then where do I put this?" he asked, holding up the shelf.

"Above a snug," replied Declan, matter-of-factly.

"A what?" asked Tony, dumfounded.

"Snug."

"Snug?"

"Snug!"

"What the hell is a snug?"

Declan looked me straight in the eye. "Let me shoot him, Jed. Please let me shoot him."

Just then Melvin entered the pub, stepping carefully over the construction equipment and the beam joists scattered across the floor.

"Jaysus Christ, not this bloody bollocks," muttered Declan.

"You know what he did. Show some respect." I offered my hand to Melvin. He shook it while glancing around the pub.

"This place looks like shit," he said. I could almost see the hair on the back of Declan's neck rising like the fur of an angered wolf.

"Come on, Melvin. My pop is waiting." I snapped my fingers at Declan. "You play nice."

"*Póg mo thóin*," replied my cousin, which was Gaelic for *"kiss my ass."*

"Oh, and Tony ..." I said. "A snug is a booth."

"Well why couldn't he have just said that instead?" he asked incredulously. I half expected to hear a gunshot while Melvin followed me up the stairs.

My old man spun around in the chair of his newly refurbished office and slipped off his reading glasses. "Melvin Van Lowe," he said, standing to shake his hand. "I owe you a great deal of thanks." Melvin shifted uncomfortably.

"It was no big deal. Jed did all the work, really. Who knew a pro wrestler could turn out to be such a badass?" Melvin snickered, but neither my father nor I found his comment amusing.

"Nobody," replied my father. "And it's going to stay that way." Melvin all but crumpled under my father's stern stare.

"Yeah, no, of course. Who am I going to tell anyway? And let's not forget I deal in the confidentiality business."

"Speaking of which," said my old man, before handing Melvin a large manila envelope.

"Those are some solid clients," I said. "Play your cards right and a few of them could become repeat customers."

"No shit? Like who?" asked Melvin.

"Lawyers. Insurance adjusters. People who tend to need serious investigative work more than snapshots of sleazy sex." Melvin grinned so wide he looked like a saber-toothed squirrel.

"Holy shit," he said, his eyes darting behind me. "Is that for real?" Melvin pointed to the newly installed frosted glass on the door to my father's office.

"Yeah," I replied. "Licence pending."

The words on the door read *OUNSTEAD & SON INVESTIGATIONS*.

"I couldn't wait for him to apply to the PI Association," crowed my old man proudly.

"I guess I better make the most out of these contacts while I can," grumbled Melvin. I escorted Melvin downstairs but when I reached the main floor I discovered that I had a visitor.

Rya. She was dressed in a tan pantsuit with a crème coloured blouse, looking more attractive than ever. She and Declan were chatting at the bar, but when my cousin saw me he whistled at Tony, who had started to fasten the shelf to the wall above one of the booths.

"Oi, gobshite! Take a break." Declan didn't have to tell Tony twice. Melvin followed them out the door and suddenly Rya and I were alone.

"Hi," I said, making my way over to her so slowly it was as if I was afraid I'd scare her off like a doe in the forest.

"Hi," she said.

"You never called me back."

"I seem to remember you doing the same once."

"Look, Rya—"

"Why, Jed?"

"Why?"

"Why didn't you wait for me at the hospital?"

"I didn't have a choice."

"Yes, you did."

"I couldn't risk the chance that you'd involve Cornish or Sankey or the ERT."

"You know what Frank means to me. Do you really think I would have done that?"

"I don't know. Maybe. Your style is pretty by-the-book." I regretted the words immediately. Rya looked at me like I had just slapped her across the face.

"My style gave you, a civilian, access to an active homicide investigation. It also allowed you to interview a potential suspect in a police interrogation room. There's nothing by-the-book about that."

"You're right. I'm sorry. I was wrong."

"You were."

"I should have trusted you."

"You should have."

"It won't happen again."

She looked at me, her eyes still betraying hurt. A strand of hair hung down in front of her face. I reached out gently and brushed it aside. My hand lingered and slowly cupped her cheek. I tilted my head and leaned forward until I felt her hand press against my chest.

"I know what really happened," she said softly.

"What?"

"The press can spin the story all they want and Frank can deny it for the rest of his days. But I know it was you who caused that accident and shot and killed those men."

"I don't know what you're talking about." Rya's eyes narrowed. The hurt was gone, replaced by anger.

"You don't?" I leaned on the mahogany bar, struggling to find the right words.

"Even if I did, those bastards deserved it. They killed Johnny. They nearly killed Declan. And they would have killed my father."

"You could have died, Jed. There was no need for you to take such a stupid risk all by yourself." Rya turned and strode toward the door, finding a way to appear graceful despite stepping across a floor cluttered with tools and timber.

"How did you figure it out?" I asked. She paused in the doorway and looked back at me like she had the morning I awoke in her guest bed. I would have given anything for the chance to go back to that moment.

"Because I don't get caught up in the hype and sensationalism like everybody else, including my fellow officers. And that allows me to see things other cops miss. Like how it's impossible that a man who is handcuffed would be able to fire a shotgun and hit his target with his wrists being only inches apart." And with that, she was gone.

FORTY-FIVE

It's amazing how much weight you can lose when you cut back on the drinking. And just to be clear, I'm talking about booze—not milkshakes. No diet or workout regimen in the world could get me to give up those. Of course, I had also stepped up my workouts and replaced my usual lifting split with high-intensity circuit training, and I even added some intervals into the mix in order to really tighten up my midsection. The result was that I still wasn't quite as ripped as I had been back in the day, but I was getting there, and it was nice not feeling embarrassed about going shirtless again.

I finished lacing up my boots and took a look at myself in the mirror. I had kept my promise to myself and had gotten that haircut and shave, and now when I stared at my reflection I saw a glimmer of the man I used to be. I checked out my side profile and was pleased to see that I had managed to fit comfortably into the old pair of black pants I was wearing. They were still tight and snug, but then again, they were supposed to be.

I looked at the clock. Five minutes to go. A wave of nausea washed over me and I ran to the washroom and braced myself against a sink. After a few moments the feeling passed, and I returned to the bench and took a seat.

"Ounstead," he said, walking into the room. "You ready?"

"As I'll ever be."

"It's fucking nuts out there."

"Yeah, well, I'm going a little nuts in here."

He took a seat next to me on the bench. "You regret your decision?"

"No."

"Good. C'mon, it's time." I jumped to my feet and bounced on my toes, swinging my arms in circles and from side to side. Bert Grasby crossed his chubby arms over his belly and eyed me curiously.

"There's still one thing I don't understand about our arrangement," he said.

"I thought it was pretty clear."

"The SUV."

"What about it?"

"Why did it have to be no older than 1998?"

"Airbags," I replied. "That's the year they became standard issue."

Grasby smirked. "You know, if I had known what a crazy son-of-a-bitch you were I never would have come after you in the first place."

"I guess I underestimated you too. That was a pretty shrewd move renegotiating our terms. I was dead set on this being a one-time only kind of deal."

"So what's a few more? Besides, it's better for everybody. Wouldn't you rather be here than that dumpy community centre?"

"I don't care about the venue."

"Well, I sure as shit do. I'm making such a killing off this whole thing it actually makes me grateful I took that beating."

I followed Grasby out of the locker room and down one of the long dark hallways within the bowels of the PNE Agrodome. The rustic sports arena had a five-thousand-seat capacity when configured for the type of event it was hosting on this particular evening, and the musty air was still thick with smells of sawdust and horse manure from the previous night's equestrian show.

An announcer's voice boomed in the distance. The hallway around me seemed to constrict the closer I got to the red velvet curtain.

"*— and the reigning XCCW champion, hailing from Tijuana, Mexico, 'The Original Baja Bad Boy', 'The Tequila Tornado', the one, the only ... EL GUAPO!*"

Latino rap pounded out of the building's sound system as the crowd erupted, a mixture of cheers and boos. I took a deep breath and closed my eyes, trying to ignore the hammering of my heart against my rib cage. I gripped the weakened two-by-four piece of wood in my hand tightly and waited for the announcer to continue.

"*And introducing the challenger, a hometown boy, hailing from Vancouver, British Columbia, making his first return to the ring in nearly three years, 'The Best From The West,' 'The Thunder With Lumber,' the former Tag-Team and Intercontinental Champion of the world ... 'HAMMERHEAD' JED OUNSTEAD!*"

The crowd exploded into a thunderous ovation. Chants of "*Ham-mer-head! Ham-mer-head!*" broke out amidst the ravenous applause. The sound of Jeff Beck's wailing guitar blared as his instrumental rock song "Hammerhead" stirred the wrestling fans even more. I waited for my customary cue, and when the song's bass kicked in I gave Grasby the nod and he pulled back the curtain. I stepped out into the sports arena and strode toward the ring, just as I had done so many times before.

ACKNOWLEDGEMENTS

*Writing this book, and being fortunate enough to get it pub-*lished, has been the culmination of a long personal journey for me. As a result, I would be remiss if I didn't take this opportunity to properly thank the people who were vital in making my dream of seeing the character of "Hammerhead" Jed Ounstead on bookshelves a reality. I have many more Jed stories that I would like to tell, and the ending of the book you just read also feels like a beginning to me.

The name Ounstead has a special meaning in my heart, as it was the surname of my grandparents neighbours and dear friends who spent many of my childhood birthdays knitting me sweaters or keeping me stocked up on socks and underwear. Phonetically, they pronounced their name *"OW-n-STED,"* so if I'm lucky enough to have you join Jed and me for future adventures I wanted to share how I hear his name in my head.

I must start by thanking my late professor, mentor, and great friend Leonard Schrader, to whom this book is dedicated. I would also like to thank his wife Chieko Schrader for all of her years of support. Leonard's influence is all over this book and to this day I still hear his voice when I write. Without Leonard's years of sharing his wisdom, nurturing my work, and collaboration *Cobra Clutch* simply wouldn't exist. I would also like to thank Anna Thomas, as if it were not for her pushing me in her writing workshops at The American Film Institute many years ago the character of Rya would not have become the take-no-crap badass that she is.

Fellow Chapman University alumni, Schrader protégé, and award-winning crime writer Theresa Schwegel has been unbelievably generous to me over the years, and I am indebted to her for her astute guidance as I followed in her footsteps and navigated my way from screenwriting to crime writing. Author David Russell has been a stalwart friend who has helped me acclimate to Canadian crime writing, and his witty protagonist Winston Patrick from his own series of mysteries was also an inspiration for Jed's sense of humour.

Thank you to BC crime authors Sam Wiebe, Cathy Ace, R.M. Greenaway, Elle Wild, Sheena Kamal, Eileen Cook, Debra Purdy Kong and all my Canadian crime writing colleagues who have been so supportive and patient, despite me spending years popping up at author event after author event, peppering them with questions or simply learning by their example. Thank you to Crime Writers of Canada as well as everyone who read and wrote a blurb for *Cobra Clutch* and I hope to return the favour in the future.

Thank you to Sean O'Brien, my long-time best friend and ambassador of my quan, whose friendship has never meant more to me than it does now. Thank you to Andrey and Nina Schmidt, Andrew Huzar, Nancy Johnston, Caleb Harder, Mike Smith and everyone who read early drafts of *Cobra Clutch* and gave me valuable feedback. And a special thank you to Darren "The Rocket" Stein, "Hammerhead" Jed Ounstead's biggest fan, whose continued support and passion for the character motivates me so very much.

Thank you to my amazing publisher NeWest Press. It's an honour to be part of the NeWest family and I will do my best to make you proud. In particular, thank you to the talented Claire Kelly for the endless amount of effort she puts forth for her authors as Marketing and Production Coordinator. Thank you to my outstanding editor Merrill Distad, whose unparalleled experience and sagacity immediately elevated my work to another level (there's another Scrabble word for you, Merrill!). And a monumental thank you to NeWest Press General Manager Matt Bowes, who believed in *Cobra Clutch* from the start, and saw something when other agents and publishers did not.

Thank you to my friend and neighbour, retired VPD Sergeant 1314 Joel Johnston. Not only was Joel's input absolutely invaluable with regards to accurately depicting the Vancouver Police Department, but also the ride-along I took with him and the VPD Beat Enforcement Team around the Downtown Eastside was a remarkable experience that allowed me to better understand, capture, and reflect the city in which Jed lives. Thank you to my cousin Jamey Gillis and Rob Ancell of *Ancell Marketing* for helping me with my social media (#ajdevlinauthor) and designing my website (ajdevlin.com). And thank you to my photographer Gina Spanos, who made taking author headshots as much fun as when my family and I take our annual photos.

Thank you to the world of professional wrestling, particularly indy wrestling. Thank you to pro-wrestler Tony Baroni and ECCW in Vancouver for putting on regular shows that I could attend for research and for inspiring the creation of XCCW in *Cobra Clutch*. Thank you to every pro-wrestler out there who pulls up his or her tights, night in and night out, only to beat the hell out of their bodies just to entertain the fans.

Finally, thank you to all of my friends and family for the never-ending love and support. Thank you to my sister and parents for never giving up on me, and a special thanks to my Kindle-loving mother Dianne who takes it upon herself to keep me apprised of the latest in crime fiction (whether I ask her to or not). Thank you to my late grandfather Bill Gillis, who took a chance on a naïve but hungry nineteen-year-old kid and cut a tuition cheque because he didn't want his grandson to ever look back and regret not having chased his dreams, despite how improbable they may have been. Thank you to my two beautiful children, who not only make me a better writer, but who also truly give my life purpose. And last but not least, thank you to my wonderful wife Susie. I love you and our children so very much, and while I will spend the rest of my life trying, I can never fully repay you for the years of support, encouragement, faith, and patience that you have so generously and lovingly shown me.

—A.J.D.

A.J. Devlin grew up in Greater Vancouver before moving to Southern California for six years where he earned a Bachelor of Fine Arts in Screenwriting from Chapman University and a Master of Fine Arts in Screenwriting from The American Film Institute. After working as a screenwriter in Hollywood he moved back home to Port Moody, BC, where he now lives with his wife and two children.